Minsk

RUSSIAN EMPIRE

Lukas, Michael
David.

The Oracle of
Stamboul.

$24.99

DATE			

ROMANIA
Bucharest
Const

BULGARIA

S

Sea of

Caspian Sea

Tabriz

PERSIA

dad

BAKER & TAYLOR

EGYPT   Cairo

The

Oracle

of

Stamboul

The
Oracle
of
Stamboul

A Novel

MICHAEL DAVID LUKAS

An Imprint of HarperCollinsPublishers
www.harpercollins.com

HarperCollins books may be purchased for educational, business, or sales promotional use. For information, please write: Special Markets Department, HarperCollins Publishers, 10 East 53rd Street, New York, NY 10022.

FIRST EDITION

Designed by Leah Carlson-Stanisic

Endpaper map by Nick Springer, Springer Cartographics LLC

Library of Congress Cataloging-in-Publication Data

Lukas, Michael David.
    The Oracle of Stamboul / by Michael David Lukas.
        p.   cm.
    ISBN 978-0-06-201209-8 (hardcover : alk paper)
1. Girls—Turkey—Fiction. 2. Oracles—Turkey—Fiction. 3. Sultans—
Turkey—Fiction. 4. Istanbul (Turkey)—History—19th century—Fiction.
I. Title.
    PS3612.U258O73 2010
    813'.6—dc22
                                    2010014810

11 12 13 14 15   OV/RRD   10 9 8 7 6 5 4 3 2 1

TO MY SIBLINGS—

Adam AND *Anna*, *Coleman* AND *Allison*—

FOR REMINDING ME WHAT MATTERS;

AND TO *Haley*,

FOR EVERYTHING

Acknowledgments

This book owes its existence to the wisdom, generosity, patience, love, and support of many people. At the top of the list is the best agent/editor team anyone could ask for. Thanks to Nicole Aragi, who is not just a wonderful literary agent, but also a wonderful person; and to Terry Karten, whose wisdom, kindness, and dedication are a consistent inspiration. Thanks also to Jane Beirn, Olga Gardner Galvin, Sarah Odell, Christie Hauser, Jocelyn Kalmus, Jim Hanks, Katherine Levy, and everyone at HarperCollins, for all their hard work and enthusiasm.

I am enormously grateful for the patience, passion, and encouragement of my mentors: Engin Akarli, Marilyn Booth, Maud Casey, Elliott Colla, Michael Collier, John Keene, Joan Nathan, Howard Norman, Ben Percy, and Michael Ray.

Much thanks to the National Endowment for the Arts, Elizabeth George Foundation, Ludwig Vogelstein Foundation, Napa Valley Writers' Conference, Squaw Valley Community of Writers, Bread Loaf Writers' Conference, Hall Farm Center, William J. Fulbright Foundation, New York State Summer Writers' Institute, and Rotary Foundation, whose generosity allowed me the time and space to write.

Endless thanks to the friends, family, and fellow writers who read previous incarnations of this book and whose insights helped make it what it is now: Adam Akullian, Anna Akullian, Jenny Asarnow, Lillie Brum, Jonah Charney-Sirott, Avery

Cohn, Nava Et Shalom, Bucky Fazen, Kevin Fingerman, Danny Fingerman, Leah Fisher, Cooper Funk, Daniela Gerson, Billy Karp, Ben Lavender, Krys Lee, Cheryl Ossola, Ethan Pomerance, Robby Rapoport, Ana Maria Santos, Charles Shaw, Seth Shonkoff, and Nomi Stone.

Thanks to the Lukases, the Colemans, the Colmans, the Brums, and the Akullians for being the best family ever and for not asking too many times when I was going to get a real job. Thanks to my Dad, for dreams, for teaching me how to take things apart and how to put them back together again; and Wendy, for Narnia, Dickens, and Harriet the Spy. Thanks to my Mom, for chicken soup, Super Mario 3, and everything in between; and Dave, for Uncle Gaby, Baby Bobby, and Inspiration Point. Finally, thanks to Haley, for all of the above and more.

"Ah, Stamboul! Of all the names that can enchant me, this one remains the most magical."

–Pierre Loti

Chapter One

�֎

Eleonora Cohen came into this world on a Thursday, late in the summer of 1877. Those who rose early that morning would recall noticing a flock of purple-and-white hoopoes circling above the harbor, looping and darting about as if in an attempt to mend a tear in the firmament. Whether or not they were successful, the birds eventually slowed their swoop and settled in around the city, on the steps of the courthouse, the red tile roof of the Constanta Hotel, and the bell tower atop St. Basil's Academy. They roosted in the lantern room of the lighthouse, the octagonal stone minaret of the mosque, and the forward deck of a steamer coughing puffs of smoke into an otherwise clear horizon. Hoopoes coated the town like frosting, piped in along the rain gutters of the governor's mansion and slathered on the gilt dome of the Orthodox church. In the trees around Yakob and Leah Cohen's house the flock seemed especially excited, chattering, flapping their wings, and hopping from branch to branch like a crowd of peasants lining the streets of the capital for an imperial parade. The hoopoes would probably have been regarded as an auspicious sign, were it not for the unfortunate events that coincided with Eleonora's birth.

Early that morning, the Third Division of Tsar Alexander II's Royal Cavalry rode in from the north and assembled on a hilltop overlooking the town square: 612 men, 537 horses, three cannons, two dozen dull gray canvas tents, a field kitchen, and the yellow-and-black-striped standard of the tsar. They had been riding for the better part of a fortnight with reduced rations and little rest, through Kiliya, Tulcea, and Babadag, the blueberry marshlands of the Danube Delta, and vast wheat fields left fallow since winter. Their ultimate objective was Pleven, a trading post in the bosom of the Danubian Plain where General Osman Pasha and seven thousand Ottoman troops were attempting to make a stand. It would be an important battle, perhaps even a turning point in the war, but Pleven was still ten days off and the men of the Third Division were restless.

Laid out below them like a feast, Constanta had been left almost entirely without defenses. Not more than a dozen meters from the edge of the hilltop lay the rubble of an ancient Roman wall. In centuries past, these dull, rose-colored stones had protected the city from wild boars, bandits, and the Thracian barbarians who periodically attempted to raid the port. Rebuilt twice by Rome and once again by the Byzantines, the wall was in complete disrepair when the Ottomans arrived in Constanta at the end of the fifteenth century. And so it was left to crumble, its better stones carted off to build roads, palaces, and other walls around other, more strategic cities. Had anyone thought to restore the wall, it might have shielded the city from the brutality of the Third Division, but in its current state it was little more than a stumbling block.

All that morning and late into the afternoon, the men of the Third Division rode rampant through the streets of Constanta, breaking shop windows, terrorizing stray dogs, and pulling down whatever statues they could find. They torched the governor's mansion, ransacked the courthouse, and shattered the stained glass above the entrance to St. Basil's Academy. The goldsmith's was gutted, the cobbler's picked clean, and the dry-goods store strewn with broken eggs and tea. They shattered the front window of Yakob Cohen's carpet shop and punched holes in the wall with their bayonets. Apart from the Orthodox church, which at the end of the day stood untouched, as if God himself had protected it, the library was the only municipal building that survived the Third Division unscathed. Not because of any special regard for knowledge. The survival of Constanta's library was due entirely to the bravery of its keeper. While the rest of the townspeople cowered under their beds or huddled together in basements and closets, the librarian stood boldly on the front steps of his domain, holding a battered copy of *Eugene Onegin* above his head like a talisman. Although they were almost exclusively illiterate, the men of the Third Division could recognize the shape of their native Cyrillic and that, apparently, was enough for them to spare the building.

Meanwhile, in a small gray stone house near the top of East Hill, Leah Cohen was heavy in the throes of labor. The living room smelled of witch hazel, alcohol, and sweat. The linen chest was thrown open and a pile of iodine-stained bedsheets lay on the table. Because the town's sole trained physician was otherwise disposed, Leah was attended by a pair of Tartar midwives who lived in a village nearby. Providence had brought them to the Cohens' doorstep at the moment they were needed most. They had read the signs, they said: a sea of horses, a conference of birds, the north star in alignment with the moon. It was a prophecy, they said, that their last king had given on his death-watch, but there was no time to explain. They asked to be shown to the bedroom. They asked for clean sheets, alcohol, and boiling water. Then they closed the door behind them. Every twenty minutes or so, the younger of the two scuttled out with an empty pot or an armful of soiled sheets. Apart from these brief forays, the door remained closed.

With nothing for him to do and nothing else to occupy his mind, Leah's husband, Yakob, gave himself over to worry. A large man with unruly black hair and bright blue eyes, he busied himself tugging at the ends of his beard, shuffling his receipts, and packing his pipe. Every so often he heard a scream, some muffled encouragement to push, or the distant sound of gunshots and horses. He was not a particularly religious man, nor superstitious. Still, he murmured what he could remember of the prayer for childbirth and knocked three times three times three on wood to ward off the evil eye. He tried his best not to worry, but what else can an expectant father do?

Just after twilight, in that ethereal hour when the sky moves through purple to darkness, the hoopoes fell silent. The gunshots ceased and the rumbling of hoofbeats whittled to nothing. It was as if the entire world had paused to take a breath. In that moment, a weary groan choked out of the bedroom, followed by a fleshy slap and the cry of a newborn child. Then the older midwife, Mrs. Damakan, emerged with a bundle in the crook of her arm. Apart from a soft infant gurgle, the room was silent.

"Thank God," Yakob whispered, and he bent forward to kiss his daughter on the forehead. She was magnificent, raw and glowing with new life. He reached out to take her into his own arms, but the midwife stopped him.

"Mr. Cohen."

He looked up at the tight line of her mouth.

"There is some trouble."

Leah's bleeding had not stopped. She was gravely weak. Just a few hours after giving birth, she succumbed. Her last word was to name her newborn daughter, and as she spoke it, the sky opened.

It was a downpour unlike anyone in Constanta had ever seen, an endless cavalcade of rain and thunder. In torrents, waves, and steely sheets, it strangled fires, erased roads, and wrapped the town square in a blanket of wet smoke. Through the worst of the storm, the hoopoes concealed themselves in entryways and the hollows of dead trees. For their part, the men of the Third Division rode south toward Pleven, their plunder lashed like spider nests to the backs of their horses. It rained for four days straight, during which time Mrs. Damakan and the young woman, her niece, cared for the newborn child. Leah was buried in a mass grave with a dozen or so men killed trying to defend their property, and Yakob filled the house with wails. By the end of the week, refuse clogged the harbor and the town square was strewn with soggy cinders.

Life, however, must continue. When the clouds finally retreated, Yakob Cohen took a coach to Tulcea and sent two telegrams: one to Leah's sister in Bucharest and the second to his friend and business partner in Stamboul, a Turk by the name of Moncef Barcous who had recently been granted the title of Bey. The first telegram informed his sister-in-law of the tragedy, and requested any assistance she could provide. The second message was sent at the behest of Mrs. Damakan, and recommended her and her niece for any open positions Moncef Bey might have in his household. As with most of the Tartars living in the villages around Constanta, Mrs. Damakan and her niece planned to leave soon and seek a new life in Stamboul, which would be more hospitable to Muslims. In the meantime, they agreed to stay with Yakob and assist him as best they could.

Moncef Bey's response arrived a few days later. In it, he indicated that he would be glad to meet Mrs. Damakan and, in fact, was in search of a new handmaid.

The reply to Yakob's other telegram came a week later, in the form of Leah's older sister, Ruxandra. It was six o'clock in the evening when her carriage pulled up to the harbor. An angular woman in traveling clothes and a dark green felt hat, Ruxandra was possessed of a sharp nose, a weak chin, and a mole in the middle of her left cheek, which looked like the tip of a volcano on the verge of eruption. Portmanteau in her left hand and a sweaty, crumpled telegram in her right, she disembarked, paid the driver, and began up the hill to her brother-in-law's house.

Mounting the front steps of the Cohens' house, Ruxandra adjusted her hat and peered back at the sheen of bird droppings coating the front walk. She glared at the flock of purple-and-white hoopoes perched in the plane tree overhead, then turned back to the door and knocked. When no one answered, she knocked again, leaning forward to listen for any stirrings inside. Again, there was no answer. Not one to wait outside in the cold, she straightened her hat and let herself in.

The entirety of the Cohens' house was not much larger than the dining room of Ruxandra and Leah's childhood home in Bucharest. There were three bedrooms, a pantry, a kitchen, and a living room, the walls of which were bare apart from a small charcoal drawing of Leah's above the hearth. In one corner of the main room was a cupboard and a pockmarked birch dining table covered with a nest of dirty dishes. In the other, a pair of worn leather armchairs sat watching the fireplace. The floor of the living room was drowned in a sea of oriental carpets, laid out with no discernible regard for color or style, and sometimes as many as three deep, like an ancient city built on the ruins of even older civilizations.

Stepping gingerly over the threshold, Ruxandra set her portmanteau down and closed the front door behind her.

"Hello," she called out. "Is anyone there?"

Yakob had been sitting at the table the entire time, his head in his arms behind a stack of papers. When he stood to greet her, it was apparent how badly Ruxandra's assistance was needed. His frock coat was stained in a number of places, his beard had gone to seed, and his eyes were shot through with red.

"Ruxandra," he said, shocked to see her standing in his living room. "Please, sit down."

She pulled a chair out from the head of the table and sat.

"You requested assistance," she said, flattening his telegram on the table as proof. "Here I am."

"Of course," he said. "How are you?"

"Considering the circumstances, I am fine. Thank you. But it has been a long journey and I would appreciate very much a cup of tea."

As Ruxandra spoke, Mrs. Damakan pushed backward out of the kitchen, a thread hanging from her mouth and Eleonora swaddled in the crook of her arm. She was sleeping, Eleonora was, her eyelashes fluttering like dragonfly wings, and hands clasped serenely at the center of her chest.

"She has her mother's mouth," said Ruxandra, bending over the bundle. Then she looked up. "This is her nurse, I assume."

"Yes, in a way," said Yakob. "Mrs. Damakan and her niece attended Eleonora's birth, and they have been good enough to assist me for the past few weeks."

"I see," said Ruxandra. "Mrs. Dalaman, is it? Would you mind fixing me a cup of tea. Strong, if you please. It has been a long journey."

Ruxandra retook her seat and watched Mrs. Damakan step out of the room.

"In general," said Ruxandra, "I prefer to come at things directly, whether or not that is the most polite route. This is something you should know about me."

Yakob nodded.

"I received your telegram," she began. "And I have come to offer the assistance you requested. In that role, I am prepared to stay in Constanta for at least a month, to help with general housekeeping and such."

She looked around the living room.

"You said that Mrs. Dalmatian will be leaving soon?"

"Yes," said Yakob. "She and her niece are moving to Stamboul."

"A filthy city," Ruxandra spat. "Filled with Turks."

"They are Turks themselves," said Yakob. "Tartars, to be precise."

"Well, whatever they are," said Ruxandra. "They will be gone soon, won't they?"

"They are planning to leave at the end of the week, though their arrangements are somewhat tenuous."

"As I mentioned," Ruxandra said, "I am happy to stay here for a month, perhaps even two, to offer the assistance you requested. However, if you expect me to stay more than a few months, I should think that we will need to be married."

Ruxandra had always been the selfless one, the dutiful daughter. She had nursed her parents through sickness, old age, and death while her younger sister went to school and married herself off. By the time their father died, a bit more than a year previous, Ruxandra was dangerously close to thirty, wrung out by life, and profoundly resentful. In spite of the sizeable dowry she had inherited, she had been unable to find a suitable match. At this point, she had no pretensions to romance. She just wanted a hearth of her own and a competent husband to exchange pleasantries with after dinner.

"You won't mind," Yakob said, after a long silence, "if I reserve my response until I have had some time to consider."

"Not at all."

"And what about your things? Is this all?"

Ruxandra smiled and looked at the small, leather-covered chest resting against her shins.

"There's no need to worry about my things," she said. "I've already made arrangements."

The next morning, two steamer trunks arrived from Bucharest and Ruxandra began to make herself at home. After unpacking her trunks in the second bedroom, she enlisted Mrs. Damakan's niece to help her scrub the countertops, wash the windows, beat the carpets, dust the bookcases, and sweep the fireplace. When they were finished with these chores, Ruxandra washed the front walk and attempted to shoo away the flock of hoopoes that had taken up residence in the plane tree next to the house. As much as she waved her arms, however, as many rocks as she threw, the hoopoes were devoted to their roost. And three days later, the walk was covered again with bird droppings. In spite of this minor annoyance, Ruxandra settled well into her new situation. She cooked, cleaned, and when Mrs. Damakan and her niece were otherwise engaged with planning their voyage south along the Black Sea coast, she cared for Eleonora. When the midwives left, at the end of Ruxandra's second week in Constanta, she assumed entirely the duties of the household. At the end of her third week, Yakob knocked on her bedroom door and said that he agreed, in the interest of everyone involved, that it would be best if they were married.

The ceremony was performed in Tulcea, as the synagogue in Constanta was still undergoing repairs. Yakob and Ruxandra stood at the front of the room with the rabbi, a young man with a large red beard. The rabbi's two youngest brothers served as witnesses and, at the back of the room, Eleonora was crying in the arms of the rabbi's wife. After the ceremony, Yakob saw to some business in Tulcea and they took the six o'clock hackney back to Constanta, the hoopoes following at a respectful distance overhead.

Chapter Two

The Sultan of the Ottoman Empire, Servant to the Holy Cities, Caliph of Islam, Commander of the Faithful, and Supreme Padishah of Various Realms, His Excellency Abdulhamid II gazed up at a sea of interlocking green and blue ceiling tiles while the palace barber lathered his face with soap. In a nearby room, he could hear the plucking of an oud and the languid chatter of concubines. A bulbul sang out from its cage and, dappled through latticework, the mid-morning sun fell in a heap at his feet. Abdulhamid shut his eyes and, inhaling the soapy scent of jasmine, listened to the blade work up his neck.

This same man had shaved Abdulhamid every morning for the past thirty years, since the initial wisps of manhood first sprouted on his royal chin. Prior to that, he had served seven years in the court of Abdulhamid's father. He was an old man, the barber, but his hand was steady as a calligrapher's and, even after so many years of practice, he still approached each morning's shave as if it were the most important task of his life. This was a gravity Abdulhamid dearly appreciated. With so much intrigue and conspiracy swirling about the palace, one needed to trust one's barber completely. It was not unprecedented for a member of the Sultan's court to attempt regicide. In fact, three of his distant relatives—Murat II, Mustafa Duzme, and Ibrahim I—had been assassinated by supposedly devoted members of their staff: Murat by his cook, Mustafa by his bodyguard, and Ibrahim by his barber.

Abdulhamid opened his eyes and watched the barber wipe his blade on a strip of leather. Then, shutting them again, he sank ever deeper into his chair, allowing the distant music of the oud to wash over him like sea water. There was such sadness in those strings, so many years of sorrow. It was al-Farabi, if he remembered correctly, who related the story of the oud's invention, its bowed neck inspired by a skeleton hung from a carob tree. Whose skeleton it was Abdulhamid couldn't recall—Lamech, or possibly one of Noah's sons. In any case, it was an ancient instrument with roots in grief.

In the midst of these thoughts, the Sultan sensed a presence hovering over him.

"Your Excellency?"

It was the Grand Vizier, Jamaludin Pasha, his face red from exertion and his mustache laced with what looked like a string of saliva.

"Your Excellency," he said, wiping his face. "I am sorry to interrupt your shave, but I have a most disturbing piece of information."

"Please," said the Sultan, indicating for the barber to continue. "News of my domains is no interruption."

"Your Excellency, Pleven fell three days ago to the Russians. Osman Pasha and what is left of his men have pulled back to Gabrovo."

This was most disturbing news indeed, not especially surprising but troubling nevertheless. The Sultan sighed, watching in his peripheral vision as the barber tweezed out the hairs along his cheekbone. Pleven was the latest in a long string of military embarrassments. Most likely, it would mean the end of the war, then another conference of the Great Powers, another excuse to carve up his empire. Not that he minded losing hold of Bulgaria or Romania. They could sink into the earth for all he cared, as could Greece and the Balkans. It wasn't the land that bothered him, it was the shame, the slavering chops of the Great Powers circling his house like wolves. He couldn't care less about Bulgaria and Romania, but he knew it wouldn't end there. The Russians wanted Kars, the French had long coveted the Levant, and the Greeks wouldn't stop until they got their grimy paws on Stamboul.

"Osman Pasha thinks it would be best to withdraw his men to Adrianople, but he won't do so without your approval."

The Sultan considered his advisor. A squat, tomato-faced man, Jamaludin Pasha bore a prodigiously large nose set on either side with eyes like the hurried marks of a fountain pen and underlined by a thin mustache.

"And what is your view?"

"In this case, I must agree with Osman Pasha. Adrianople is the ideal location from which to defend the capital, if that is needed. And I fear it might be."

"Such is your view."

"Such is my view, Your Excellency. I can give no other."

This was the great limitation of Jamaludin Pasha. Although he was far and away superior to Abdulhamid's previous Grand Vizier, in counsel and in loyalty, he was much too caught up in the rush of events as they happened, too enamored with his own place in history. To him, every revolt was the beginning of a revolution, every spy a sign of a coup, every war the tipping point in the balance of power. As intelligent as he was, Jamaludin Pasha was unable to see the long view, to step back and consider his position. In this particular case, however, he was right. One needed to defend Stamboul at all costs.

"Very well," said Abdulhamid. "Osman Pasha is free to withdraw his troops to Adrianople, or anywhere else he may see fit. Now tell me, Jamaludin Pasha, what other news is there?"

Righting his turban, the Grand Vizier glanced at the small black notebook he kept in his breast pocket and began reciting the previous day's events.

"We are continuing our investigation into the officers' revolt. The new Rector of Robert's College arrived in Stamboul two days ago. There have been numerous reports of intercommunal unrest in the Sanjak of Novi Pazar."

Abdulhamid felt the tickle of the blade under his nose and blinked to stifle a sneeze.

"Tell me more about this new Rector."

"As you requested, Your Excellency, we have tried not to inconvenience him or arouse any suspicions. Thus, our investigation was not as thorough as it might otherwise have been. We know the basic facts, however, and they are as follows: he was born and schooled in a state called Connecticut; after he completed his schooling, he took a position at the American University in Beirut, and he has been there for the past seven years, serving most recently as dean of students."

The Grand Vizier paused to look at his notebook.

"There are rumors," he continued. "But they are entirely unsubstantiated as of yet. Some of our contacts indicated that he is an American spy, others that he is a homosexual."

"Not that those two occupations are mutually exclusive."

"No, Your Excellency, they are not."

"Though they both seem somewhat at odds with his profession."

"Indeed, Your Excellency. Also, Madame Corvel, one of our contacts in the American Consulate, swears she met him before, under an entirely different name, when she was living in New York. However, she cannot remember what his name was at the time, nor the circumstances under which they met."

"Continue monitoring his movements," said the Sultan. "And apprise me if you uncover anything interesting."

"I will, Your Excellency."

While the barber prepared a fresh bowl of lather, Abdulhamid leaned back and crossed his legs in front of him. As he did so, he noticed that he had neglected to change out of his bed slippers. It was a minor breach of etiquette to wear slippers in this area of the palace, but if the Grand Vizier had noticed, he kept it to himself.

"Before I take my leave, Your Excellency, there is one additional matter that may be of interest."

"Please."

"There have been reports that Moncef Barcous Bey has recently incorporated a new secret society. This is the same Moncef Bey who, as you will recall, was active in agitating for the constitution brought out under the reign of your predecessor."

"Moncef Bey," said the Sultan pensively. "I do remember that name. I thought we granted him a posting of some sort in Diyarbakir."

"That is correct, Your Excellency. You might also remember that his post was transferred at the last moment to Constanta."

"Which is now under the control of the Russians."

"Precisely. Though unfortunately Moncef Bey's term ended last year and he has since returned to Stamboul."

Watching the light weave a yellow-red tapestry on his eyelids, Abdulhamid nodded vaguely and exhaled.

"Do we know the nature of this new group? Is it dangerous? Or just another theosophical reading circle?"

"It is difficult to know, Your Excellency."

"Let us wait, and see how things develop."

"Very well, Your Excellency. Again, I am sorry to interrupt your shave."

"Not at all."

Before taking his leave, Jamaludin Pasha gave the Sultan one final piece of intelligence. Her Majesty, he said, leaning in to whisper, His Excellency's mother, had been searching for him all morning and was apparently quite upset. Touching the smooth curve of his jaw, Abdulhamid thanked his advisor for this information and rose abruptly to seek a more discreet locale. Not that he was avoiding his mother. He merely wanted to consider the fall of Pleven and its various ramifications in private before he attended to anyone else's concerns. Leaving the bath complex through a side door, the Sultan made his way around the edge of the harem gardens, past the walls of the palace prison, and through the northern stables to what was known, for reasons obscure to him, as the Garden of the Elephant.

His intended destination was a narrow swath of apricot and sour cherry trees in the northernmost corner of the garden, a secluded grove where he often went to think. Planted nearly two centuries previous at the behest of Sultan Ahmet II, the trees had become over the years a favorite chattering place for squirrels and small birds. Abdulhamid had discovered the grove, which was almost always empty of human visitors, as a young prince in his father's court. Now that he was Sultan himself, now that his word was law from Selonika to Basra, Abdulhamid would often escape there to read and watch the birds along the water.

Contemplating the consequences of Osman Pasha's withdrawal, the Sultan shaded his eyes from the sun and looked out on the twinkle of the Bosporus, hoping he might catch an early mustering of storks or an improbability of shearwaters. He followed a flock of swifts curving over the straits, from the Galata Tower to the new Haydarpasa train station in Kadikoy. Aside from the swifts, there was nothing of particular interest, just the usual assortment of gulls, cormorants, and swallows.

"There you are."

There was no need to turn. He could recognize his mother's voice anywhere. Regardless, he did turn and, kissing her hand, moved to make room for her on the bench. For although she had willfully disrupted his thoughts, although she had neglected again to address him by his proper title, she was his mother.

"Good morning, Mother. It is a wonderful morning, is it not?"

"It is," she said, continuing to stand. "And I do sincerely regret disrupting your enjoyment of it."

"Please, Mother, sit. You are only adding to my enjoyment."

"Your Excellency," she said. "I have but a small request and will be on my way."

His mother was quite beautiful, even in her old age. She had lost her figure, of course, and her face was lined with experience, but he could still see the remnants of what had drawn his father to her so intensely.

"As you know," she began, holding her hands behind her back, "the palace is hosting a dinner next week in honor of the French Ambassador and his wife."

Abdulhamid furrowed his brow. The French Ambassador was such a haughty man, so painfully transparent in his purposes. And his wife was no better, a plump ninny hen who devoted her life to throwing parties and repaying social slights.

"I know you are not partial to him," she said. "But the dinner is long overdue and we need all the support we can muster if we wish to counterbalance the Russians."

"Yes," said the Sultan. "Indeed, we do."

He could not tell from his mother's comment whether she had received word of Osman Pasha's defeat at Pleven. In case she had not, he kept his thoughts to himself.

"As you may recall," she continued, "the Ambassador is particularly fond of beluga caviar. He often mentions this fact in his correspondence with myself and the Grand Vizier."

"Yes, I do think I remember him mentioning something about caviar. You will, I trust, make sure to serve it at his dinner."

"It is already on the menu, Your Excellency. Unfortunately, Musa Bey informed me this morning that there is no beluga caviar in the storeroom. He said a new shipment has been ordered, but it is delayed due to hostilities in the region and won't arrive until after the party."

"That is most unfortunate, Mother."

The conflict between the Sultan's mother and Musa Bey, the warden of the palace storerooms, had been festering since he was a young prince. As palace conflicts went, it was relatively benign, a war of attrition in which each side desired little more than to aggrieve their adversary. Recently, Abdulhamid had begun to suspect that his mother's general distaste for Jews had sprung from her years of battle with Musa Bey, though it could just as easily be the other way around.

"There are ten tins of sterlet in the storeroom," she said.

"Sterlet should do."

"That is the worst-case scenario," his mother continued. "Which, in the grand scheme of suffering, is not so very bad. However, seeing that the Ambassador praised the beluga caviar specifically and seeing that we may need the support of his government in the near future, I thought I might rummage for a few tins in your private larder. Musa Bey, however, will not allow me access. He said that such access requires an express request from His Excellency himself."

The Sultan grazed his fingers against the grain of the bench. Why did people always bring him such trivial concerns? Did the Sultan of the Ottoman Empire really need to bother with a few tins of caviar? He had more important matters to attend to, matters of state, matters of war and international diplomacy.

"I will ask him," said the Sultan, trying his best to contain his annoyance. "Expressly."

"There is one more thing, Your Excellency."

"What is that, Mother?"

"Your slippers," she said, glancing at his feet, "appear to have been damaged by the dampness of the gardens. If you would like me to fetch you another pair, or a pair of shoes, I am at your service."

"No, Mother, thank you, but I think I will be fine for the present."

"Very well," she said, and, bowing, turned to leave.

Chapter Three

In spite of Ruxandra's repeated efforts to shoo them away, the hoopoes that had attended Eleonora's birth settled permanently in a fig tree outside the Cohens' house, as a result of which the front walk was perpetually splattered with a slick coat of green-and-white bird droppings. It was not clear at first why the flock was so intent on inhabiting this particular tree, why they would tolerate broom, bleach, and boiling water when there were any number of more hospitable roosts nearby. With time, however, it became apparent that their attraction was connected in some way to Eleonora. It was almost as if they regarded her as part of their flock, the queen without which their lives had no purpose. They slept when she slept, stood guard while she bathed, and when she left the house, a small contingency broke off to follow along overhead. They were strange birds, in both appearance and behavior, but eventually Eleonora's flock became a part of daily life, a familiar fixture atop East Hill. The townspeople paid them no more attention than they did the pigeons lined up along the gutters of the Constanta Hotel, and Ruxandra ultimately resigned herself to scrubbing the front walk every week with hot water and bleach.

The hoopoes would have been more surprising perhaps if Eleonora were not such an extraordinary creature herself. Even when she was an infant in her nurse's arms, one could already discern the first shoots of what would later blossom into a stunning and demure beauty, her pleasant flushing cheeks crowned with a nest of curls, wide green eyes the color of sea glass, and milk teeth like tiny cubes of ivory. She rarely cried, took her first steps at eight months, and was speaking in complete sentences by the age of two. She brought a childish, though astonishingly precise, logic to bear on the world around her, and the intensity of her presence, that indescribable inner radiance and clarity, drew people to her from across the marketplace with no more desire than to kiss her on the forehead. In spite of this undeniable uniqueness, Eleonora's early childhood was, for the most part, rather normal. She spent her days sleeping, eating, and exploring the world around her, playing wooden spoons on pots in the kitchen or lost in concentration of a pattern on one of the carpets in the living room.

Among Eleonora's earliest memories were the stories her father told sometimes after dinner. Climbing into his lap, she could feel the scratchy wool of his jacket against her arm. There was the crackle of the fire settling, the worn leather smell of the armchair, and Ruxandra darning in the corner of the room. Before he began his story, Yakob would reach into his coat pocket, pinch out a dram of shredded tobacco, and pack it into his pipe with the flat of his thumb. The mouth of the pipe was a tawny-gold lion's head, carved from a stone called meerschaum. Eleonora held her breath as her father took the matchbox from his coat pocket, struck one, and held it to the crown of the lion's head. It was as if this act were some ancient rite and they the sole remaining keepers of its secrets. After two or three preparatory puffs, he would lay a hand on the ridge of her shoulder and ask if she wanted to hear a story. Of course, she always did.

Her father's stories told of wise men, travelers, merchants, and fools. They were stories of Bucharest, Paris, Vienna, and all the other faraway cities he had visited as a young man. Cities with names like Lanzhou, Andizhan, Persepolis, and Samarkand; cities with hanging gardens, towers as tall as the sky, and more people than you could ever imagine; cities with tigers lurking in the shadows and elephants tromping down the middle of the street; cities as old as the mountains, teeming with magic both good and evil. He had been all over the world, her father had, and seen more places than he could count, but his favorite city of all was that ancient hinge of continents, home of Io and Justinian, envy of Constantine and Selim, the pearl of the Bosporus, that dazzling jewel at the center of the Ottoman Empire. His favorite city was Stamboul and all his best stories took place there.

Apart from her father's stories, Eleonora's first memory was of an incident that took place just after her fourth birthday. It was on that halcyon blue afternoon in early fall that she first realized the power of her concentration. Barefoot and dressed in a simple red cotton smock, Eleonora sat cross-legged under the tomato vines, digging a hole in the wet, clumpy earth with her fingers. There was a warm breeze blowing up the hill, the hoopoes were chattering among themselves, and from the back steps one could see all the way to Navodari. She had just scooped up a shiny gray pill bug and was watching it unfurl itself in her palm when she heard a rustling at the edge of the garden. It was a deer, tentatively poking its head out from the forest. She watched it take a step forward into the onion patch, then half a step back. To see a deer in the garden was not unusual, but there was something about this particular young buck that caught her attention. After observing the animal through the tomato vines for a few moments, she decided to investigate.

Brushing the pill bug back into its hole, Eleonora stood and crossed the garden. The deer did not move, though it seemed anxious being in such close proximity to a human. Standing at the edge of the onion patch, less than an arm's length away from it, she could feel its warm, sour breath on her forehead. She looked up into the polished granite of its eyes and brought her hand, slowly, to rest at the base of its neck. Still it did not move. Beyond the quivering of its nostrils and the soft rise of her own breath, both stood completely still.

Then, in one motion, the buck stepped back and lowered its antlers, lifting its left leg like a soldier presenting his weapon for inspection. Eleonora immediately saw the cause of the animal's distress and she knew what she would need to do. Just above the hoof lay a barb, a twisted piece of metal buried deep in the flesh. It looked as if it had snapped off of a fence, or perhaps some hunting implement. Brushing a strand of hair out of her eyes, Eleonora took the injured limb in her hand and inspected the wound. The veins around it were pulsing frantically, and a white froth bubbled up against the metal. The deer's leg hair bristled as she brought her free hand toward it. She blinked and, with one swift tug, removed the barb.

Watching the deer bound off through the forest, Eleonora quivered at the thought of what she had just done. The hoopoes above her broke into a chorus of throaty chirps, and the very crunch of the underbrush sounded like subtle applause. Her ovation, however, was not long to last. A moment later, she was caught up by her armpits and carried to the bathroom.

"You must never," Ruxandra said, pulling her frock up over her head, "ever do that again. If this gets out—"

She stood hunched over herself, shivering in the middle of the bathroom while Ruxandra prepared a washcloth. Eleonora had never seen her aunt like this. She seemed shaken, scared almost.

"What do you mean, Ruxandra? What did I do?"

In lieu of a reply, Ruxandra began scrubbing vigorously with a soapy washcloth, first the arms then the hands, especially between the fingers.

"Please," Eleonora whined. "Tell me what I did wrong. I can't be better if I don't know what I did."

Ruxandra stopped scrubbing.

"It's not normal to cavort with animals. We have enough trouble as it is, being Jews and your father constantly shipping carpets to Stamboul. The last thing we need is to attract more attention."

"But it was hurt," Eleonora said. "There was a piece of metal in its leg. It wanted me to help."

Ruxandra dunked the washcloth in cold water and began scrubbing again.

"I don't care what you think that deer wanted. I don't ever want to see you doing anything like that again. And I don't want you to tell anyone about this, not even your father. Do you understand me?"

Eleonora knew better than to protest. When the bath was over, she told Ruxandra she was very sorry for what she had done and would never cavort with animals again. That, she supposed, was the end of that. And, in a way, she was right. Her aunt never mentioned the incident again. Even so, Eleonora couldn't help but think there was a connection between the deer and Ruxandra's announcement the next morning at breakfast. It was high time, she declared, that Eleonora begin to learn the art of housekeeping. These skills would serve her well for the rest of her life. They would help her attract a good husband. And, what was more, empty hands invite the devil. Although Yakob expressed some reservations about the plan, he deferred his authority on the matter to Ruxandra, who assured him that Eleonora was more than up to the task. With that, it was decided.

"The first lesson," Ruxandra proclaimed, "will be sewing."

She reached into the front pocket of her apron and produced one of Yakob's old handkerchiefs, along with a needle and a spool of thread.

"Do you see this?"

She leaned over Eleonora's shoulder and pointed at the blue fishbone stitching along the outside edge of the fabric. Eleonora nodded. She propped her elbows on the table and let her chin rest in the cradle of her palms.

"Repeat the same pattern along the inside. If you have any questions, I'll be in the kitchen."

Eleonora looked down at the needle and thread, coiled like a snake in the middle of the fabric. This was not going to be fun at all, but there wasn't much she could do to protest. Taking the needle between her thumb and forefinger, she stared through its eye. Squinting slightly, she pinched the end of the thread between the thumb and forefinger of her other hand. With a fierce concentration, she slipped it through. Once the needle was threaded, sewing was easy. Careful to avoid poking herself, she made her first stitch and pulled the thread tight. Then she made another, and another, and another. The pattern wasn't particularly difficult, just the same two lines over and over, repeating around the edge of the fabric. It was boring work, but not especially difficult.

Such was Eleonora's life in the months following the incident with the deer: boring, but not especially difficult. She helped Ruxandra around the house, sewing and peeling vegetables, dusting and cleaning the front walk. On Wednesdays they scrubbed the floors, Sundays they did the wash, and every Monday they walked down the hill to market, where Ruxandra initiated her into the fine art of bargaining. Housekeeping was not quite as bad as Eleonora had expected and, no matter what she had to do during the morning and afternoon, she could always look forward to six o'clock, that delightful hour when, without fail, she heard the clank of the door handle and the squeak of her father stepping over the threshold. Running to him, she would bury her face in his jacket and inhale the dusty smell of wool mixed with hibiscus tea. In these moments, she knew everything would be fine.

It was in the spring before Eleonora's sixth birthday, by which time she had learned the basics of housekeeping tolerably well, that Ruxandra suggested they might proceed with her academic education. Men these days wanted a woman who could read and write and figure, a woman who could do the books and order from catalogs. Yakob saw nothing wrong in expanding the scope of his daughter's instruction, and so it was decided. They began that very morning with the first reader of Ruxandra's youth, a small green book in surprisingly good condition. By lunch, Eleonora had mastered the alphabet, the special shape of each letter and the various sounds it could make in different situations. By dinner, she was piecing together sentences. And that evening, she memorized her first lesson, a discourse on the habits of crocodiles. With her back to the fireplace and her hands clasped in front of her, Eleonora repeated the lesson in its entirety for her father and Ruxandra.

"Was that correct?"

She looked to her aunt, who had been following along in the reader.

"Yes," she said, her face the pale color of astonishment. "Precisely."

Yakob removed the pipe from his mouth and examined his daughter curiously, as if he had met her somewhere a long time ago and was trying to remember her name.

"When did you learn that lesson, Ellie?"

"Just today, Tata, after dinner."

"And you learned that entire passage just now?"

She looked from her father to Ruxandra and back again.

"Did I say something wrong?"

The fire felt warm on the backs of her legs as she waited for a response.

"No, Ellie. Not at all. It's just that we were surprised, or at least I was, by how quickly you were able to learn your lesson."

"It doesn't make sense," said Ruxandra, flipping through the reader. "This should have taken at least a month, perhaps two weeks for a particularly bright child."

Yakob drew deeply on his pipe, then turned back to his daughter.

"Tell us how you did it, Ellie."

She didn't know what to say. How could she explain something so simple? She had learned the letters and, with a bit of concentration, there it was.

"Once I learned the sound each letter makes," she said, taking a small step away from the fire, which had become quite uncomfortably hot, "once I knew that, I looked at the words and heard them in my head. And once I could hear the words in my head, it was easy to memorize the lesson."

That night Eleonora overheard a quarrel between her father and her aunt. She couldn't hear exactly what they were saying, but between the pounding of fists and slamming of doors, she understood that her father was in favor of continuing her education while Ruxandra was opposed. The next morning at breakfast, her father announced that he would be taking over her academic education while Ruxandra would remain in charge of the domestic instruction. Buttering a piece of bread, Ruxandra nodded tersely. From that morning forward, Eleonora's days were split between these two spheres. Her mornings and afternoons continued to be occupied by needles and thread, feather dusters, and scrub brushes, while her evenings were kept solely for academic pursuits.

For the first few weeks, Eleonora's academic education consisted primarily of memorizing lessons from the reader, descriptions of famous capitals, discourses on the habits of various animals, and short stories about children tempted by mischief. However, it soon became clear that she was ready for more advanced reading materials. At that point, they moved on to the bookcase in the corner of the living room, an imposing elm structure ornamented on either side by Chinese ceramic cats. The shelves of the bookcase were stuffed with a cascading multiplicity of books, bound in red, blue, green, and black leather: tall, skinny, plump, short, and embossed with all manner of writing on the spine. Over the next six months, Eleonora read through much of the bottom shelf, sitting in her father's lap while he smoked his pipe and occasionally ran a hand through her hair. She read *Aesop's Fables*, *Gulliver's Travels*, *The Three Musketeers*, *Robinson Crusoe*, and *The Arabian Nights*. In addition to her reading, Eleonora's father also introduced her to writing, arithmetic, and the rudiments of Turkish, each of which subjects she mastered with astonishing ease.

In deference to what her father called Ruxandra's concerns, Eleonora was told repeatedly that she should not, under any circumstances, speak of her lessons outside the home. She did not understand the purpose of this rule, but she followed it nonetheless, having learned long ago that it was best to abide Ruxandra's concerns, whether they made sense or not. In any case, it was not a particularly difficult rule to follow. Aside from holidays and the occasional picnic, Eleonora only left the house once a week, when Ruxandra brought her shopping at the Monday market.

One such Monday, in the early spring of Eleonora's seventh year, Eleonora and Ruxandra were finishing up their shopping at Mr. Seydamet's dry goods store when it began to rain, a sudden and heavy storm that drove the entire market toward cover. The fruit vendors found refuge in a small arcade off the town square. The hoopoes that had followed Eleonora down the hill huddled under the awning of the Constanta Hotel. And a number of people crowded into Mr. Seydamet's shop, pretending to consider this jar of beets or that tin of roe. The store smelled like a forest of wet pants, and the empty barrel next to the door brimmed with umbrellas.

"Good afternoon," Ruxandra announced, pulling Eleonora up to the counter. Craning her neck, Ruxandra caught the eye of a young clerk named Laurentiu.

"Good afternoon, Mrs. Cohen," he said and, bending over the counter, gave Eleonora a hard candy. "And a very good afternoon to you, Miss Cohen."

A stringy, mop-haired boy with an easy smile, Laurentiu had worked in Mr. Seydamet's store for as long as Eleonora could remember. He was a kind soul, though somewhat slow. On more than one occasion, he had wrapped the wrong item into their package and they were forced to walk down the hill again to replace it.

"We would like one kilogram of kidney beans, two bars of that green soap over there, a kilo of yellow lentils, and," Ruxandra paused, glancing down at her list, "two spools of thread, a tin of sweetmeats, and a hundred grams of cumin."

"Is that all, Mrs. Cohen?"

"Yes, it is."

Repeating the list to himself, Laurentiu went about the store, gathering everything Ruxandra had requested, piling it into the cradle of his left arm while he bagged the bulk goods with his right. He returned a few moments later with their package, neatly wrapped in brown paper and tied with a string.

"Two rubles even."

Ruxandra pulled her coin purse out and was counting the money into her hand when Eleonora reached up to tug at the sleeve of her dress.

"It should be one and a half rubles, Aunt Ruxandra."

Pretending not to hear, Ruxandra handed over the coins.

"Thank you, Laurentiu."

"But Aunt Ruxandra," Eleonora persisted, pulling hard on the sleeve of her dress. "It should only be one and a half."

"Don't be silly," Ruxandra said, raising her voice. "You think you know the prices better than Laurentiu?"

Conscious now of the other customers, Ruxandra grabbed hold of Eleonora by the scruff of her dress and began toward the door. They were stopped, however, by a voice from the other counter.

"How much did you say it should be?"

It was Mr. Seydamet, a cork-faced Dobrujan who occasionally visited their house to drink tea after dinner with Yakob.

"How much did you say it should be?" he repeated, bowing graciously in their direction. "We wouldn't want to charge you the wrong price, Mrs. Cohen."

Eleonora felt the grip on her collar relax.

"Go on," said Ruxandra, her lips pursed to a hyphen. "Tell him what you said."

Eleonora glanced up again at her aunt before she began.

"It should only be one and a half rubles," she said, straightening out her dress. "The kidney beans are forty kopek per kilogram, soap is ten a piece, yellow lentils are thirty-five, the thread is two for ten, sweetmeats are fifteen, and a hundred grams of cumin is thirty. That makes one-fifty."

Mr. Seydamet took a moment to check the math in his head.

"She's right," he said, addressing the onlookers as much as those involved in the transaction. "It should be one-fifty. Laurentiu, please give Mrs. Cohen her money back."

With an apologetic shrug, Laurentiu dug into the register and held a half-ruble coin over the counter, but Ruxandra was already on her way out of the store.

"I'm sorry," she said, pulling Eleonora through the crowd. "She doesn't know what she's talking about."

It was still raining hard when they left Mr. Seydamet's store, the sky dark with clouds and the road muddy up to their ankles, but Ruxandra was in no mood to notice the rain. She walked quickly with her head high and her packages tucked under her arm, paying as little heed to the puddles as she did to Eleonora. She didn't look back once and she didn't say a word until they arrived home.

"This is precisely," she said, slamming the door with such force that the ceramic cats shook in their pedestals, "this is precisely what I said would happen. This is exactly why I said these lessons should be clipped at the bud. Now the whole town will be talking about us. And the last thing we need is to draw more attention to ourselves. The widower and his barren sister-in-law, Jews, doing business with Turks. And now the girl, doing figures in her head, correcting shop boys."

"But Aunt Ruxandra, I just thought the money—"

"The money," Ruxandra said, snorting a laugh through her nose. "You and your father both with the money. I can tell you one thing, Miss Cohen. Your lessons are over. You broke the rule, the only rule there was and you broke it."

"But," Eleonora objected, her voice straining, "I didn't break the rule. I didn't say anything about my lessons."

"You broke the rule in both spirit and in letter. Now go to your room and don't come out until I say you can."

When she awoke—who knew how much later—Eleonora was lying on top of her quilt, the pillow pulled over her head and her thumb stuck to the roof of her mouth. It was cold, and the sky outside her window was a steely blue. She felt as if she were in a different world, or at least a different person in the same world. Pulling her head out from under the pillow, she removed her thumb from her mouth and smacked at the paste of dried saliva. She could smell fried potatoes and mince pie. She heard Ruxandra laugh and the sound of chairs scraping against the floor. They were talking, but she couldn't quite understand what they were saying. In order to hear more clearly, she slid off her bed and put her ear to the door.

"And furthermore it's for her own good," said Ruxandra. "You remember the story of my great-aunt Sheidel. Couldn't stop her from reading, spent all her time in the library, and when the time came to find a husband no one wanted her. The matchmaker treated her like a cripple. Is that what you want for her? Is that what you want for your daughter?"

There was a short pause and Eleonora could hear the sound of meat being cut.

"I just want Ellie to be happy."

"We all want Ellie to be happy. But the fact of the matter is she broke the rule."

"Maybe," her father said, through a mouthful of meat, "we could continue with the lessons every other day, or once a week."

"She broke the rule. There was only one rule and she broke it."

Her father didn't respond.

"There is something strange about her, you said so yourself. And now everyone knows, now everyone has seen it."

After a few moments of silence, Eleonora heard a chair scrape back from the table and her father cleared his throat.

"I'll be in the living room."

Eleonora continued listening at the keyhole while her father's pipe smoke mixed with the sound of Ruxandra clearing the dishes. After a few moments of this uneasy quiet, she returned to bed and, lying curled up on her side, looked about her little room. She let her gaze drift from the rickety three-legged washstand to the flaw in the windowpane and the squat dresser beneath it. She hadn't intended to break the rule, nor had she intended to upset Ruxandra. She just wanted to do what was right. Rolling onto her back, Eleonora stared up at the ceiling and watched the shadows move across her room. Was there really something strange about her? She didn't feel strange, or different, or anything beyond what she imagined was normal. Closing her eyes, she listened to the faint cooing of her flock and drifted off to thoughts of Robinson Crusoe, stranded alone on his desert island of despair. If she couldn't continue her lessons, if she couldn't finish the book, he would be stranded there in her mind forever.

Chapter Four

The fate of Eleonora's lessons was not a matter for debate. She had broken the most important rule, the only rule there was, and no amount of reason or pleading would convince her aunt to relent. However, in acknowledgment of her dutiful behavior in the months following the episode at Mr. Seydamet's store, Eleonora was permitted to read for pleasure at the pace of one book per month. Anything more than a book a month, her aunt reasoned, would cease to be pleasurable. While Eleonora did not agree with this sentiment, she savored her monthly ration without protest, limiting herself as best she could to a set number of pages each night. Toward the end of the month, Eleonora would expend an enormous amount of time and energy selecting the next book. Whole evenings were spent under the blank gaze of the ceramic cats, contemplating the contents of the bookcase. She paid especially close attention to the books themselves, to the hue and texture of the binding, the quality of the paper, and the shape of the letters on the spine, as if these external traits might somehow reveal the story within.

One drizzly morning toward the end of September, a bit more than a month after her eighth birthday, Eleonora was considering the bookcase in this same manner while waiting for the iron to become hot. Starting at the bottom shelf, she went book by book, lifting the iron off the coals every so often to check its progress. As she grew older and proved her competence, Eleonora had gradually been entrusted with a few of the more difficult household tasks, such as chopping vegetables and knitting. Ironing was the most recent addition to her repertoire, and had quickly become one of her favorites. She liked the greasy black smell of the coals, the smooth wood of the handle, and the crisp lines she made pressing her father's pants. It was a big responsibility, but she was up to the task. She had never once burned any of her father's clothes and was always exceedingly careful when extracting the coals from the stove. What was more, the location of the ironing board afforded her an excellent view of the bookcase.

When the iron was hot enough, Eleonora took a pair of her father's pants from the pile at the end of the board and laid them flat. She sprinkled a handful of water over the left cuff, touched the bottom of the iron with her wet fingertips, and, watching the sizzle disappear, began to work. When she finished with the left leg, she put the iron back onto the coals and glanced up again at the bookcase. Having spent August on *Jane Eyre* and most of September deep in the fortunes of David Copperfield, she was particularly excited about her prospects for October. Scanning the top shelf, she took in her options. *Swiss Family Robinson* she had read in April. There was a volume of short stories by Nicolai Gogol, which looked interesting, but it was too short to justify a whole month. *Tristram Shandy*. She lifted the iron off the coals and a hissing sheet of steam brushed her forehead. The iron was more than hot enough. She sprinkled water on the cuff of the right leg and was about to begin pressing when she looked up again at the shelf. *Tristram Shandy*. It was an intriguing title and certainly big enough to last the month.

Setting the iron aside, Eleonora reached up onto her tiptoes and pulled *Tristram Shandy* off the top shelf. After reading the

first few pages, she decided it probably wasn't what she was looking for, not this month at least. As she reached up again to put
it back in its place, she noticed another book peeking out of the
space between, a dark blue volume with thin silver writing on
the spine. Bracing a palm against the wall, she raised her foot to
the second shelf and pushed herself up to the level of the ceramic
cats. From this vantage point, she could see that the book was
part of a larger set. It was the fourth volume, the spine indicated,
of *The Hourglass*. Hidden behind a stretch of Dostoyevsky were
the other six volumes, the complete set, waiting patiently to be
discovered. Eleonora pulled down volume four, opened it to a
thin wooden bookmark in the middle of the twelfth chapter, and
began to read.

*It was not without a small piece of remorse that Lieutenant Brashov
reported that next morning to his garrison. Walking to the streetcar,
his heels clacking against the cobblestones, he more than once looked
back over his shoulder to admire his new wife in the doorway. More
than anything, he wanted to turn around and run back into her arms,
to share that stuffy spring morning with her, to share with her the
rest of the day. But alas, life is not all dancing and kisses. There are
papers to sign, cases to argue, products to manufacture, and wars to
fight. It was unfortunate, he thought. But true. There will always be
wars to fight.*

At the smell of burning wool, Eleonora looked up from the
book. The iron had fallen, she saw, and singed her father's pants.
As she stared at the mark she had made, a discoloration in the
cuff about the size of a strawberry, tears swelled up and collected
along the cusp of her eyelash. Ruxandra was right. She was too
distractible, too much lost in her own thoughts. There would be
a scene, no doubt. And Eleonora would likely never be allowed
to iron again. She would probably be punished in other ways

as well. Perhaps she would be sent to her room without dinner; maybe her reading privileges would be taken away. All this for such a small mistake, for a mark her father wouldn't even notice. Even if he did notice, he wouldn't care. And wasn't it his opinion that mattered? They weren't Ruxandra's pants.

With this logic and the heavy pounding of her heart, Eleonora finished pressing the pants, folded them, and laid a new pair out on the ironing board. A moment later, she heard the back door open and Ruxandra walked in with a bunch of green onions in her hand. She looked as if she were going to say something about the onions, then paused and sniffed in the direction of the ironing board.

"What's that smell?"

Eleonora sniffed in either direction and scrunched up her nose.

"What smell?"

Ruxandra brought her face closer to the board.

"It smells like burning wool."

Eleonora sniffed at the new pants, the air above them, and the iron itself, squinting as if trying to make out the source of the smell.

"I think it might be the iron."

Ruxandra brought her nose to the same three places and looked to be on the verge of making a final judgment when she noticed volume four of *The Hourglass* lying open on a stool next to the ironing board.

"*The Hourglass*," she said, as if she had encountered an old friend in a strange country. "Where did you find this?"

Eleonora indicated the top shelf of the bookcase.

"Behind *Tristram Shandy*," she said. "The fat green one. There's a whole set up there, behind the others."

Ruxandra picked the book up by its back cover and flipped to the frontispiece. As she turned the vellum, it crinkled like a sheet of phyllo dough.

"This used to be my favorite book, when I was younger."

She ran a finger down the inside cover.

"Where did you find this?"

Eleonora pointed again to the top shelf of the bookcase.

"Behind *Tristram Shandy*."

Ruxandra stood silently contemplating the cover of the book for a long while before Eleonora ventured a question.

"Are they yours?"

"They're your mother's," Ruxandra said. "My father gave this set to her for her fourteenth birthday. She was always his baby—his little turnip, he called her. In any case, she must have taken them with her when she married Yakob."

Ruxandra put the onions on the stool where the book had been and flipped back to the frontispiece.

"Leah Mendelssohn," she said, reading her sister's maiden name aloud.

Hearing Ruxandra speak her mother's name sent a chill down the back of Eleonora's leg. So rarely spoken, the very sound of her name had become almost sacred. Like the name of God, uttered only on the holiest of days, only in the holiest of chambers, by the high priest in the temple in the holiest city of Jerusalem, her mother's name served in her mind as a sort of incantation, a spell possessed of unknown power. Eleonora stood silently behind the ironing board until Ruxandra left. When she was alone again, she sat down with the book and opened it to the frontispiece. It was an etching of a shield and two swords, below which the words *ex libris, Leah Mendelssohn* were written in a childish hand she could only assume was her mother's. She shivered and closed the book.

Eleonora began reading volume one of *The Hourglass* that next Tuesday, the first of October. Like anyone who has had the pleasure of reading that magical seven-volume chronicle of a notable Bucharest family in decline, Eleonora was quickly swept up in the current of events, the parties, the war, the revenge, the tragedy, and love affairs too numerous to count. Being so young, she was particularly affected by the novel. Other books had a significant influence on her imagination, but none affected her quite so much as *The Hourglass*. Staring at the page, Eleonora felt sometimes as if she were a peasant pressed up against the windows of a great house in hopes of catching a glimpse of the ball. It was as if she had discovered the door to another world, a world filled with action and sudden violent reversals of fortune, greed, capriciousness, and desire. If only, she thought sometimes, if only I were a baroness, if only I had grown up in Bucharest and spent my evenings in a literary salon. That October and far into November, Eleonora was perpetually with her nose in the book. She read before breakfast, after dinner, and anytime she could steal in between. She slipped sentences between stitches and pilfered whole paragraphs beneath potato peels. She was so engrossed in the book, so caught up in the death of Miss Holvert's parents, in Count Olaf's betrayal, and in Miss Ionescu's dwindling marriage prospects that she didn't realize there were decisions being made around her.

She had overheard pieces of conversation about a trip, and more than once raised her eyes from the page at the mention of Stamboul, but Eleonora was wholly unprepared for the news brought down on her that evening in late November. She was sitting at the dinner table with volume three—and had just arrived at the famous scene where General Krzab calls the remaining members of his family together to berate them and distribute the

fortune he had uncovered at the back of his mother's closet—
when her father pulled up to the front door in a donkey cart
laden with four steamer trunks. As he and the driver finished
unloading the trunks in the corner of the living room, Eleonora
looked up at him with a curious tilt.

"What are all those trunks for, Tata?"

"They're for my trip."

She laid the book facedown on the dinner table and they
looked at each other with mutual confusion.

"Don't you remember?" he said. "I'm going to Stamboul next
month."

"Stamboul?"

To her ears, Stamboul was not a place you could just up and
visit. It was a city of legends, a ruined metropolis shimmering
at the edge of the desert, the lost capital of an ancient civiliza-
tion, ossified over centuries of neglect or buried somewhere at
the bottom of the ocean.

"I'm going to sell carpets," he explained. "Maybe buy some.
Business hasn't been very good these past few years and I think
I would do better in Stamboul."

"How long will you be gone?"

"It's not such a long journey," he said. "Maybe a week or a
week and a half, depending on the weather. But I'll need to stay
there at least two weeks, perhaps more. Luckily, my contact
there is very hospitable."

What could she say to such news? While Eleonora tried her
best to swallow the idea, Ruxandra emerged from the kitchen
with a pot of chicken soup and served out three bowls. Eleonora
stared down at her bowl and stirred it with her spoon. Slices of
carrot, celery, onion, and eddies of dried parsley swam in languid circles under an oily film. Letting a pinkish-white piece of

chicken breast float into the well of her spoon, Eleonora tried to imagine a month without her father, a month alone with Ruxandra. Just the thought of it made her sick to her stomach.

"Tata," she blurted out. "I don't want you to leave."

Her father put down his spoon and looked at her as he chewed on a gristly joint. She hid her face in her forearms. If only there were something she could say to make him stay, but she knew there wasn't. It had already been decided.

"I'll miss you, Ellie," he said. Reaching across the table, he put his hand on her back. "But I will only be a month."

"It will only be a month," Ruxandra repeated. "And there will be plenty for us to do around the house in the meantime. He'll be back before you know it."

Eleonora looked up at her father and her aunt Ruxandra. She felt as if the whole world were falling apart around her, as if it had been disintegrating for weeks and she was only just now being informed of the situation. She swallowed hard and bit her bottom lip. A month was such a long time, thirty days, maybe thirty-one, and it was a dangerous journey. There were thieves, wild animals, landslides, and bandits. What if something happened? Then where would she be? The sadness rose up into her throat like a salty wave, but she knew that crying would not solve anything. It would just make things worse. Instead of succumbing to the sadness, Eleonora put the feeling out of her head. She recalled the words Miss Holvert said to her cousin after the tragic death of her parents. *Why should I not decide myself how to feel? They are, after all, my feelings. If I want to cry some other time, I will cry some other time. I do not want to today.*

After dinner, Eleonora excused herself and went straight to bed. Lying on her back with her quilt tucked under her heels, she listened to the house sounds die down. She watched the shadows move across the ceiling, her breath tracking the rustle of night animals. It's a different world, night, the bottom of the well, a hole from which we might never emerge. At one point, in what might have been a dream, a deer glanced past her window, its eyes reflecting some hidden luminosity like a string of lighthouses multiplied along the shore. Then it was gone, off again into darkness.

The next morning, when she awoke, Eleonora knew exactly what she would have to do. There was no other option. Over the next few weeks, she continued with her life as normal. She read, peeled vegetables, scrubbed the floors, and even listened to a few of her father's stories. All the while, however, she was planning the details of her escape. The most important thing, she decided, was to prepare a sack of provisions to sustain herself during the first few days, until she was able to figure out some means of procuring food. For the sack she used an old pillowcase, a pale blue cotton fabric with a row of yellow flowers embroidered along the top. Obtaining the supplies was much easier than she had imagined. She saved candle stumps, slipped uneaten pieces of cheese into her pocket, and, when the opportunity presented itself, pilfered unnoticeables from the pantry. All these preparations had to be carried out in the utmost secrecy. If her father or Ruxandra had even the slightest inkling of what she was planning to do, everything would be ruined.

The closest call came the day before Yakob was set to leave. It was a crystalline afternoon, the first clear day in weeks, and Ruxandra announced she was going outside to beat the carpets. After watching her aunt carry what seemed like an endless stream of carpets, one by one, out to the garden, Eleonora took a stool into the pantry and pulled herself up to survey the goods: smoked meat, wheels stacked upon wheels of cheese, preserves of all types, dried fruit, and a massive mince pie. There was enough food in there to feed her for a month. Eventually, Eleonora decided on a jar of blackberry jam and a length of salt cod. She had already taken the jam under her arm and was reaching for the cod when she felt the doorway darken.

"Thought you might pinch a bit of jam?"

Startled, Eleonora dropped the jar. She and Ruxandra both looked down at the mess of shattered glass and blackberry jam, oozing like a squashed slug.

"While I was busy in the garden, working, you thought you might make yourself a jam sandwich? That was the last jar of blackberry jam, you know."

As Ruxandra spoke, Eleonora stepped down from the stool and hung her head in surrender. She had been caught, but Ruxandra had no idea what she intended to do with the jam, and it was the motive that mattered.

"I'm sorry, Aunt Ruxandra," she said. A smile fluttered to her lips, but she held them tight. "I was hungry."

"Well, you'll be hungry until dinner. Now clean this up and I had better not see you poking around the pantry again."

That night, Ruxandra prepared Yakob's favorite autumn meal: squash soup, chicken with plum sauce, and apple pie. Although Eleonora was quite hungry, she was too excited to eat. In less than twelve hours, she would be stowed away on the boat to Stamboul. Stomach churning with the thought, she listened to her father and Ruxandra discuss the last-minute details of his trip: when the carriage was coming to pick him up, what time the steamer left, whether the Viennese brocade had arrived, who his cabin mate might be, and so on. All the while, Eleonora's mind was racing with pictures of Stamboul, details of her plan, and everything that could possibly go wrong.

After dinner, having hardly touched her food, she asked to be excused. She wasn't feeling well, she said. Her father, who was involved in a bit of last-minute packing, told her he would come in to check on her when he was finished. As always, he was true to his word.

"Ellie," he said, poking his head into the room. "Are you awake?"

She rolled over onto her side and blinked. Though she hadn't slept, she figured it was best to pretend that she had. Her father was wearing his usual gray wool suit, but it looked crisper than normal. His mustache was freshly trimmed, and there was a sparkle of anticipation in his voice.

"I brought this for you," he said, placing a piece of pie on her dresser. "In case you're hungry. I noticed you didn't eat much at dinner."

Eleonora could hear her stomach growling, gurgling up around her lungs like an impatient volcano.

"Thank you, Tata."

"I'm leaving tomorrow," he said, stroking her forehead. "I thought I should say good-bye now so I don't wake you in the morning."

Eleonora looked up at her father, leaning over her bed. The light from the open door made a halo around his head. For a moment, he looked as if he wanted to say something, but he didn't.

"I'll miss you, Ellie."

"I'll miss you too, Tata."

A tear grew against his lashes like rainwater collecting at the edge of a leaf, and he stood to leave.

"Good night."

Eleonora did not feel good about deceiving her father, but she knew it was for the best. When she finally revealed herself, on the boat to Stamboul, too far out to turn back, he would take her up into his arms and thank her. She knew he would. If there was one thing she had learned from *The Hourglass*, it was that you should always follow the dictates of your own personal heart. That was how Miss Ionescu had put it. *There is no sage wiser than the dictates of your own personal heart.* She considered for a moment whether Miss Ionescu's dictum contradicted Miss Holvert's. She decided that it did not. Indeed, both pressed the reader toward the same ultimate end: to look inside one's own personal heart, determine what was right, and do it without regret.

Many restless hours later, when she was sure that her father and Ruxandra were asleep, Eleonora slipped out of bed, changed silently into her traveling clothes, and made straight for the row of steamer trunks next to the front door. With a twist, she unlatched the trunk closest to her and pushed up on the lid. Just as she had imagined, it was stuffed full with rugs. Looping her arms underneath a large purple Hereke, she braced herself against the foot of the trunk and, with the full thrust of her weight, jerked it onto the floor. Moving as quickly and quietly as possible, she dragged the carpet across the living room and into her bedroom. With all her strength, she pulled it onto her bed and tucked it under the blankets. Stepping back, she examined the tableaux. It wasn't perfect, but it would have to work.

As she was about to leave, Eleonora paused to look back at her room one last time. There was her dresser, her bed, and there, on the nightstand, was volume five of *The Hourglass*. For a moment she thought about taking it with her, but there was no room for extra baggage. Instead, she opened the book and removed the wooden bookmark she had found in volume four. Then, she was off. Throwing the sack of provisions over her shoulder, she crept out into the living room and scrunched herself into the battered old steamer trunk almost, but not entirely, filled with carpets her father planned to sell when they arrived.

Chapter Five

Lifting his foot to the edge of his bed, Reverend James Muehler bent over himself to tie his laces. *Rabbit around the tree and into its hole.* He was nearly forty, a distinguished scholar and educator, yet here he was, humming a song he had memorized more than thirty years previous. There was an article there, on the connection between melody and memory, or perhaps an investigation into the childish rituals of great men, another article he didn't have time to write. Brushing a piece of lint off the tip of his shoe, he stood and shrugged into his coat. The schedule for the day indicated that they would be stopping in Constanta briefly to take on new passengers and, according to the card on his door, his new bunk mate, a Mr. Yakob Cohen, would be among them. Mr. Cohen was a Jew, no doubt, which was fine with the Reverend. He had known his fair share of the chosen in New Haven, though of course this particular Mr. Cohen would not be a Yalie. Patting his breast pocket for cigarettes, he glanced about the cabin and, seeing nothing particularly embarrassing or revealing, proceeded up to the deck.

It was a bright winter day, cold but otherwise quite pleasant. The smell of burned coal mixed with pine and the docks bustled with activity. A horde of stevedores humped trunks from carriage to hull. There were a few teary good-byes and a carriage driver gesticulating wildly over what was likely no more than a pittance. Beyond the docks, the remainder of Constanta arranged itself along the ridge of two hills, a few hundred gray stone houses gathered in a semicircle about an unremarkable town square. Inhaling deeply, James took a cigarette out of his coat pocket and lit it with a small flourish. Constanta wouldn't be a terrible place to live for someone who didn't know any better. The climate was pleasant enough and, if he remembered correctly, it had played a role of some importance toward the end of the Roman Empire. He took a long drag and tapped off his ash before recalling what it was: Ovid had spent the final, unhappy years of his life in Constanta, then known as Tomis. *The last outback at the world's end*, he called it, and so it must have seemed to that sweet, witty soul in exile.

As he finished his cigarette, Reverend Muehler noticed a curious bird perched rather close to him on the railing. It looked to be a hoopoe, though its coloration was unlike any he had ever seen, light purple with bright white streaks along the wings and breast. Hoopoes tended to be reticent of human contact, yet this one held his gaze with an unnatural intensity, almost as if it were requesting something. He returned its gaze, focusing on the patch of purple just above its thin, pointed beak. After a few moments, the bird flew off to join two of its brethren perched on the top seat of a carriage waiting to be unloaded. James dropped the butt of his cigarette into the harbor and leaned over the wooden rail, watching stevedores unload the carriage's luggage compartment while a stout man with a thick black beard looked on. The man was a merchant, no doubt, and looked to be a Jew. Perhaps this was Mr. Yakob Cohen. Perhaps it was just another Jew. When the final trunk was stored safely in the hull, the bearded man boarded ship and the hoopoes took off up the hill.

Straightening himself up, Reverend Muehler shivered and pulled his coat close around him. He had been away from Stamboul for an entire semester and a mess of work would be waiting for him when he returned. The new term would begin just four days after he was set to arrive. There were three new teachers in the upper school. And he would have to write a speech for convocation. In addition to his responsibilities at Robert's College, he had a paper pending for the *Annals of Education*, and the American Vice Consul was anxious to receive his report on the condition of religious minorities under the new capitulatory system. On top of all this, he was a disappointment to his handlers from the Department of War. It had been more than a few years already, and he was still unable to uncover any actionable intelligence regarding German influence in Stamboul. This final, covert charge worried him more than anything else. He knew how to write a report, how to train new teachers, how to edit a paper for publication, but he had no clue how to go about gathering intelligence. He was not a spy, or at least had not received any formal training in the art. His successes in Beirut, as he readily admitted, were nothing more than good luck, but the higher-ups in the department had taken his candor for modesty, and now here he was, beholden to them for his position at Robert's and unable to provide what they wanted.

He lit a second cigarette and allowed his thoughts to wander back to the warm fires of Yalta, its windy esplanade and the melancholy facade of empty summer homes. Yalta had been the perfect respite from Stamboul, far from its parties, far from all the treachery and intrigue, but he knew all along that he would have to return. Butting his cigarette on the rail, he watched impassively as a handful of new passengers boarded and, amid a flurry of handkerchiefs, the ship puffed away from the harbor. He was beginning to regret not taking the direct service from Sevastopol to Stamboul. This local steamer docked at least once a day and, more to the point, there was no one on board with whom he could have a decent conversation. He would be spending New Year's Eve on the ship, he had realized that morning, not that anyone on board followed the Gregorian calendar. James forced a grin as he recalled his dear mother's favorite maxim: *We can only but make the best of the situation the Lord gives us.* Patting his breast pocket, he bid a hearty though somewhat sardonic farewell to those few souls remaining on the docks, then ducked below deck to meet his new cabin mate.

Mr. Yakob Cohen, as it turned out, was indeed the same stout bearded fellow Reverend Muehler had observed from above deck. Upon entering their shared cabin, he found the man engaged in unpacking a battered portmanteau.

"Hello there."

Mr. Cohen turned and stuck out a paw.

"Mr. Muehler?"

"You can call me James," the Reverend said, as he did when people neglected his title. "Or Reverend Muehler, if you please."

"Yakob Cohen," his cabin mate said, and they shook hands. "I'm on my way to Stamboul."

"Well then." James smiled. "I can attest that you are on the right ship."

Mr. Cohen spoke English tolerably, as well as some French and a smattering of Russian. After trying on these and a few other languages, they settled on Turkish as the best conduit between them. While his new bunk mate unpacked, James seated himself at the table in the corner of the cabin and they chatted loosely about their journeys. As he had guessed, Mr. Cohen was visiting Stamboul on business. Specifically, he was engaged in the textile trade and intended to sell off some excess stock. Although Constanta was no longer under Ottoman political control, Stamboul exerted a residual economic influence over the region. The pull was especially strong, Mr. Cohen explained, in the textile trade. While Constantans and Russians appreciated oriental carpets as much as anyone else in Europe, certain more sophisticated styles were easier to sell in Stamboul, or so he hoped.

Reverend Muehler was pleasantly surprised to find that Mr. Cohen was much more intelligent and worldly than he appeared. He had spent much of his youth traveling about Central Asia and the Middle East, using a small inheritance to acquire the germ around which he built his business. He had visited dozens of countries and, although his formal education did not extend much beyond the age of thirteen, he was as well-read and informed as any of the teachers at Robert's College. They probably would have continued their conversation through lunch had Mr. Cohen not become suddenly and violently sick in the cabin's tiny sink. Excusing himself profusely, he explained that he was cursed with a debilitating seasickness and, waving away all offers of assistance, insisted that the best remedy was to lie down and rest until the seas calmed.

James took this opportunity to go outside for a turn and write a few letters in the library. When he returned to their cabin just before dinner, he found Mr. Cohen lying with his back to the door in the upper berth of the bunk bed. The room smelled of dry sweat and the lingering tang of sickness. Approaching the bed, James put a hand on Mr. Cohen's shoulder and lightly roused him.

"Mr. Cohen," he said. "Welcome to the world of the awake."

"Mr. Muehler," Yakob mumbled, rolling onto his back.

"It's James," the Reverend corrected. "Or Reverend Muehler, if you please."

Yakob blinked and tasted the inside of his mouth.

"Excuse me."

"Not a problem," James replied and seated himself on the bottom bunk. "Not a problem at all. Tell me, sir, how are you feeling?"

"Not so bad as before."

"That's good to hear."

As they spoke, James took off his shoes and slipped on a fresh pair of slacks.

"What time is it?" asked Mr. Cohen.

"It's seven o'clock on the dot," said James, taking out his pocket watch to confirm. "Dinner will be served in half an hour."

Washing his hands briskly, James splashed a bit of water on his face and glanced at himself in the mirror.

"I was planning to go up early and secure a table," he said as he slipped into his dinner jacket. "If you would like to join me, however, I'll gladly wait."

With some exertion, Yakob sat up and dangled his legs over the edge of the bed, bending forward slightly at the hip to avoid knocking his head on the ceiling. He looked like a gypsy, dressed as he was in an undershirt and crumpled trousers. His hair was disheveled and his bright blue eyes jumped about the room.

"Yes," he said, rubbing his face. "That would be nice. Thank you."

Rung by rung, Yakob climbed down the thin metal ladder and took his place in front of the mirror. It wasn't a particularly promising foundation, but with a splash of water, a comb through his hair, and a change of clothes, Mr. Cohen was able to transform himself into a rather presentable-looking fellow, at least by the standards of the ship. Although breakfast and lunch were informal affairs, the crew did their best to instill a sense of elegance at dinner. Because it was a primarily second-class ship, there were no tails or tuxedos, no glint of emerald brooches or crystal chandeliers. With some red bunting, however, crisp white table-cloths, and an endlessly resourceful chef, the proceedings came off rather well.

James and Yakob spent much of dinner that first night com-paring stories from their travels. It goes without saying, perhaps, that a missionary and a carpet dealer would encounter vastly dif-ferent segments of a city's population; still, James was astounded at just how dissimilar their anecdotes were. In all his visits to Shiraz, he had never once met a fortune-teller or a professional thief, yet in Yakob's telling, the city was teeming with both. On the other hand, Yakob had never dined with a Head of State or an Ambassador, though he insisted he had become close with Moncef Barcous Bey when he was the Ottoman governor in Constanta. This divergence of experience was not a stumbling block to conversation; indeed, it was what made the conversa-tion interesting. After dinner, the two men retired to a makeshift drawing room known as the smoking lounge, and, over a bottle of port, they continued in this same manner until quite late.

More than anything, James was impressed by his bunk mate's knowledge of textiles. He could spot a flaw in a piece of fabric across the room and knew more about the history of carpet-making than any dealer in the Grand Bazaar. His most re-markable skill, however, was as a salesman. Although his wares were stored safely in the hull of the ship and could not be brought up for display, Yakob's descriptions of his carpets, their vibrant colors, classical designs, and the elegance of their workmanship convinced more than one passenger to put a down payment on a piece for later delivery. Even James, who saw through the sales pitch and, moreover, was tight on money after such a long vacation, was convinced to put down 10 percent on a magnificent purple-and-white Hereke that Yakob was sure would fit beautifully in his office.

Their relationship was a perfect example of the friendships one forms on ships, when there is nothing much to do but talk, and one need not consider issues of status or class. It was a pure and simple bond, of the sort James had not known since his early days as an undergraduate. He kept his darker secrets to himself, of course, but as the week progressed, he shared with Yakob the story of his father's death, some of the worst humiliations he had encountered upon arriving in New Haven, and the events leading up to his decision to pursue a degree at the Divinity School. For his part, Yakob shared some of the harsher details of his upbringing, the tragic story of his first wife's death, and the loveless marriage that ensued. It wasn't until the final night of the trip, however, that he revealed anything about his daughter, Eleonora.

In addition to being the last night on the ship, it was also the last night of the Year of Our Lord 1885, and they were celebrating accordingly. They had retired to the smoking lounge, drinking the last bottle of Reverend Muehler's port and smoking a few crumbs of Yakob's tobacco. It was quite late already—or early, as the case may be—and they had the room to themselves. A bluish pipe smoke hung thick above their heads, and only the brightest stars peeked through the foggy portholes.

"There is something," Yakob began, straightening himself up in his chair, "I would like to ask your advice about."

"Of course," said James, crossing his ankles as he leaned back to listen.

"It concerns my daughter."

"Yes, you mentioned her the other day. Eleanor, right?"

"Eleonora."

Yakob was silent for a moment, staring into the bowl of his pipe.

"I have mentioned her," he said. "But I haven't told you anything about her."

James took a sip of port and raised his eyebrows.

"Eleonora is—" Yakob paused, looking down at his hands. "If you met her you would know right away. You might call her a genius, or a savant. I don't know what the right word is to describe her."

Reverend Muehler leaned forward, resting his elbows on his knees. He had encountered a number of supposedly extraordinary children over the course of his career, children who had learned to read early, could perform difficult sums in their heads, or took easily to foreign languages. The subject was of some interest, both professional and personal, and he had often considered compiling a compendium of savants throughout history. However, the majority of the children he had encountered were not geniuses, at least not in the mold of Bentham, Mendelssohn, or Mill.

"You said before that you entered university at the age of sixteen?"

"Yes," said James. "Just shy of my seventeenth birthday."

"I believe that with the proper training and direction, Eleonora might be able to enter university in two years, maybe three. Not that I would want her to, but I believe she could."

"How old is she?"

"She turned eight in August."

"That would be astonishing."

James trusted his bunk mate, he was an honest man with little pretense or pride, but it was difficult not to be skeptical of such claims. They spoke for a long while about Eleonora's many achievements, the lessons Yakob had devised for her, and Ruxandra's concerns about the child's future as well as her fears of how the townspeople would react if they knew the full extent of Eleonora's powers. James did his best to support his friend, but as much as he wanted to believe him, he couldn't help but express some skepticism. Every time he did, Yakob would take a long puff on his pipe and shake his head.

"If only you could meet her," he said. "You would know in a moment."

Chapter Six

✦

Pressed in on either side by a scratchy velvet darkness, her knees collapsed and arms folded into useless flippers, Eleonora stared into the blackness, unable to make out even the walls of the trunk she was trapped inside. Somewhere in the depths of the ship, the clack and groan of a steam engine rose, bellowed, and fell like a restless giant snoring in its cave. The paste between her lips tasted of stomach acid and coal dust. A needling cramp blossomed beneath her shoulder blade. And her thigh muscles fluttered anxiously, as if there were butterflies trapped under the skin. Wiggling her fingers, Eleonora felt a new cramp fan out from her shoulder. She closed her eyes against the pain and swallowed a greasy taste of bile. She had not eaten since noon the day before and her provisions were out of reach behind the cross of her ankles. If she could maneuver herself into a new position, she would be able to ease the cramp in her back, and it was possible she might find herself within an arm's length of the provisions. Exhaling, she squirmed her left arm out from under her rib cage and canted her shoulder into the empty space left behind. From this new position, however, the best she could do was a desperate lurch into an even more awkward arrangement. At the end of it all, she was fortunate to be able to squirm back to her original fetal pose.

This was not how she had imagined her journey, not at all. Though what exactly she had imagined she couldn't recall. As much as she had thought through the various and minute details

of her plan, as many times as she checked and double-checked
her list, Eleonora had never truly considered what it meant to
shut oneself inside a trunk. When she had thought about it at all,
she had always imagined that time would pass quickly, that, like
the tedious parts of a novel, she could skim through the journey
and arrive no worse for the wear in Stamboul. This, of course,
was not the case. If anything, time moved more slowly, dragging
its hooves like a weary pack horse forced to travel long days at
the edge of its strength. If her estimations were correct, she had
been in the trunk for a bit more than seven hours. In the grand
scheme of one's life, seven hours was not a particularly long period of time, but these seven hours felt like a week of years.

At first, she had been overcome with apprehension, worried
that she would be caught, that she would sneeze or cough or swallow and her father or Ruxandra would discover her. Eventually,
however, she must have fallen asleep, because the next thing she
remembered she was being loaded into the luggage compartment
of a hackney carriage and jolted down the hill. After waiting for
a long while in what she assumed was a customs inspection line,
Eleonora felt the luggage compartment open. There was a shaft
of light coming through the crack in the lid, and she thought she
heard her father's voice. A bustle of men crowded about the carriage, and the trunk was passed from hand to hand like a sandbag.
Her father's luggage must have been among the last on board,
because, soon after she was loaded, the hull closed with a creak
of iron chains, the engine sprang to life, and the ship puffed away
from the harbor. It was only at this point that Eleonora allowed
herself to exhale and take stock of her circumstances. The first
part of her plan had been an unmitigated success, but now here
she was, trapped, a cramp blooming across her back, and hunger
bubbling into her mouth like lava.

"Hello?" she called out, her voice scratching against the top of her throat. "Hello? Is anyone there?"

It was no use. There was no one there and, even if there had been, they wouldn't be able to hear her over the growl of the engine. She kicked hard once against the base of the trunk, partly in frustration and partly in the wild hope that she might kick her way out. Although the wood held true, something fell out of Eleonora's front pocket in the jerk and thrust of her kick. She wriggled her arm out from under herself and ran her thumb along the edge of the object. It was the bookmark, one of the few personal effects her mother had taken with her from Bucharest to Constanta, or at least one of the few that remained. A thin piece of oak carved with overlapping hexagons, it seemed to possess an inner light, to pierce almost through the darkness. Eleonora imagined her mother absently twirling her hair around the bookmark as she reread a favorite passage in *The Hourglass*. Twirling it herself between thumb and forefinger, Eleonora remembered the scene in which the elder Mrs. Holvert escaped from her great-uncle's prison by picking her handcuffs with a hairpin clenched between her teeth.

It was worth a try, if only because there was nothing else left. Bending her wrist in on itself like a chicken, Eleonora pressed her chin to her chest and bit down. With the clench of her teeth and the guiding tip of her tongue, she was able to maneuver the bookmark with surprising dexterity. After a few minutes, she succeeded in slipping it through the crack between the lid and the body of the trunk. Eyes tight in concentration, she ran it back and forth along the length of the groove until it caught purchase on the locking mechanism and, with the release of a spring, the lid gave way.

With the bookmark still between her teeth, Eleonora sat up

blinking in the dim coal-dusted luggage room. By the distant flicker of the furnace, she could see the outline of her own trunk and a handful of others around her fading into a grainy black. She could make out shapes but not colors, smells but not their source. With some effort, she stepped out onto the warm metal floor, stretched her arms over her head, and bent forward to touch her toes. She worried the epicenter of her cramp with the knuckle of her thumb and, quivering, rolled out her neck. When she was fully stretched, Eleonora sat down on a nearby trunk. Fishing out her sack of provisions, she began to eat, handing bread ends and cheese rinds into her mouth like a hungry raccoon.

As her eyes began to adjust to the sooty darkness of the hull, she saw that she was surrounded by a metropolis of luggage, row upon row of trunks, crates, and baggage lit only by the glow of the furnace. Surveying the ruined landscape, she searched for indications of which trunks might be hiding sardines and crackers, dried cherries, walnuts, or minced meat. In one sitting, she had eaten more than half of her provisions, and still her stomach persisted. Surely none of these people whose names were written on the luggage would object to giving a starving child a small portion of their food. Using the bookmark as a pick, Eleonora went trunk to trunk, jimmying those locks she could and moving on from those she could not, rummaging through clothes, books, jewelry, and perfume in search of sustenance. She found a set of fancy engraved stationery, crystal glassware, the clockwork of an enormous timepiece, and a portmanteau stuffed full with love letters, but she found nothing to eat.

Eventually, she came upon a line of five wooden crates, aloof from the rest of the luggage in a far corner of the hull. Each was as tall as Eleonora herself and stamped in gold with a calligraphic seal. In spite of their nobility, or perhaps because of it, the crates had no locks or bolts. Their only fortification was a wooden latch and pin. The first crate she opened was filled with books, novels mainly, written in French, German, and English. Glancing over the titles, she closed the lid and moved on. They may be of interest later, but now she wanted food. The second crate was filled with Crimean rose water, and the third stacked full of caviar, smoked fish, and herring, hundreds of red and golden tins stamped with a few words of Russian or a picture of a fish. Looking over her shoulder, Eleonora removed one of the tins from the top row and, twisting off its lid, revealed a sheet of glistening black spheres. She touched the fish eggs suspiciously with the tip of her pinkie and brought it to her lips. Her nose tensed in revulsion. The pungent, salty flavor was not what she had hoped for, but it was food. In less than an hour, Eleonora consumed an entire bottle of rose water and three tins of the caviar, scooping hand after hand into her mouth until she was drunk with roe.

She made her bed that night with the thick pile of a Shushan carpet and a bolt of velvet. Laying her head on a folded-up corner of the carpet, she pulled the velvet around her shoulders, closed her eyes, and began to drift. Her mind swam with fear and doubt, but as scared as she was, as much as she questioned the wisdom of her decision to run away, Eleonora was also very tired. As the grumbling of her stomach subsided and the furnace settled into a steady pulse, her mind slipped into that warm, salty ocean of sleep: white caps and waves, gulls gliding overhead, and, every so often, a distant glimpse of land. As she drifted further, the sea became a country road: a lonely cow regurgitating weeds, the occasional stone cottage, a stand of cypress trees, and, beyond that, vast tracts of yellow-green farmland. Soon the cottages turned to villages, the villages to cities, and the cities grew taller, with wide boulevards, crystal domes, and night gardens redolent of roses and jasmine.

In the belly of the ship, Eleonora lost all track of time. The sway of the waves and sporadic coughing sputter of the furnace were her only indications it was passing at all. She slept when she was tired, ate when she was hungry, and relieved herself in a vacant corner of the hull like some feral animal trapped in a basement. In time, her eyes adjusted to the dim, sooty light of the furnace and, although she was attacked every so often by fits of coughing, she became accustomed to the coal dust. More than once she pulled a book down from the Sultan's crate and tried to read, but the words blurred and fled across the page, allowing no more than a paragraph or so before she was overcome with a debilitating headache. With reading impossible, no sun, and no chores, Eleonora occupied herself by looking through other passengers' luggage, thinking back over her favorite books, and wondering, like David Copperfield, whether she would turn out to be the hero of her own life or if that station would be held by someone else.

Eleonora did not know that the ship was to stop twice before Stamboul, and so, when the engine slowed that first time and a horn blew above deck, her heart lurched. Had it been a week already? To be safe, she stashed her bed in the trunk and scrambled behind the Sultan's crates. With a snap and creak, the hull door began to open. It was midday and sunlight cut deep through the widening crack, the light pouring into her cave like a barrage of flaming arrows. She stifled a sneeze as a trio of stevedores began loading and unloading trunks from the front of the hull. As they were bringing in the last of the baggage to be loaded, one of them sniffed at the air and barked a few words over his shoulder. His companion barked back and laughed. Although she didn't understand what they said, the sound of their voices made her pulse flutter in her neck.

As the great door closed, the hold water rushing out and iron chains clanking precariously, one of Eleonora's hoopoes flapped into the hull. She saw the bird only for a moment, out of the corner of her eye, but there was no mistaking that it was a member of her flock. It circled the hull once and departed just as the door clanged shut. When the ship pulled out again to sea, Eleonora found that the bird had left a gift for her, an orange, placed perfectly in the middle of her trunk. Complete with stem and leaves, it glowed in the bowl of her hands like a tiny sun. For a long while she just held it, letting its warmth flow through to her extremities. With this fruit in her hands, she knew her flock was with her still. They had left their roost in Constanta to follow her across the sea, to watch over her in her journey. When she became hungry, Eleonora peeled and ate the orange, section by section, savoring the explosion of each juicy corpuscle between her tongue and the roof of her mouth.

Thus was her life in the hull. Although her most basic needs were accounted for, it was not a pleasant way to live, and Eleonora was often overcome with an unbearable longing for home, for her father, even for Ruxandra. In those moments, she wanted nothing more than to reveal herself, to find her way above deck and collapse into her father's arms. She knew, however, that if she revealed herself too early, her plan would be ruined. Her father would put off with her at the next port of call, Ruxandra would be telegraphed, and all her preparations, all her suffering, would amount to no more than a few days' delay. The question, then, was how she would know that the time was right. With no clock or calendar, and only a vague understanding of the ship's course, she had only her intuition to guide her, only a hazy sense of her position in the world.

It was the last night of their journey, the night before they were set to dock in Stamboul, when Eleonora decided to reveal herself. She did not know, of course, that the ship would enter the mouth of the Bosporus that morning, but she had sensed a subtle change in the strength of the waves, a flag in the power of the furnace, and not a minute too soon. After seven long days in the hull of the ship, she was dirty, her lungs were filled with coal dust, and she was beginning to develop a pain in her abdomen. Imagining how she must look, she considered trying to clean herself up, to wash herself somehow or fashion a new dress from a bolt of fabric, but there was no soap in the hull and any dress she could fashion would ruin more of her father's merchandise. She would have to present herself as she was.

Pulling her hair back, she straightened her dress, tidied up around the trunk, and made her way over the familiar landscape of luggage to the great iron door that led out of the hull. Standing before it, Eleonora ran her fingers over the surface of the metal, its dents like the pockmarks in the door leading up to Mrs. Brashov's attic. Behind this door lay her father, all manner of food and bedding, hot soup, feather pillows, and the crystal air of the sea. A shiver of anticipation ran down to her fingertips and she paused to steady her breath. This was it. She was more scared than she had expected, scared of her father's reaction, of being caught before she could find him, of any number of horrible outcomes she couldn't even imagine, but there was no other choice, no other way out. She inhaled to calm herself. Grasping the doorknob with both hands, she pushed into a damp and vacant hallway, dim by most standards though quite bright compared to the darkness of the hull.

She rubbed the glare out of her eyes and followed the hallway a few meters to a room filled with buttons, levers, and wheels, all hissing and clacking like a crowded café. As she stood deciding which of the three available doors she should take, Eleonora heard a string of disembodied words float past her, naked and swift as angels. She listened to the voices grow closer and closer until she could hear them just outside the room.

"It must be in here somewhere," said a man's voice as the door swung open.

From behind a tangle of pipes, she could make out the profile of two men, one much larger than the other. Their mustaches and turbans cast a crooked shadow on the open door behind them.

"Where did he say it was?"

As the second man spoke, Eleonora realized that they were speaking in Turkish. She had only ever heard the language in her lessons with her father, but she found that, with a bit of concentration, she could understand it quite well.

"He said it was in here."

"Where in here?"

"If I knew, we wouldn't be looking for it."

The first man took a half-step back and lifted the lantern so that it shone across the room.

"Did you see that?"

"No."

There was a long silence and Eleonora could feel herself trembling, the anticipation of being caught like metal on the back of her tongue.

"I don't see anything," said the first man, turning to leave. "It's too dark to see anything in here."

When she stepped out from behind the pipes, Eleonora was still quivering. If those men had seen her, who knows what trouble she might have found herself in. She took a few moments to catch her pulse, then, counting to thirty, made her way through the door they had taken, presuming they would be going back to the main part of the ship. Passing under a jungle of leaky pipes and soot-blackened lanterns, she found herself eventually in a much brighter hallway. This new hall was lined with carpet, wood paneling, and a row of doors, each of which was stamped with a circular window and a numbered brass plaque. Doors 16 to 30 were all closed. As she made her way down the hall, Eleonora could hear the soft, persistent sounds of sleep, the muttering, snoring, and turning over that mark our fitful journeys through the world of dreams.

She had reached the end of the hallway, and was readying herself to climb a flight of metal stairs, when one of the doors behind her creaked open. She froze and hunched her shoulders, bracing for an accusatory shout, the opening of other doors, and a gathering of curious passengers arguing over what should be done with this filthy little stowaway. The only sound she heard, however, was the soft patter of footsteps interlaced by a thin mumbling. Eleonora inched her chin toward her shoulder, craning her eyes toward the source of the noise. It was an old man, gaunt in his nightgown and with a mess of thick gray hair. He was walking toward the stairway, shuffling his slippers against the carpet, but he did not seem to notice her. Slowly, so as not to draw attention, Eleonora turned to face the man. Although his eyes were open, they were lifeless and glossy, devoid of any recognition. She caught her breath in her throat and swallowed. As he approached, she could hear he was mumbling through a series of nervous questions. He stopped just in front of her and, as if sensing her presence, fell silent. Eleonora inhaled the old man's sleep smell, the accretion of a week's perspiration on his nightgown. She looked up into the heavy lines of his face and reached her hand out, but did not touch him.

"It's okay," she said. "Turn around. Go back to your room."

A glint of recognition shot across his eyes, then the old man turned and walked back toward his room. Eleonora waited for him to close the door behind him before she exhaled, then turned herself and, heart pounding in her neck, climbed the stairs.

She emerged at the entrance of what seemed to be the dining room. Pushing a strand of hair over her ear, she surveyed the empty room. The tables were folded and stacked for docking. A contingent of potted plants huddled in the corner, and the piano stood flush against the wall like a disobedient student. Eleonora's mouth watered at the thought of food and, hoping that those leather double doors by the piano might lead to a kitchen, she crossed the room to investigate. As she approached, she could hear the sound of voices coming from inside the room, which, according to a brass plaque on the wall, was the smoking lounge. Drawing yet closer, she smelled a trace of her father's pipe smoke. It could have been anyone's pipe smoke, really, but Eleonora was not in a position to quibble. Putting aside her hesitations, she pushed through the doors. There he was, just as she had imagined. Dressed in the same jacket he had been wearing the night before he left, her father was seated in a narrow armchair, drinking a glass of wine with a red-faced man in a dark blue suit.

"Tata!"

In the long stretch of silence that followed, Eleonora noticed a reflection of herself in the mirror next to her father's head. Her dress was caked with food and her stockings torn at both knees. Her face was smeared with coal dust and a clump of dirty hair hung over her eyes. She looked like Cupid returning home from a battle, beaten down, dragged chin-first through the mire, and with wings clumped with mud. She opened her mouth to explain, but everything she had practiced, all of her justifications and reason, slipped away. Instead, she rushed across the room and threw herself into her father's lap, causing him to drop his glass and spill wine all over the rug.

"Ellie," he said, his voice betraying his wonder and no small amount of displeasure. "What on earth are you doing here?"

Chapter Seven

That next morning, Eleonora and her father sat together on the front deck of the ship, watching Stamboul rise out of the sea. At first glimpse, the city was a haze, no more corporeal than a specter sleeping under fog, but as they drew closer, she could see an outline of the city, its street lamps blinking like a conference of fallen stars. It was not yet dawn, and Eleonora was wrapped in a scratchy wool blanket on the edge of her father's lap. He was still cross with her. She could feel his irritation in the tense posture of his forearms and the steady inhalation he used to calm his thoughts. What these thoughts were she could not say. He had not spoken more than a dozen words to her since she had revealed herself. She did not know whether he planned to send her back to Constanta or whether he might allow her to stay on with him in Stamboul. Unfamiliar as she was with the contours of her father's anger, Eleonora had no tools to judge its shape or magnitude. She knew, however, that it would be best not to break the silence.

In its time, the sun rose unsteady from a distant corner of the sky, and with it the fog lifted. Already the Bosporus was teeming, packed with fishing boats, caïques, and the occasional lumbering steamer. On the shore, under the shade of cypress trees, miniature people hawked and haggled, bustled, bargained, and prayed. Three gargantuan turtle-domed mosques glinted in the rising sun, their minarets piercing the sky like bayonets, and

there, at the confluence of waters, was the most glorious building Eleonora had ever seen. Gardens upon gardens, arches, bal-
ustrades, and clerestories ringed by a gleaming white marble
wall and watched over by a regiment of glassy towers, Topkapi
Palace, the residence of His Excellency Sultan Abdulhamid II,
sat perched on the rim of the Golden Horn, a testament to incon-
ceivable wealth and power.

As they pulled into the docks, the captain's horn sounded
and a chorus of shouts went up from the deck. A team of dock
boys tied down the ropes, the hull cranked open, and a mass of
stevedores descended on the ship, strapping trunks, crates, and
barrels to their backs like so many mules. Just across from the
new train station, the docks were a frantic crush of humanity, a
jumble of fezzes, turbans, suit jackets, and robes. Barefoot beggars jostled with hawkers waving their wares over their heads
and, at the outskirts of the crowd, carriages jockeyed for position
with camels and stray dogs. This was what Miss Ionescu meant
when she called the train station in Bucharest *an unwashed tumult
of men clawing and rasping at each other for a slightly more advanta-
geous position in the crowd*. As Eleonora glimpsed what appeared
to be the backside of an elephant disappearing around the corner, a fight broke out between two stevedores and she could feel
her father's arms tighten protectively around her. Settling herself
deeper into his lap, she inhaled the familiar smell of hibiscus and
pipe smoke before daring a question.

"Tata," she said, looking up at the dense underside of his
beard. "Where are we going now?"

He exhaled and pulled a pouch of tobacco from his jacket
pocket.

"The first thing we're going to do," he said, "is send a telegram to Ruxandra. Then, my friend Moncef Bey will pick us

up in his carriage and bring us to his house. I was planning on staying with him for the entirety of my trip. Hopefully, he will be able to accommodate you as well."

Yakob lit his pipe, letting the import of these words sink in.

"I don't know how you got it into your head that this would be a good idea," he said, drawing through the tobacco.

While her father smoked, a pungent salty smell wafted up from the docks and Eleonora thought back to the hull. Shuddering, she pushed the thought to the back of her mind. Her father had not asked her any questions about what had transpired in the hull, and she was glad of it. Some things were better left undiscussed, she knew that now for sure. When her father finished his pipe, he stood, took his portmanteau in one hand, and with the other led her down to the docks.

"Ride, sir? Room? Take your bags?"

Even before they stepped off the plank, they were swarmed by a push of touts, oily-faced men waving postcards and grabbing at her father's bag.

"No thank you," Yakob said, brushing past. "No. No, thank you."

"A nice girl there," one of them said with a hint of menace. "She your daughter?"

Yakob pulled Eleonora past the touts to a less crowded area near the train station and set his portmanteau down. Reverend Muehler was nowhere to be seen and, from the looks of it, Moncef Bey hadn't arrived yet either. Eleonora thought to ask her father whether they were going to send the telegram to Ruxandra, but he seemed tense and she didn't want to aggravate him with her questions. He searched the crowd once more before he nudged her in the direction of a small café.

"Here, Ellie. Let's sit down and have a cup of tea."

They had just ordered when a carriage glided up to the front of
the café, scattering a flock of sea gulls and a few unseemly lurk-
ers. A stately oak-paneled contraption led by four gray Arabian
horses, the carriage stood for a moment before its door swung
open and a tall, broad-chested man stepped out. This, Eleonora
surmised, must be Moncef Bey. Dressed in a dark blue suit and a
red fez, he had thick black hair and the delicately arched features
of a Persian miniature. He seemed like the kind of person one
might encounter in *The Hourglass*, the kind of person one would
not be surprised to find discussing matters of great importance
in Count Olaf's drawing room or enjoying himself in the Von
Hertzogs' private box at the opera.

"Moncef Bey!"

He smiled and embraced her father heartily.

"My dear Yakob. It has been much too long."

"Indeed," her father said. "Indeed it has."

They embraced again, then the Bey turned his attention toward Eleonora, who was still seated at the table.

"And this?" he inquired. "Who is this lovely girl?"

Eleonora felt the color rise around her ears. She looked up
from her lap and gave the Bey the best smile she could muster.

"This," said Yakob, "is my daughter, Eleonora. I sincerely
hope that she won't be any inconvenience. I would have tele-
grammed ahead, but I must admit, she was a surprise for me as
well."

"Not at all," said the Bey, dismissing Yakob's concerns with
a flick of the wrist. Turning on his heels, he motioned for them
to follow. "A child will do us good, especially such a charming
young girl."

And that was that. Once Yakob's trunks were loaded, Moncef Bey said a few words to the driver and they were off. Like

most carriages in Stamboul, the Bey's coach was equipped with wooden latticework screens in place of windows. It was a contrivance, he explained, which shaded the passengers from the sun and, more important, prevented people from seeing the ladies of the house as they went about town. Fortunately, it did not prevent those inside from seeing out. As Eleonora settled into the red velvet seat, she crossed her hands in her lap and fixed her gaze on the screen opposite her, following a kaleidoscope of mosques and municipal buildings, creaky wooden mansions, plane trees, vegetable carts, and what appeared to be her flock, circling triumphantly above them.

"The city has changed a great deal," said Yakob, crossing an ankle over his knee. "Of course, it has been nearly a decade since I was last here."

The Bey looked over his guests' shoulders and seemed to lose himself for a moment in the passing scenery.

"There are new buildings every day," he said. "New cafés and shops, new schools, mosques, and markets, but the essential character of the city remains unchanged. No matter who sits on the throne, no matter how many new railroad stations are built, no matter which country's warships patrol the Bosporus, Stamboul will always be Stamboul, from now until the end of time."

"Well put," said Yakob and raised his right hand as if making a toast. "Here's to Stamboul."

Soon the carriage pulled up to the front entrance of the Bey's house, and a team of coachmen began unloading Yakob's luggage, unlatching the horses and leading them to their stables. An enormous yellow-and-white mansion seated on the edge of the water, the Bey's house faced the passing boat traffic with the languid elegance of an old man in a three-piece suit feeding pigeons from a park bench. As Moncef Bey led his guests to the front door, he gave a curious glance to Eleonora's flock, which had found roost in a large linden tree hanging over the drive.

"They followed you," her father said. "The whole flock, they followed you."

Eleonora had never doubted the fidelity of her flock; still, it was a long way from Constanta to Stamboul. She was imagining their journey across the water—drafting sea birds and secreting themselves away in empty life rafts—as she entered the antechamber of the Bey's house and her attention was drawn to a colossal crystal chandelier hanging from the middle of the ceiling. A dense forest of reflection, it looked as if it might at any moment buckle under its own weight and come crashing down on the marble staircase below. Just inside the front door, to her immediate right, was a side table scattered with visiting cards. To her left, a suit of armor stood permanent guard over the room. And at her feet, stretching more than eight meters from the front door to the foot of the staircase, lay an enormous red, blue, and green silk Hereke carpet. It was the most magnificent carpet she had ever seen, the many-flowered border surrounding a trio of telescoped medallions, within which she was able to make out depictions of Noah's Ark, the Garden of Eden, and all seven days of Creation.

"Unfortunately," said the Bey, removing his pince-nez and wiping it on the hem of his jacket, "the women's quarters are shuttered. We have not had ladies living here for some time now. But if Miss Cohen doesn't mind staying on the male side of the house, I have a room in mind that should suit her perfectly."

He paused and glanced at Eleonora for approval. His eyes flashed with a glint of moonlight when he smiled.

"Yes," she said. "I would be much obliged."

"Excellent. She is obliged. Then it is decided. Monsieur Karom, please show Miss Cohen to the Red Room."

At this, the butler emerged from his corner and, with the up-turned palm of a white glove, showed Eleonora up the stairs.

"Your room, Miss Cohen," he said, holding the door for her. "I will knock for dinner at eight."

The Red Room was, true to its name, covered with a deep-red wallpaper the same shade as kidney beans. To mitigate this crush of red, the room's wainscoting was painted a creamy white, as was the ceiling and the trim on the two sixteen-pane bay windows opposite the door. To Eleonora's left lay a four-poster bed, draped in lace curtains like an imperial litter. In front of her, just below the windows, sat a caramel-colored suede armchair and an oak writing table topped with a crystal inkwell. To her right stood the bureau and a dressing table, each with more drawers than she could think of what to put inside. She remained in the doorway for quite a long while, examining the room, its furniture, and the brilliant blue-green Tabrizi underfoot. After a week in the hull, she found it difficult to reconcile herself to the presence of such luxury, and even more so to the notion that this room, which could easily have contained their entire house in Constanta, was, for the time being at least, hers.

With careful steps, Eleonora walked along the edge of the carpet to the dressing table and leaned her face close to the mirror. She watched her breath form and vanish on the silver surface, scrunched her face up around her nose, and puffed out her cheeks. Drawing back from the mirror, she smoothed down a cowlick, smiled charmingly, and tilted her head to the left. Eleonora had seen her reflection before, at the tailor's shop in Constanta, but she had never had the chance to examine herself so closely. She leaned forward again and rested her nose on the surface of the mirror so that she could see only her eyes and the top half of her face. She tried to focus, but the harder she looked, the more blurry things became. Taking a step back, she wiped her breath off the glass and considered herself from a distance. She had no doubt that she was beautiful—people had told her so her whole life—but at the moment she did look somewhat ragged. Although she had bathed the night before, washed her clothes, and slept on a proper bed, her hair was matted, her eyes withdrawn into their sockets, and her dress little more than a formless sack.

On the off chance that she might find a more suitable dress there, Eleonora crossed the room to investigate what appeared to be a closet. Turning the knob, she opened the door a crack and found that it was indeed a closet, empty but for a suit jacket, a pair of pants, and a fez that looked to be about the right size for a boy her age. She reached a hand out to touch the fabric of the fez when she heard the door open. Breath trapped in her throat, Eleonora turned slowly and saw that the noise was caused by a wrinkled old woman in a dark blue dress. The old woman did not appear angry at her for snooping in the Bey's closet; in fact, she seemed somewhat frightened herself. Setting a stack of towels on one of the chairs next to the door, she pushed her kerchief up over a tangle of white hair and wiped her forehead with her sleeve.

"Eleonora," she said in a low voice. "You have arrived."

Eleonora was not sure how to respond to this observation, so she did not.

"I am Mrs. Damakan," said the old woman, crossing the room. "I knew your father in Constanta. Now I work for the Bey."

She took Eleonora's hand between her palms and held it for a moment before seeming to remember her purpose.

"He said you might need a change of clothes, your father did."

"Yes," Eleonora said. "I think I do."

"And it looks as if a bath wouldn't hurt either."

Mrs. Damakan smiled and led Eleonora through a connecting door to the bathroom. Covered with blue and white tiles, the room was enveloped in a damp swampy heat and the smell of birch. A porcelain tub took up one corner of the room, and in the other sat a large copper pot. Scratching the base of her neck, the handmaid mumbled a few words of delicacy before she bent down and raised Eleonora's dress over her head. She then took the copper pot under her arm and said she would return shortly, leaving Eleonora naked and alone in the middle of the bathroom. Although she was not particularly cold, Eleonora shivered and clutched her arms around her chest. Staring at the ghost of her reflection in a blue tile, she sat on the edge of the tub and waited for Mrs. Damakan to return. When she did, it was with a scrubbing cloth and a pot full of hot water.

"When I left Constanta," she said, sloshing the water into the tub, "you were no longer than my arm. Now look at you."

Eleonora looked down at herself and blushed. It had been a long while since anyone had seen her so naked. Except for the first few years of her life, she had always bathed herself, and when she changed, it was usually alone in her room. This bashfulness, however, soon dissipated in the warmth of Mrs. Damakan's presence. Holding herself on the cold porcelain rim, Eleonora lowered her legs into the tub. The bathwater was much warmer than she had expected, but after a few moments of prickly discomfort, she slid back and began to enjoy the steam on her face, the clean smell of olive oil soap, and the hot water thawing into her bones. Gently at first, cautiously almost, then with increasing force, Mrs. Damakan scrubbed her with a soapy washcloth, working her back, legs, arms, neck, and stomach with the vigor of a scullery maid scouring rice off the bottom of a pot.

Afterward, wrapped up in a thick white towel, Eleonora felt like a newborn baby, as if all the discomfort and worry of the past week had been scrubbed away and was swirling down the drain with the bathwater. She was still tired and her hip bones stuck out like tent poles, but she felt like a new person.

"Now let us hope this fits."

Eleonora turned and saw Mrs. Damakan standing behind her, a beautiful blue velvet dress draped over her arm. Handing Eleonora a fresh set of underclothes, she helped her into the dress and buttoned it up the back. As Mrs. Damakan secured the last clasp, the butler, Monsieur Karom, knocked at the open door. He conducted Eleonora wordlessly downstairs to the dining room. Her father and the Bey were already seated, but both rose as she entered.

"Stunning," said the Bey. He pulled out the chair next to him and motioned for her to be seated. "That dress really does suit you beautifully."

Timid in the light of the Bey's compliments, Eleonora pulled the lace collar of her dress away from her neck and glanced at her father. He had changed into his best suit. A proud smile rose under his freshly trimmed mustache as he reached across the table to squeeze her hand.

"You look beautiful, Ellie."

A moment later, Monsieur Karom emerged from the kitchen with three roasted game hens crouched on beds of saffron rice. Eleonora normally would have paid more attention to the conversation, about business and the political scene in Stamboul, but famished as she was, her concentration was reserved for her game hen and the tiny, plump currants buried in the rice. She did, however, overhear a piece of the conversation in which her

father and the Bey discussed the circumstances of Mrs. Damakan's niece. She had been with the Bey for a number of years
before marrying a young Tartar man who made his living as a
blacksmith outside Smyrna. The dress Eleonora was wearing,
in fact, had once belonged to Mrs. Damakan's niece. The two
women had brought it and a few other pieces of clothing to sell
when they arrived in Stamboul, though for some reason this particular dress never found its way to the clothing bazaar. After
a dessert of quince pudding, the men retired to the library and
Eleonora, exhausted, went upstairs to bed.

The next morning, rested and revived, they took the Bey's
carriage to the Galata station, posted a telegram to Ruxandra,
and rode a red lacquer funicular car up the hill to Le Grande Rue
de Pera. Standing at the base of the gently sloping boulevard,
Eleonora felt as if she had been dropped into the middle of Bucharest or Paris, as if she had stepped into the pages of *The Hourglass*
or some other equally elegant book. Watching the fashionable
European ladies fan out into the crowd, Eleonora closed her eyes
and inhaled the sweet, tannic smell of sugared almonds drifting
down the street from a vendor in front of Café Europa.

"Come, Miss Cohen," said the Bey, his heels clicking against
the cobblestones. "I think you will take a special interest in our
destination."

In his gray three-piece suit and red wool fez, Moncef Bey cut
a striking figure. Even the European ladies watched with silent
approval as he led Eleonora and Yakob up the street—past a
haberdasher, a pharmacist, and a photography studio—stopping
finally in front of a shop with the words *Madame Poiret, Dress-
maker* written across the window in gold. As they entered, a bell
tinkled and the woman at the counter, presumably Mme. Poiret
herself, looked down at them over her eyeglasses.

"Good afternoon," she said. "May I help you?"

"We would like to have a dress made," said the Bey, sitting on a divan in front of a triptych of mirrors. "For the young lady."

The young lady, Eleonora realized, was herself.

"Really." Her father coughed into his handkerchief. "Moncef. There's no need."

"Oh, but I object," said the Bey. "There is every need."

"She needs new clothes, of course, but I think this shop is a bit beyond our means."

Mme. Poiret raised her eyebrows and ran a hand through her graying brown hair.

"I can tell that your products are of the finest quality," Yakob continued, addressing himself now to Mme. Poiret. "But she's just a little girl and we are, well, we don't want to be any trouble to anyone."

Still seated on the divan, the Bey crossed his legs and, pulling out a gold pocket watch, flipped it open to glance at the time.

"I insist," he said. "And truly, it's no trouble. We were lucky Mrs. Damakan had this dress on hand, but every girl should have at least three beautiful dresses. Don't you agree, Miss Cohen?"

Eleonora fiddled with the ruffles at her waist. It was true. She couldn't very well wear the same dress for the rest of her time in Stamboul, and the samples in the window really were quite beautiful. More than a new dress, though, Eleonora most wanted not to upset anyone, not her father and certainly not the Bey.

"Of course," Mme. Poiret interjected finally. "A young lady without a beautiful dress is like a swan without feathers, and one can't very well think she will do with just one or two. Now, Miss Cohen, if you will have a seat, we can choose the fabric that best suits you."

"Very well," said her father, seating himself next to Eleonora. "I have been overruled."

They emerged quite some time later with a stack of white paper packages and rode the funicular back down the hill. In addition to a more formal silk evening gown with puffed sleeves and a large bow, Moncef Bey bought Eleonora three everyday dresses, two pairs of shoes, and a raft of what Mme. Poiret called the necessary accessories. The dresses would be finished within a few days, but the shoes and accessories they could take with them.

"Thank you, Moncef," her father said as they clattered over the Galata Bridge. "We can settle up after our visit to Haci Bekir."

"Yes," said Eleonora. "Thank you. I really do appreciate it."

"Not at all," said the Bey, waving them both off. "Not at all."

Just before the entrance to the Egyptian Bazaar, the carriage turned up a steep alleyway crammed with market stalls, stevedores, and mules. They turned left, right, and left again, before stopping at the top of a dingy cul-de-sac rowed in on either side by gold merchants. Disembarking, they walked past a line of old men fingering prayer beads over tea and backgammon. At the base of the cul-de-sac was a battered green door that led into the storeroom of the most important carpet dealer in the city, a Syrian by the name of Haci Bekir. Eleonora had heard stories from her father about Haci Bekir and his hoard of carpets, but to see the storeroom with her own eyes was something else entirely. Lit with a single gas lamp and whatever sun could make its way through the dirty windows overhead, the cavernous room was lined on either side with piles and piles of carpets, each as tall as a man. There must have been at least a thousand carpets in that room alone and many more in the catacombs that adjoined it.

"Moncef Bey."

An obese, pockmarked man dressed in an immaculate white robe and green fez appeared from behind one of the piles. Haci Bekir raised his arm in greeting before lumbering across the room.

"Mr. Cohen," said the Bey, coughing into his fist. "I would like you to meet my friend and business partner, the esteemed Haci Abelaziz Ibrahim Bekir."

Nodding, Haci Bekir reached out and violently shook Yakob's hand. Then, motioning to the bench that ran along one wall of the store, he clasped his hands together and said a few words to the Bey. Since Haci Bekir spoke only Arabic, Moncef Bey was compelled to translate.

"If you don't mind," he said, "Haci Bekir would like to examine the carpets you have brought."

"Yes, of course."

Stroking the ends of his mustache, Eleonora's father watched impassively as the shop boy unlatched his trunks and began removing their contents. In the time it took to drink the small glasses of tea that Haci Bekir offered them, the boy had removed all of the carpets. At Haci Bekir's direction, the boy laid them out into two piles. Sucking his teeth, Haci Bekir pulled down on his jowls and glanced at the carpets lining the walls of his storeroom. Then, clearing his throat, he pointed to the smaller of the two piles and said a few words to the Bey. Somewhat taken aback, the Bey began to ask a question, but Haci Bekir shook his head and repeated those same three words, blowing up toward his nose as if trying to get a mosquito off his face.

"Haci Bekir says that your carpets are very beautiful," the Bey began. "But at this time he would like only the pieces on his left. He can offer five hundred pounds for the lot."

Eleonora watched her father's reaction closely. Five hundred pounds was a great deal of money, but she could tell from his face that the carpets were worth much more than that. At the same time, she thought he might agree to the price. Haci Bekir did not seem like the kind of man one would want to push too far. He had twice snapped at the shop boy and raised a hand to strike him before remembering the assembled company. Eleonora troubled a loose fringe of carpet with the toe of her shoe as she watched her father rise from the bench and amble toward the center of the room. Without so much as a glance at Haci Bekir, he squatted down next to the carpets in question, lifted them off the pile, and laid them out gently, one by one, like a farmer tending his crop. Whereas Haci Bekir had given each piece no more than ten or fifteen seconds, Yakob took his time, turning up the corners and bringing the weave to his nose. When he was finished inspecting the carpets, he spread his legs and pressed his lips together. The two men stared at each other for quite some time before Yakob spoke.

"I will sell them for no less than nine hundred."

The Bey began to translate, but he was cut short. Snorting in disbelief, in mock pain and insult, Haci Bekir repeated his previous offer, then said he could raise it to six hundred. This was his final offer, he said, through the Bey.

"Eight hundred," said Yakob.

When the Bey translated this counteroffer, Haci Bekir bit his bottom lip and muttered something under his breath. The Bey flinched.

"What did he say?" Yakob asked.

"Nothing of importance," said the Bey. "He was just speaking to himself."

The haggling went on for nearly an hour, Haci Bekir shouting and waving his arms in the air while Eleonora's father stood rooted to eight hundred.

"That is what they are worth," he said over and again as Haci Bekir raised his price in erratic fits and starts.

Finally, when it looked as if Haci Bekir was on the verge of collapse, his face red and wheezing, when they had reached an unsurpassable barrier, Yakob relented.

"Seven hundred and fifty."

At that, Haci Bekir sprang from his corner and, shaking Yakob's hand, began barking orders at the shop boy. Before there was time for a second thought, the carpets were packed up, the money was exchanged, and they were on their way out the door.

On the carriage ride home, after being rebuffed again in his offers to repay the Bey for the dresses, Yakob asked what it was that Haci Bekir had muttered under his breath.

"You don't want to know," said the Bey.

Yakob considered this and, nodding, glanced at Eleonora.

"You're right," he said. "We probably don't."

Chapter Eight

The ceiling of the Sultan's audience chamber was decorated with a gilt, purple, and green design, an interlooping nest of circles that always reminded him of a peacock's tail unfurled in sunlight. By the standards of the palace, it was a relatively small room, no larger than the quarters of the head physician or the confectioners' kitchen, but the audience chamber played an essential role in the affairs of the empire. It was here that the Sultan heard the concerns and requests brought to him by his subjects, here that he came in contact with the daily existence of his dominion. Flanked on either side by a pair of deaf palace guards, His Excellency Sultan Abdulhamid II sat cross-legged on his divan, leaning forward to listen to the Sanjak Bey of Novi Pazar present his appeal. Apparently, a provincial tax collector had been set upon by a mob of landowners and strung up in the town square. In light of these events, the Sanjak Bey was requesting military assistance from the palace; a battalion or two would be sufficient, he said, to preserve order.

It was not at all likely that imperial troops would be committed to such a distant and irrelevant conflagration, but seeing as the Sanjak Bey had come all the way from Novi Pazar to make his request in person, it seemed only right to let him present his petition. Making the case for immediate action, the goat-faced former military officer trampled about the audience chamber, pausing occasionally to scratch the back of his head or wipe a fleck of spittle from his lips. Before being tapped to administer the territory of Novi Pazar, the Sanjak Bey had served for thirty years in the Third Division of the Ottoman Army, where he was known primarily for his brutality. It was rumored, for example, that he had ordered the massacre of an entire Bulgarian town for refusing to quarter his troops. As far as Abdulhamid was concerned, such behavior should not be rewarded, but General Sipahoğlu had suggested the Sanjak Bey specifically for the position and the Grand Vizier had concurred. Unfortunately, the Sanjak Bey had proven inept so far as an administrator, unable to put down even the simplest tax revolt. It was yet another instance in which the Sultan would have done best to keep his own counsel, another instance in which he was failed by his advisors.

Leaning back onto his elbow, Abdulhamid examined the sleeve of his caftan and, rubbing the fabric between his thumb and middle finger, felt the individual cords of silk against each other. There were so many other, more important matters he and Jamaludin Pasha could be attending to. As they listened to the Sanjak Bey's increasingly irksome appeal, the Serbo-Bulgarian War was intensifying, Jews and Poles were being expelled en masse from Prussia. Why should he concern himself with a distant tax revolt? He was much more worried about the Greek nationalist cell Jamaludin Pasha had uncovered in Selonika, or the rising clamor of the constitutionalists advocating for a new parliament. As he abided this barbarian in administrator's clothing, the Sultan let his mind wander back over the previous year, landing as he often did on that maddening conference of Great Powers in Berlin. At the personal request of Bismarck, Abdulhamid had sent a team of his best diplomats to aid Sadoullah Bey in Berlin, but his men turned out to be nothing more than pawns, extra votes in support of the Prussian position. While the Great

Powers divided the spoils of a continent, his emissaries smoked and drank aquavit with the representatives of Sweden-Norway. The once great Ottoman Empire, its territory stretched from the gates of Vienna to the shores of the Persian Gulf, respected and feared around the world, was equal now to a middling nation of fishermen and drunks.

"As you know," said Jamaludin Pasha, finally interrupting the Sanjak Bey's appeal, "we have in the past ordered troops to facilitate the collection of taxes, in the Levant and in parts of Bosnia. You will appreciate, however, that our troops are a limited resource and thus we cannot pursue this policy in every case."

"Of course."

"In an ideal world," the Grand Vizier continued, smoothing down the ends of his mustache, "we would like to be able to assist with every predicament that is brought to us, we would like to be able to send aid wherever aid is needed, but as you know, this is not an ideal world."

"Far from it."

Jamaludin Pasha paused to write a few words in his notebook.

"I hope you will not interpret our inaction as a slight."

"Not at all."

"It is not that we are not concerned with the recent events in Novi Pazar, or the collection of taxes. To the contrary, we are very concerned with both. Given the best of circumstances, there is no doubt that we would send the troops you requested forthwith. However, in a world of not-unlimited resources, we must prioritize."

"Of course," said the Sanjak Bey. "Thank you, Jamaludin Pasha, for allowing me to voice my concerns."

"You are most welcome."

"And thank you," said the Sanjak Bey, bowing deeply to the Sultan. "Your Excellency, I am honored you would deign to accept an audience with someone as humble as myself."

"I am always eager to advance the condition of my subjects," said the Sultan. "Especially those in the more distant provinces."

"Yes, Your Excellency. You can have every confidence that the citizens of Novi Pazar are advancing apace."

"I am glad to hear that," said the Sultan. "And please excuse us for cutting your audience short."

With that, a palace guard saw the Sanjak Bey of Novi Pazar out of the audience chamber and the door was closed behind him.

The Sultan reorganized himself on the divan before turning to the Grand Vizier.

"Tell me," he said. "What further business needs attending to before lunch?"

"We have received another letter from von Siemens."

Abdulhamid released a puff of breath through his nose and closed his eyes. It was beneath his station to attend constantly to these bankers and industrialists. And yet, he knew the Baghdad Railway could not be built without their backing.

"How do you suggest we respond?"

"I would recommend inviting him to the palace. You can speak with him briefly, in general terms, and leave the details to the chairs of the Treasury and the Public Debt Administration."

The Sultan ran his thumb along the edge of the cushion.

"They will be involved?" he asked. "The Public Debt Administration."

"I imagine they would like to be."

Abdulhamid pursed his lips and nodded. This Public Debt Administration was a clear violation of his sovereignty, but there was nothing he could do to drive it away. The empire was underwater in debt and these were the terms they had worked out to pay the money back. Or, rather, these were the terms imposed upon them.

"If we want to modernize the hinterlands," Jamaludin Pasha interjected, "we must facilitate a steady flow of goods."

"I am aware," said the Sultan, sharply, "of the arguments in favor of building the railroad. Just as I am aware of Berlin's desire for a Stamboul-Baghdad link. Just as I am aware of your predilection toward the Kaiser. I will ask, however, that you not interrupt my thoughts."

"Forgive me, Your Excellency, I apologize."

"You can send the invitation," the Sultan said. "See to it immediately."

"Very well," said the Grand Vizier, standing. "Your Excellency, I will."

Although the Sultan knew there was no need to stand on ceremony with his advisors, he felt somewhat restless following this exchange and was struck by a strong desire to get outside into the clear air. Nodding to the palace guards on either side of his divan, the Sultan ducked out the back door of the audience chamber and, retrieving his new field glasses from the Library of Ahmet III, slipped through the pages' quarters to the Tulip Garden. It was an unseasonably bright morning and, although none of the tulips were in bloom, the constant glow of the sun warmed the earth like an old lover. The air was brusque on his face as he wandered through the dormant tulip beds and around the inside of the Baghdad Kiosk to the Elephant Garden. An effective ruler needed, more than anything, to maintain a proper distance from the events that occurred within his domain. If he allowed himself to fret over the particulars of every battle and infrastructure project, he would never be able to focus on the decisions that truly mattered. Unfortunately, the Grand Vizier had proven time and again unable to understand this concept.

Pausing to adjust his caftan, Abdulhamid seated himself on the bench beneath his favorite sour cherry trees. It was not a particularly good time of year for bird-watching, but one never knew. Unlatching the blue silk-lined case, he removed his field glasses and scanned the length of the straits. These new field glasses, made on special order by Emil Busch himself, were far and away clearer than any he had ever used; still, there wasn't much to see. A few gulls hovered around the squat, crenellated bulk of Galata Tower and a white-tailed eagle was perched on the minaret of Ali Pasha Mosque. The Sultan was about to put down the glasses when he saw something strange: a flock of what looked like hoopoes, of a peculiar purple-and-white coloring, congregated around a house near the Beşiktaş Pier. He watched them for a few minutes, wondering what might have attracted the flock to this particular roost. Aside from the bright yellow-and-white of its facade, he could think of no reason why the flock should be drawn to this house, especially not at this time of year.

When the Sultan put his glasses back in their case, he was surprised to find a pair of the same purple-and-white hoopoes perched in the branches of the tree above him. They were talking among themselves and pecking at the lonely white buds tricked by the warmth of the previous few days into believing it was spring. Peering up at the birds, Abdulhamid followed their fluttering movement from branch to branch. He had always been enamored with the hoopoe, ever since his first bird-watching excursions as a young prince. It was a portentous and regal bird, with all the pomp and finery of a sovereign. Yet, at the same time, it was one of the more sensible members of the aviary, not above bathing in dust or fashioning its home from feces. It was a hoopoe, he recalled, that brought word of Sheba to King Solomon and a hoopoe that, in Farid il-din Attar's famous poem, persuaded the other birds to go off in search of the great Simurgh. Abdulhamid was not usually very good with Latin names, but he could always remember the name for hoopoe, *Upupa Epops*.

He said the name aloud and, as he did, the smaller of the two birds hopped down to a branch just above his head. The two stared at each other for a long moment before the hoopoe fluttered down and alighted next to him on the bench. Tilting its head, as if in expectation or inquiry, the bird hopped closer to him. Not sure what the hoopoe wanted, Abdulhamid snapped a bud off the branch above him and held it out. Hopping twice, the bird took the bud in its mouth and, as if that was precisely what it had been waiting for, it flew off across the straits.

Chapter Nine

※

The remainder of Eleonora's and her father's days in Stamboul were spent in much the same manner as the first. Each morning after a breakfast of flatbread, honey, olives, and crumbly white cheese, they set out in Moncef Bey's carriage and rode the funicular up the hill to La Grande Rue de Pera, where the Bey insisted on buying yet more presents for Eleonora and even some for Yakob. It was a situation they were both somewhat uncomfortable with at first, Eleonora because she had never received presents from anyone, and her father because he didn't, as he said repeatedly, want to inconvenience their host. Yakob tried more than once to repay the Bey for his kindnesses, but such gestures were firmly repulsed. Moncef Bey insisted that shopping was no inconvenience at all; in fact, it was a pleasure. Having no children, nephews, nieces, or anyone else to buy presents for, he relished the opportunity to spend his money on such a fine young lady. What, after all, was money for? When they finished shopping, they would gather up their packages and pause for lunch at one of the more fashionable restaurants on the boulevard, sampling borek and iskander, grilled fish, kofte rolled in crushed pistachios, and a crunchy orange-dusted pastry called kunafa. Then it was back down the hill to Eminounu, where Moncef Bey had arranged a string of appointments for Yakob, primarily in the textile bazaar but also in the sun-dappled porticos of the Grand Bazaar. In the late afternoon, they returned finally to the Bey's house and rested, each savoring a short spell of privacy.

Eleonora typically passed this time upstairs in her room, reading the Bey's copy of *The Hourglass* deep in the armchair next to the bay window. She had come upon the book quite by accident, poking around the library on her second night in Stamboul. She was halfway up the stacks on a ladder, browsing through the Bey's prodigious collection of atlases, when the familiar blue-and-silver binding of *The Hourglass* caught her eye. She spent the rest of that evening, and every evening afterward, ensconced in what is known as the late, or Trieste, volumes of the epic novel. Sitting curled up in her armchair, with *The Hourglass* balanced on the edge of her knee, Eleonora truly could not have been more content. What a joy it was to read in freedom, to fall into a book without the fear of Ruxandra peering over her shoulder. Consumed though she was by the book, Eleonora would glance up occasionally at the window, following the flutter of her flock from eaves to branch or the stacks of a steamer as it floated past the dimming orange hills.

She finished the final volume of *The Hourglass* just a few days before she and her father were set to leave Stamboul. Although a considerable piece of her wanted to dive back into the first volume and read the entire book again, this time with the eventual fate of its characters in mind, she decided it would be best to take the night off. Dinner that evening was an eggplant and lamb stew with béchamel sauce, following which the Bey led them down the hall to the library and they sat ranged around the fireplace in a trio of light-brown suede armchairs. A dark, wood-paneled space decorated with antique globes and navigational instruments, the library was lined from floor to ceiling with books: philological treatises, geographies, encyclopedias, biographical dictionaries, poems, novels, and more than a few religious tracts, all bound in red, blue, green, and brown morocco leather. Monsieur Karom served pistachio baklava and tulip-shaped glasses of black tea while the Bey set up a game of backgammon for Yakob and himself. Adorned with a sunburst of tiny cedar rhombuses, the Bey's backgammon board was a masterwork of craftsmanship and elegance. Watching his large hands glide over the surface of the board, pushing the agate and glass pieces into formation, Eleonora tried to make sense of the game, why the pieces were arranged as they were and how they might move about the board.

"Have you ever played?" the Bey asked, meeting her gaze.

Eleonora felt the color rise to her cheeks.

"No."

"I could teach you if you like. It won't take long."

"Thank you," she said. "But I think I'll just watch for now, if that's not too much of a bother."

She looked up at the Bey and then to her father, who was engaged in clipping off the end of a cigar.

"No bother at all, Ellie. If you have any questions just ask."

Although they were gentle men, Moncef Bey and Yakob played backgammon with unrestrained force, slapping the board with their pieces and throwing the ivory dice hard into corners. Every so often they would pause to take a sip of tea or exhale a cloud of cigar smoke, but their rhythm was the game, the clatter of ivory on wood, the shuffle of agate and glass. They played without stopping to consider their moves, with the careless confidence of a blacksmith who has pounded the same mold thousands of times. Neither of them spoke until the final roll of the game.

"I forgot to mention," said Moncef Bey, rubbing the dice between his palms. "I was invited to a cruise tomorrow in honor of the American Vice Consul's seventy-fifth birthday."

Eleonora's father tapped a finger of ash into the silver tray next to him.

"I'm sure Ellie and I can find a way to occupy ourselves while you are on the cruise," he said. "Perhaps we can visit Kiz Kulesi or Rumelihisarı."

"No," the Bey said as he threw a double-four, winning the game. "What I meant to say is that I would like for you and Miss Cohen to join me. I don't usually attend such events, but I thought that perhaps you would enjoy it. And I can assure you, it is no inconvenience. Under normal circumstances, it's true, I probably wouldn't attend, but it will be good for me to show my face in society."

Yakob picked up a die and clicked the edge of his thumbnail against it.

"We truly do appreciate all you've done for us," he said, looking to Eleonora for concurrence. "I know both of us will be very sad to leave Stamboul."

Eleonora narrowed her eyes and tilted her head. She knew all along that they would, at some point, have to leave the Bey and Stamboul and the routine she had so quickly become accustomed to, but knowing one has to leave is much different than being faced with an impending departure. At some point, everyone must leave this world, but who is ready to go? Eleonora looked down at her new black patent-leather shoes and tapped the heels together.

"Will you play a game with me, Tata?"

She asked not so much because she wanted to play but because she was worried that this would be her last chance to play on the Bey's board. As the question hung in the air between them, her mind swarmed with other last chances, unlikely prospects, and never-agains.

"I'll play," the Bey interjected. "That is, Yakob, if you don't mind."

"No, no, of course not. There's nothing wrong with a little backgammon. It's just, it's been a long couple of weeks."

"Naturally," said the Bey and, rotating the table, began setting up for a new game. "Are you quite certain you understand the rules?"

"Yes," said Eleonora, staring hard at the board. "I think so."

He handed her the dice, which she took and, after a moment's pause, feeling the cool ivory in her palm, she rolled, a one-two, the worst opening possible. With a glance at her father, Eleonora leaned forward. Considering her options, she slid one of her pieces three spaces to the left.

"Are you sure you want to do that?" the Bey asked. "It leaves you open to attack."

She nodded.

"You see," he continued, hypothetically moving his pieces onto hers. "If I roll either a two or a four, I can bump you."

"I'm quite sure."

Shrugging, the Bey picked up the dice and rolled, a three-five.

"Well then," he said, taking the last sip of his tea. "I stand corrected."

By the end of the first game, Yakob was snoring, a gentle, grumbling reminder of how late it was. Still, they finished the game, which Eleonora won, and another, which she won as well, before deciding that it was time for bed.

Guided by the flicker of an oil lamp, Eleonora trudged upstairs to her room, to the room she would soon have to leave. In less than forty-eight hours, she would bid farewell to this house, the Bey, the entire city. And for what? A boat ride home and the tedious drudgery of life in Constanta. Stepping over the threshold, Eleonora noticed one of the windows in her room was open. A dark breeze rustled the flame of her lamp and she shivered. As she turned to close the door behind her, a bird swooped down from one of the bedposts and alighted on the open windowsill. It was a member of her flock, and it seemed to want something. Setting the lamp on the bed stand, Eleonora crossed her room and knelt down in front of the windowsill, resting her chin in the valley of her arms. The hoopoe had brought with it a precipitate cherry bud, green mostly, with a peek of white petals visible at the top. Instead of flying away, it looked directly at her, jerking the purple-and-white-streaked feathers of its crown.

She picked up the cherry bud and brought it to her nose.

"Why can't we stay in Stamboul?" she asked aloud.

At the sound of her voice, the hoopoe cocked its head to the side, as if to listen more carefully. Eleonora looked out at the hazy city, sparkling like an errant school of stars caught up in the dark net of the straits. As she inhaled to speak, the city fell into an expectant hush. The earth slowed on its axis.

"I wish I could stay. I wish I could stay in Stamboul forever."

At this, her visitor hopped to the edge of the sill and flew off into darkness. Pumping its wings, it banked down toward the water and, joining the rest of the flock, disappeared into the night.

She woke that next morning to Mrs. Damakan standing in the doorway of her room with a stack of towels and a copper cauldron filled with hot water. Although Eleonora had been somewhat reticent of her first bath, she had come to look forward to Mrs. Damakan's visits, the prickly-hot water, the soft smell of jasmine soap, and the crisp, warm towel at the end. Her favorite part of their routine came after the bath itself. When Eleonora was dried and dressed, Mrs. Damakan would sit her on one of the red velvet chairs next to the door and comb out her hair, humming Tartar folk songs that tugged at Eleonora's earliest memories like the shadow of a partially reconstructed dream. It was not until she was dressed and ready for breakfast that Eleonora realized this might be the last time Mrs. Damakan bathed her.

When Eleonora, her father, and the Bey arrived at the Beşiktaş Pier, her entire flock of hoopoes was waiting silently in the branches of a tree overhanging the ferry building. After the guests of the Vice Consul boarded and the boat pushed away from the pier, a small contingent of the flock broke off and followed along overhead, but even then they kept a wary distance. Moncef Bey glanced up at the birds, then up the shore toward his house, where they had spent much of the past few weeks. It seemed as if he were about to say something, then held himself back.

There was a sharp breeze blowing along the Bosporus and the sky was the same bright blue color as the tiles inside Sultan Ahmed Mosque. Holding the rail with one hand, Eleonora waved her father's handkerchief to the dock workers and boatmen milling about the ferry building. She was wearing a pale green gown with short puffy sleeves and a ruffle of taffeta cascading down the front, an adaptation of a style displayed in Mme. Poiret's shop window. How long ago that first trip to Pera seemed, and yet they had been in Stamboul less than three weeks. She had seen so much of the city, of life, and now, no matter what she said, no matter how much she protested, they would be leaving soon. The thought of their impending departure was almost too much to stand. If only she could stay in Stamboul forever.

Signaling a passing waiter, the Bey lifted a pair of drinks off his tray and handed one to Yakob.

"Cheers," he said, raising his glass.

Yakob raised his as well and they clinked.

"Cheers."

Among those present that afternoon, according to Moncef Bey, were the Lady Katherine de Berg, the Prussian military attaché, an avant-garde Viennese painter of some renown, the French Ambassador, Madame Corvel, and of course the American Vice Consul. The Consul himself was not on hand, having been called away that morning on urgent business regarding the Prussian deportations. Leaning her shoulders against the rail, Eleonora took in the progress of the party, the red-coated waiters steering caviar and canapés through a crowd of tuxedos and wide-bustled dresses, drinks in every hand and in every drink a piece of ice reflecting the sun. The Bey was talking with an older American lady while Yakob, finishing his drink, picked a puffed pastry from the tray of a passing waiter. As her father popped the appetizer into his mouth, Eleonora spotted Reverend James Muehler making his way toward them through the crowd.

"My dear Mr. Cohen. What a pleasant surprise!"

They shook hands vigorously, then Yakob took the priest by his cheeks and kissed him on the forehead.

"This—" said Yakob when they finished embracing. "Moncef Bey, I would like you to meet my good friend and former cabin mate, Reverend James Muehler. He is the Rector of Robert's College and an American from the state of Connecticut."

"Pleased," said the Bey and they shook hands.

"And this, Reverend Muehler, is my most generous host, friend, and business partner, Moncef Barcous Bey. You will not find a better Turk in Stamboul."

"Moncef Barcous Bey," said the Reverend. "I have been hearing that name since the day I set foot in Stamboul. I must say, I am very happy to finally meet you in person."

"Your reputation precedes you as well, Reverend Muehler."

"All good, I hope."

The Bey took a sip of his drink and smiled.

"Mostly good."

"That's good enough for me."

"And I assume you know the young Miss Cohen," said the Bey, stepping aside to bring Eleonora into the conversation. "A very fine young lady on every account and, as I discovered last night, quite an expert backgammon player."

"Is that so?"

Eleonora averted her eyes, looking down at the contrast of her pale green shoes with the deck.

"She beat me twice in a row," said the Bey. "And soundly. I wish I could attribute her success to luck, but as we say, a person does not seek luck, luck seeks the person."

"Indeed," said the Reverend, continuing in the slightly more sonorous tone he reserved for quotations. "Luck affects everything. Let your hook always be cast. In the stream where you least expect it, there will be a fish."

"I don't think it's luck at all," Yakob interjected. "As I told you on the ship. She's read nearly every book there is."

"Every book?" Reverend Muehler repeated. He caught Eleonora's eye and grinned. "Well then, Miss Cohen, if you have read every book, which is your favorite?"

"Go on, Ellie," said her father, resting a hand on her shoulder. "Tell him your favorite."

She looked up at the trio of men, squinting a bit in the sun. The truth was, she hadn't read more than a few dozen books.

"So far," she said, "my favorite is *The Hourglass*."

"How old did you say you are?" the Reverend asked, bending down to her level.

"Eight years old."

"Eight," he repeated. "And already reading novels? That is very impressive. Very impressive."

Reverend Muehler was on the verge of expanding this thought when a bubbly young woman tapped him on the shoulder and whispered something in his ear. She was wearing a striking mandarin-colored dress, the bright orange fabric trimmed at the bodice with white lace and gathered at the back into a bustle of enormous proportions. Eleonora thought she resembled an exotic snail.

"Excuse me," said the Reverend. "Madame Corvel has reminded me of an urgent matter that we must attend to. It will only take a moment."

"Not at all," said the Bey. "In fact, I was just planning to show the Cohens the view from the stern of the boat. It is quite stunning. Feel free to join us there if you like."

"Excellent," said Reverend Muehler and, turning to Yakob, added, "My friend, we must discuss business. Don't think I've forgotten about that Tabrizi carpet you recommended for my office."

"Yes," said Yakob. "The Hereke. We can discuss that later."

"Later," said the Reverend as he was led away by Madame Corvel.

The view from the stern was indeed stunning. The light bright blue of the morning had slipped a few shades toward yellow and there were, as far as Eleonora could see, no clouds in the sky. Topkapi Palace had shrunk to the size of her thumb held out at arm's length, and all but the tips of the tallest minarets were obscured by hills. At this point, the banks of the Bosporus were overwhelmed by a thick swath of conifers, interrupted every few kilometers by a small village, a dock, and a few men in tattered fezzes drinking tea. The air was crisp and smoky, with a touch of pine. Inhaling deeply, Eleonora examined and deposited the smell in her memory. This would be the smell by which she would remember Stamboul.

Memory, however, is as fickle as fate.

Not long after the Bey brought them back to the stern, the ship hit a patch of rough water. At the first jolt, Eleonora grabbed for her father's arm and he grabbed for the rail. Swallowing a grimace, Yakob turned to ask his daughter a question. He looked as if he had been shaken by a ghost, his cheeks sunken and paled the same color as her dress. Mumbling something about seasickness, he clutched his stomach and, rushing to the head, nearly tripped over a loose oar.

"Excuse me."

As her father's footsteps fell away, the sounds of the celebration drifted back from the front deck. Eleonora blinked, and the Bey opened his mouth to speak. Then there was an explosion, the ship lurched hard to port, and, amid screams below deck, began quickly to sink.

Chapter Ten

The morning came smothered in a heap of goose down and shadows. Muffled footsteps mingled with whispers and a small flight of cormorants swept over the water like marionettes, their caws swirling with the calls of early-morning bread peddlers. In time, these lonely cries faded into the general traffic of the city, the clatter of carriages and fish mongers, a distant call to the faithful, and the plaintive ululation of stray dogs, all evidence that life and Stamboul would continue. In spite of everything, they would go on.

As the morning insinuated itself into her room, Eleonora lay curled around herself like a dried tea leaf, shrouded in a tangle of bedclothes and breathing the short, ragged breaths of restless sleep. A knock at the door drew her further from the world of sleep; still, she was only awake enough to know she wanted to go back. There was a shuffle of slippers in the doorway and the dull clank of metal against her bed stand. Then she felt the thin, calloused hand of Mrs. Damakan resting at the back of her neck. Eleonora shivered as the warmth of this other body spread through her limbs.

"Your breakfast is on the bed table," said Mrs. Damakan and she shuffled out of the room.

Eleonora waited for the click of the door closing before she rolled onto her back. The smell of hardboiled eggs and flatbread seeped under the lid of the breakfast tray, but she was not hungry, not in the least. Pulling the blanket over her head, she closed her eyes and curled back into a ball. Her head throbbed against the walls of her skull, and the lining of her stomach roiled with apprehension. She was fully awake now, but her memory of the night before was still wavy and indistinct, like a camel caravan cresting over the horizon of a massive dune. There was the cold sweetness of water, a jellyfish stinging her ankle, the hairy outstretched arm of the Bey, then, all of a sudden, the realization that her father was dead.

She gagged and felt her stomach rise into her throat. She exhaled until her lungs were empty, then let them fill again with air. It was a heavy blow. A life-shattering tragedy of the sort we comfort ourselves into thinking only happens to other people, to characters in a novel, to neighbors, or to the poor souls one reads about in the newspaper. And here it was happening to her. Clutching a pillow to her stomach, she stared up at the white lace canopy over her bed. Her father was dead, lying at the bottom of the Bosporus, in a pile of bodies on the shore, freshly buried in the earth, or somewhere else she couldn't even imagine, but dead nevertheless. She approached this same idea over and over, from hundreds of different perspectives, but the thought of it was like looking into the sun. You lost your sight trying to see.

All that morning, a swirl of malevolent questions circled her bed like ravens, landing sporadically with a thump to whisper in her ear. What about the hoopoe on the windowsill? What about her wish to stay in Stamboul? Could it be that the boat accident, her father's death and the death of nearly two dozen others, was no accident at all? Could it be that her wish, her childish desire to stay in Stamboul, had caused all this? Eleonora shivered and pulled the pillow down over her head. She wanted to fall asleep, to wake up and find everything back to normal, or at least to put these questions out of her mind for a few hours. But no matter what she wanted, the grounds of fate were fixed, and that blackening unwelcome swirl followed her into her dreams with ever more persistence and bile.

Sometime later that afternoon, or perhaps it was the next, the Bey knocked at her door and called out her name. She was awake, but she did not respond. She did not feel much like talking. She did not feel much like anything, really, but lying in bed—and even that was for lack of a better option. After knocking and calling out twice more, the Bey opened the door. He wore his usual crisp blue suit and tie, but his face was rumpled and his eyes sunken in exhaustion. He did not notice her at first, buried under a pile of blankets and pillows, like a frightened fox hidden in the hollow of a tree, but eventually their eyes met. They regarded each other for a long while before he closed the door behind him and took a seat on the red velvet chair next to her bed.

"I have attempted to contact your aunt, Ruxandra."

Eleonora poked her face out into the entrance of her hollow so she could better understand what the Bey was saying.

"I'm not sure how much you remember," he began again, clasping his hands in front of his mouth. "Of yesterday."

She felt her lip quiver as she nodded, affirming that she remembered, that she knew.

"The authorities are searching still for survivors," he said, placing a hand on the corner of her bed. "Though it's highly unlikely they will find any."

In the silence that followed, the Bey stood and walked over to the window from which Eleonora had made her wish. He scanned the activity on the water below. Then, pulling his watch out of his vest pocket, flipped it open and shut a few times.

"I have attempted to contact your aunt," he repeated, smoothing down the ends of his mustache. "Unfortunately, I haven't yet received a reply."

The Bey crossed the room and seated himself again in the chair next to her bed.

"Surely she will reply soon," he continued. "In the meantime, you are more than welcome to stay here."

Eleonora nodded. She thought she should say something, thought that saying something was in order, but the idea of talking, of articulating her thoughts into the world, was too much to bear.

"Are there any other family members I should attempt to contact?"

Her chin tensed and she could feel the tears gathering along her eyelashes. There was no one else. She was alone in the world, with no family to speak of but Ruxandra. With a whimper, Eleonora turned back into the hollow and smothered her sobs in its warm darkness. When she awoke again, the Bey was gone.

Eleonora spent that first week almost entirely in bed, slipping in and out of a restive sleep slicked with ghostly perspiration and night terrors. Every morning and every evening, Mrs. Damakan came into her room with a tray of food, then returned an hour later to remove the meal, untouched but for a corner of cheese or a nibble at the top of an egg. Eleonora left the comfort of her bed only to relieve herself and to wash her face. Other than that, she slept and did her best to drive away unwanted thoughts. She had not said a word since the crash. It was becoming a habit, the silence, a heavy garment under which to cloak herself. Beyond her bedroom, the world was a thick blur. She had no idea whether her flock was still with her or not, and she didn't much care either way. She did loosely recall glimpsing a flash of purple at the corner of her window, though that could just as well have been a dream.

One morning, toward the beginning of the second week after the accident, Mrs. Damakan came into her room carrying a towel instead of a breakfast tray. Recognizing that surrender was the path of least resistance, Eleonora allowed the old handmaid to coax her into the bathroom, strip the dirty sheets off her bed, and scrub the limp casing of her body. After the bath, Mrs. Damakan left the room and Eleonora found herself alone in front of her dressing table mirror, wearing the same itchy blue velvet dress she had worn that first night in Stamboul. She felt weak, clean but drained of all spirit and aspiration. She crossed the room, opened the bay window for the first time in a week, and, inhaling the tentative smell of early spring, remembered a passage from the second volume of *The Hourglass*, describing Miss Holvert's condition less than a month after the death of her beloved parents.

The first buds of spring blossomed without remorse, each petal a tiny knife embedded in the membrane of her most vital organs, slashing her veins like a thresher separating wheat, and reopening those scars she thought were healed. But such is the season. In spite of our best efforts to smother its growth, to lie down on the tracks of its progress, life persists. And enduring, it issues a cruel taunt to the memory of death, to memory, and to death.

Closing the window, Eleonora drew a deep breath and felt the sharpness of the air in her lungs. She then left her room and walked downstairs to the dining room. The Bey was just finishing his breakfast when she entered. Standing framed in the doorway between the antechamber and the dining room, she held a fountain pen in one hand and a sheet of paper in the other. Her mouth was a tight line and her hair still damp from the bath.

"Good morning, Miss Cohen."

Eleonora nodded and sat down in the chair across from him.

Studying his face, she uncapped her pen and wrote her reply across the top of the page.

Good morning.

The Bey read what she had written and nodded, as if it were perfectly normal to communicate in this manner.

"Would you like breakfast?"

Yes, she wrote. Then she added, *please.*

It was the same breakfast Eleonora had eaten every morning of her stay in Stamboul. Still, the sight of it on the tray in front of her made her sick. She knew, however, that she needed to eat something. Staring down at the food, she lifted an olive to her mouth, nearly gagging as she chewed and swallowed the salty, slick meat. Removing the pit from her mouth, Eleonora next attempted a bite of raspberry jam on flatbread, but the sweet seediness of the jam was an affront to her fragile taste. So, too, was the overwhelming salinity of the cheese. Despite what she had written, it was not a good morning. She could not imagine it would ever be a good morning again.

As she sat across from the Bey in that cold and vacuous dining room, memories of the accident scurried across her mind like mice on a countertop. She had been with him when the boat sank, clinging with him to an errant piece of wood. Later, wrapped in a dirty wool blanket on shore, she hung heavy to his elbow, eyes wide to the shock of the cold and the slow, descending realization that her life was forever changed. Eleonora and the Bey stayed there on the edge of the shore until late that night, shivering as the rescue parties scurried about trying to locate more survivors. As night wore on, the reality of the situation emerged. Anyone not huddled on the shore was dead. The American Vice Consul was dead, as was Madame Corvel, the French Ambassador, most of the ship's crew, a famous Russian General named Nikolay Karakozov, and her father, Yakob. They were all dead.

"There are times in life," the Bey said, then stopped and seemed to reconsider his thoughts before continuing in a slightly different tone of voice. "We still have not heard from Ruxandra. I fear she may not have received our telegrams. I want you to know that you are welcome to stay here as long as you wish. Your father was a great friend and I owe him that at least."

Clearing his throat, he swallowed a last muddy sip of coffee and turned his cup upside down on the saucer. He waited a few moments, allowing the grounds to bleed down the side of the cup. Then he lifted it off the saucer and lost himself examining the ghostly residue of striations. He stared into the grounds for a long while, shaking off the excess, tilting what remained toward a shaft of light, before he met Eleonora's gaze.

"Fortune," he said derisively and stood from his seat. "I must be off. Is there anything you want me to get while I am out, anything you need?"

She shook her head.

No, thank you.

The Bey held her eyes for a moment, as if asking the same question again, in the language of silence. She shook her head.

Wishing her a good day, the Bey left, and she was alone again. For a long while she stared into the surface of the table, watching her blurred reflection move in the gloss, the chandelier hanging over her like a crystal blade. When she looked up again, Monsieur Karom was standing next to the buffet, timid and expectant as a dog searching for a new master. He had intended to clear the breakfast dishes, it seemed, but did not want to disturb her grief.

Taking up her pen and paper, Eleonora pushed back from the

table and wandered away from the dining room. She made her way along the main hallway of the house, the walls of which were hung with the doleful faces of the Bey's ancestors. The first door she came upon was the library. She stood staring at it for a long while before she tested the handle. It gave, and the lock mechanism clicked. Closing the door behind her, she crossed the room and crumpled into the same light-brown suede armchair she had sat in the night before the accident. Could it be that her father was sitting in that very chair just a week ago, drinking tea and playing backgammon with the Bey? Could so much have changed in such a short amount of time? Releasing a sob, she pushed her nose into the crease of the chair, trying to recover her father's scent. But it was gone, masked over by the musky smell of suede.

Over the next few weeks, Eleonora developed a routine that, although it did little to diminish her sadness, succeeded at least in giving structure to her days. Each morning after her bath, she trudged downstairs to the dining room and put forth her best effort at breakfast, usually no more than a piece of flatbread or a hardboiled egg. After breakfast, when the Bey was gone and the dishes were cleared, she would occupy herself with wandering through the house, napping on the chaise lounge in the drawing room or reading upstairs in her room. She spent untold hours reading next to the bay window, *The Hourglass* propped up against her thighs and a strand of hair between her lips, whittling the afternoon away with the dull narcotic of literature. Reading the book a second time, with full knowledge of the characters' eventual fates, she had a small comfort in the sentiment that our paths in life are laid according to a plan more grandiose than we could ever conceive or comprehend. Occasionally, she glanced up from her reading and lost herself in contemplation of a passing cloud. In the later afternoon, when boat traffic hit its peak, she would let her eyes drift along with the caïques cutting across the straits or the slow progress of steamers puffing toward the Black Sea, but most of all she read. She read as a distraction, to forget herself in the distant worlds of Bucharest and Trieste, with only the call to prayer and a steady darkening of the sky to remind her that time in her own world was passing as well.

As the weeks progressed and still there was no word from Ruxandra, no answer at all, it became clear that Eleonora would be staying with Moncef Bey for an indefinite future. She was not displeased with the idea of continuing on in Stamboul, nor did she ever wish that Ruxandra would come and bring her back home to Constanta, but there was a ticklish sting in her complete lack of reply. Perhaps the Bey was right, perhaps Ruxandra had not received their telegrams; still, Eleonora could not help feeling abandoned, by her aunt, by the very hand of fate. It was as if she had been forgotten entirely, erased from the Book of Life and marooned on an exotic island in the middle of the ocean.

All that being said, Eleonora was very thankful for the Bey's generosity and she rather came to enjoy life in his house. There was no official agreement, no contract nor any conversation about the terms of their arrangement, just that she was welcome to stay as long as she pleased. They had an amicable rapport, though for the most part they each attended to their own affairs. She didn't ask too many questions and neither did he. After breakfast each morning, the Bey left the house and usually didn't return until later that evening. They ate dinner together at least three times a week. On nights that the Bey had dinner plans outside the house, Monsieur Karom brought a cold meal up to Eleonora's room, which she ate alone before snuffing out her lamp and retiring for the night.

During this period, Eleonora's closest and most constant companion was Mrs. Damakan. In addition to their morning baths, the handmaid checked on her throughout the day to see if there was anything she needed. She brought up books and tea, extra blankets and little treats from the kitchen. More than once, Eleonora awoke from a nap to find the old woman seated in the chair next to her bed. One such afternoon, she awoke to Mrs. Damakan humming a soft and distant melody.

"I used to sing that to you," she said, with a small smile.

Mrs. Damakan had stopped humming, but Eleonora could still feel the melody tugging at the frayed edges of her memory. Then it disappeared, vanished like a gull in thick fog.

Chapter Eleven

A dull iron bell rang out from the church tower above Robert's College, rousing Reverend James Muehler from his afternoon nap as it reverberated through the walls of the rectory. It was the first dinner bell, three short tolls signifying that lower school students should be in or on their way to the cafeteria. The Reverend raised his jaw onto the cold leather of the armchair he had fallen asleep in and tried to summon the details of his plan for the evening. He was dining at Moncef Bey's, that much he remembered, but he couldn't recall when. Wiping his mouth with the back of his hand, he stood, crossed the stone floor of his study, and lowered himself into his desk chair. He shuffled through his papers for a few moments before coming upon the Bey's note.

Reverend James Muehler,

I am writing to invite you to dine next Thursday
evening with myself and Miss Eleonora Cohen. As you
can imagine, Miss Cohen is exceedingly disconsolate
following the loss of her father. However, I am certain
she will be pleased to see you. Please give your response
to the courier who delivered this note. He has been
instructed to wait as long as necessary. Dinner is served at
half past seven.

Sincerely,
Moncef Barcous Bey

Half past seven was rather early for dinner, but there was little he could do to change that now. Moistening the tips of his index and middle fingers, Reverend Muehler held the note up to the yellow wash of light emanating from his desk lamp and examined it more closely. The watermark was from a posh stationer in Rome but, although the note had been composed quite recently, the paper itself was yellow at the edges. Perhaps the Bey was less comfortable than generally supposed. In any case, the invitation was an excellent stroke of luck. With ever more outrageous rumors about the cause of the boat accident swirling through the city, his handlers were becoming increasingly agitated in their desire for intelligence of any sort. The Department of War and the Grand Vizier would both be greatly pleased to have a report on Moncef Bey's domestic circumstances, and James sorely needed a success on both fronts. He did not suspect the Bey of anything more than organizing his reading groups, of riling up the intellectual classes with impassioned discourses on Rousseau, but with pressure mounting from the Americans as well as the Ottomans, even the most benign stones could use turning over.

After staring at the note a few minutes longer, the Reverend placed it aside and began leafing through a pile of documents he had acquired a few evenings previous at a dinner party hosted by the German Admiral Krupp. They did not appear to be particularly significant: a few letters, a deed for a piece of land outside of Stuttgart, and some notes in the margin of a newspaper. Still, seeing as his German was rather spotty, the Reverend thought it best to go over them with a dictionary in hand before they were discarded. One never knew in such matters. The notes in the margin of a newspaper article might allude to a secret naval training program or plans for expansion of the railroads.

The Reverend exhaled and cracked his neck to either side. In addition to this little translation project and to his regular responsibilities at Robert's, a number of inessential tasks needed tending to in the near term. His study was a mess, his books were still unalphabetized, and his desk was blanketed with at least a dozen stacks of paper, each of which warranted a careful going through. Dipping his pen in the inkstand at the top of the desk, he composed a list of tasks to accomplish within the next three days. Satisfied with his progress, he laid the list in the middle of his desk and retired to prepare himself for dinner.

When Reverend Muehler set out finally on his way, the sun was dipping orange into a convocation of pine trees behind Le Petit Champs du Mort. Pausing at the lip of a ridge overlooking the Bosporus, he shielded his eyes from the glare of the setting sun and watched a German armored frigate inching toward the Sea of Marmara. Just below him, peeking out from under the ridge, was the rubblous structure of Rumelihisarı, the tower from which Mehmet Pasha had laid siege to Stamboul more than four centuries previous. The trustees of Robert's College had chosen the location of their school well. Although they were driven, as the charter of the college grandly stated, *to teach the young men of the Ottoman Empire, instruct them in the ways of the modern world*, it was no secret that many of Robert's American staff reported regularly to the Department of War. And many of them, including himself, owed their positions to connections in the department. To the Reverend's mind, this was not a conflict of interests or intentions. If one could serve one's own country while at the same time educating the children of another, well then, all the better. His only gripe was that his intelligence-gathering drew him away sometimes from what he saw as his primary responsibility as Rector of the college.

Reverend Muehler's path snaked down the hill through an ancient graveyard disordered by gravity. It was a macabre sight, the narrow gravestones incomprehensible with age and each topped with a stone cast of the proprietor's turban or fez. Trying his best not to imagine the bones beneath his feet, or the flesh those bones once supported, he held his breath and descended the path on his heels. As James emerged from under the shadow of the graveyard, Moncef Bey's house came into view. It was a grand old waterfront behemoth painted the color of egg yolk. He had never been inside the house, but he had noticed it often from afar. For some vagary of memory, the sight of it reminded him always of the painted elephant he had ridden once in Calcutta. Such is the wonder of the mind.

As he approached, Reverend Muehler observed that the house was garlanded with a swirl of purple hoopoes nearly identical in coloration and number to the flock he had noticed on the pier that morning before the accident. He had seen this stripe of hoopoe before then even, he was sure of it, though he couldn't remember where. Near the foot of the driveway, the Reverend paused to contemplate the flock and to catch his breath. Wiping his forehead with a handkerchief, he glanced at the battered red-and-gold book he had decided at the last moment to bring with him, a translated reader of Herodotus. As he inspected the inside cover of the book, a dog barked and he started. It was a private moment, one he would not have given a second thought to had he not looked up just then and seen Eleonora watching him from her window. When she saw that he saw her, she did not wave or smile, nor did she pull away, nor pretend she had been looking elsewhere. She just continued staring with that same plain and vacant gaze. A curious child, she was. They regarded each other for a long while before the Reverend turned to knock at the front door.

"Welcome," said the butler. "Reverend Muehler, I presume?"

"Yes."

"If you please," the butler said, holding the door open. "I will alert Moncef Bey that you have arrived."

"That would be excellent."

In spite of its garish exterior, the antechamber of the Bey's house was rather tastefully decorated, a careful melding of Louis XVI and classical Ottoman styles. The Reverend adjusted his necktie and peered down the main hallway. A better spy would seize this opportunity to rifle through a few drawers or at least to examine the lock on the front door. He was not, however, a very good spy. Glancing about, he made a halfhearted attempt to poke through a pile of cards on the visiting table. Nothing of interest there, though one couldn't expect a covert operative to leave his calling card. When the Reverend looked up again, Eleonora was standing at the top of the staircase, regarding him with that same empty and vaguely accusatory gaze. Even from a distance, he could see her face was drawn and pale, her eyes sunk into their cavities and tinged with red. Holding a pen and a piece of paper in her right hand, she descended the stairs with the nervous care of an old woman.

Reverend Muehler took a step toward the base of the staircase and made a sympathetic expression of his face.

"I was so sorry to hear about your father."

Eleonora's chin shook slightly, but she did not say anything in response.

"He was an honest man," the Reverend continued. "A good man, and he cared about you very much."

She touched her lips with the tip of her finger and shook her head.

"Miss Cohen has not spoken since the crash."

Reverend Muehler turned and saw the Bey in the mouth of the grand hallway.

"When she wants to express something she writes it on a sheet of paper."

"Yes," the Reverend said. "Very well."

"It is not an ideal situation, but she is rather unwilling to speak."

They both glanced at Eleonora, who was still standing at the base of the stairs, then the Bey continued.

"Here, let me show you to the dining room."

Seating himself to the left of his host and across the table from Eleonora, the Reverend attempted to continue their conversation.

"You can write, then?" he asked her, spreading his napkin in his lap. "That is quite impressive. Who taught you to write?"

Eleonora uncapped her pen and wrote two words across the top of the page, which she turned toward the Reverend so he could read them.

My father.

"I see," he said, flattening the napkin again. "Of course, that would make sense."

Before the Reverend could ask any further questions, Monsieur Karom appeared with three silver trays and placed one in front of each of them. Dinner that evening was roast lamb and carrots served on a bed of sweet bulgur. In spite of the somewhat taciturn company, the dinner itself was rather good. The lamb was perfectly cooked, charred along the edges with a touch of blood in the middle, the carrots as soft as summer fruit, and the bulgur flavored with orange blossom water. The only thing missing was conversation. Aside from the requisite compliments and requests to pass the salt, they ate in silence, silverware clinking as the Reverend and Bey tucked into their meals.

"These are interesting times," said the Reverend, attempting to draw his host out of his shell.

"Indeed."

"I have not seen such commotion and disorder since our Civil War. Mahdists, Serbs, Armenians, Jews, all clamoring for who knows what. The whole world seems to be clamoring."

The Bey nodded philosophically.

"Clamor can be an end unto itself," he said.

"Some would say a new day is dawning."

"Some would say many things."

The Reverend cut off a piece of lamb and chewed it carefully before trying again to bait his host.

"There are those who would say that a fundamental reordering of the political system will soon be upon us."

The Bey smiled politely, but he did not bite. It was clear he did not want to engage in a political discussion, and so James turned his attention to Eleonora.

"If I remember correctly," he said, "you are quite the reader. Tell me about one of the books you've read recently."

Eleonora squirmed, but as he suspected, she was too polite not to respond.

I have been rereading The Hourglass.

"Rereading?"

Yes.

"Because you didn't fully understand it the first time?"

No, she wrote. Then, sensing that this was too curt of a response for their guest, she added: *There were some words I didn't understand, but I can usually make them out from the context.*

The Reverend mulled over this response and, instead of continuing with his original line of questioning, he brought out his old Herodotus reader. Choosing a short excerpt, he handed the book across the table to Eleonora.

"Would you mind reading that?" he said, pointing to the start of the passage.

She nodded, as if this were a perfectly normal dinnertime pursuit, and bent over the page, her finger following along under the words. Halfway through the passage, she stopped.

What does he mean when he says they say the earth and sky are full of feathers?

Reverend Muehler reached across the table and took the book from her, reading aloud for the benefit of his host.

"'Above and north of the neighbors of their country no one (they say) can see or travel further, because of showers of feathers; for earth and sky are full of feathers, and these hinder sight.'"

It was a strange passage, probably not the best to test a young student's comprehension, but it was what he had chosen. He flipped forward a few pages to where Herodotus explains the feathers.

"Here is the answer," he said, and read aloud again: "'Regarding the feathers of which the Scythians say that the air is full, so thickly that no one can see or traverse the land beyond, I have this opinion. North of that country snow falls continually, though less in summer than in winter, as is to be expected. Whoever has seen snow falling thickly near him knows himself my meaning; for snow is like feathers. I think therefore that in this story of feathers the Scythians and their neighbors only speak of snow figuratively. So, then, I have spoken of those parts that are said to be most distant.'"

He handed the book back to her and she read the new passage to herself before responding.

Why would he wait so many pages before telling us the feathers are snow? It doesn't make any sense.

"You're right," the Reverend conceded. "It doesn't make sense."

James leaned his silverware on the edge of his plate. She was a classic savant, in the mold of Lucretius and Mendelssohn, but there was something else about her as well, a certain nobility of presence, that haunted look combined with an almost total lack of self-reflection, or so it seemed. In any case, the question was not whether she was an extraordinary child. The question was what to do with her.

Unfortunately, Stamboul was not the best soil for a mind like hers. Robert's College was out of the question, for a number of reasons. And the girls' schools in Stamboul were far too unserious. The best approach would probably be to hire a private tutor, someone to teach her Greek and Latin, rhetoric, philosophy, and history. But again, the private tutors in Stamboul were all rather bad. He thought on it awhile before he realized the perfect solution. Of course. He would offer to tutor her himself. It would be intriguing to observe the spin and whir of her intellect at work. A study of her lexical acquisition alone would be worthy of a monograph. And his handlers would surely be glad for any situation that granted him regular access to Moncef Bey's house.

After the cheese course, Reverend Muehler got a chance to propose his services. The Bey granted Eleonora permission to excuse herself and suggested that the two of them retire to the library for cognac and cigars.

"I hope you enjoyed the meal," said the Bey, once they were seated.

"Yes, very much so. The lamb was truly exquisite. And the bulgur as well. Was that orange blossom water I tasted?"

The Bey swirled his cognac and watched the golden liquid recede down the walls of his glass.

"Tell me," he said, ignoring the Reverend's question. "How does Miss Cohen seem to you? In your professional opinion."

"She seems to be holding together well, considering what she has been through."

The Bey placed his glass on the table next to him.

"I appreciate your reserve," he said. "But there is a time for civility and a time for candor. She hasn't spoken since the accident. As you know, that was nearly a month ago. This type of mourning is not normal, is it?"

The Reverend took a long drag on his cigar and tapped off a flake of ash. He allowed his silence to serve as an answer, let his concern inhabit the whish of the fire, the gentle give of leather, and the pop of the Bey's knee as he recrossed his legs.

"Have you considered employing a tutor?" the Reverend said finally. "It might help her to have more serious reading material, to direct her learning."

The Bey tented his fingers in front of his nose and leaned forward.

"I was under the impression that reading was part of the problem."

"Not reading itself," the Reverend corrected. "But the nature of the reading. I have never held the novel in much esteem. It is a genre for idle women and romantic young boys. Such frivolousness, even a masterpiece such as *The Hourglass*, cannot have any real utility. But I would think that if she were given more serious reading material—philosophy, history, rhetoric—it might do her some good."

The Bey untented his fingers and poured himself another glass.

"Would you be able to suggest a tutor for her?"

James let his eyes wander over the shelves of books at the other end of the library, as if mulling carefully through the matter before he responded.

"If you like," he said, "I will take her on myself. Her father was a good man and I owe this at least to his memory."

Chapter Twelve

Lieutenant Brashov left camp at dawn, attached his saddle bags to his horse, and rode. For fourteen hours he rode through rain and rivers swollen with dead cows, past soggy field hospitals and sugar beet fields sown with salt. He rode all day and all night through rain like rice poured from a canvas bag, through muddy sodden roads and crossroads deep with clay, unable for most of the journey to see past his horse's nose. Then, the rain ceased. Without warning, the tear in the sky was stitched and a bright white moon—

"Miss Cohen."

Eleonora looked up from her book. It was Monsieur Karom.

"Reverend Muehler is downstairs," he said. "For your lesson. Shall I tell him to meet you in the library?"

Eleonora nodded and, finishing the passage at hand, shut her bookmark between the pages. She waited for Monsieur Karom to leave before she stood from the armchair and, after glancing at herself in the dressing-table mirror, made her way downstairs. She was not sure what the point of these lessons was, but she had promised Moncef Bey that she would try them for at least a month. Trailing her hand along the cold marble banister, she descended into the antechamber and crossed the room diagonally. When she came to the library, she stood for a long while in its doorway, watching her new tutor page through a book. His back was to the door, so she couldn't tell exactly what he was doing. Though it was clear he was troubling the bottom rim of his nostril with his thumb.

"Well, hello," said the Reverend, when eventually he noticed her. He had a kind and open face punctuated with watery blue eyes the color of late summer. "It is good to see you again, Miss Cohen."

There was nothing in particular to dislike about Reverend Muehler. His clothes were clean, his breath smelled of mint, and he spoke without a trace of condescension. Still, in spite of all the evidence to the contrary, Eleonora could not help but feel that they were engaged at cross-purposes.

"Please, sit down," he said, motioning to the chair beside him. "If you like."

After hesitating for a moment, Eleonora crossed the room and seated herself in the chair next to him. They were seated at the solid oak table the Bey referred to—for reasons obscure to her, though related most likely to the profession of its previous owner—as the Colonel's desk.

"Still not talking?"

She shook her head.

"It's going to be difficult for us to read aloud."

Eleonora found a sheet of paper in one of the desk drawers and took her pen out of her frock pocket.

I can listen, she wrote. *And I can read.*

"Very well."

The Reverend flipped to the fourth page of a battered red-and-gold primer much like the one he had brought to dinner the other night. He began straight away, following beneath the words with his finger.

"Mensa Mensa Mensam Mensae Mensae Mensa."

At the end of the column, he stopped and turned to Eleonora.

"Did you understand that?"

She shook her head.

"It's Latin, the language of Rome, the language of Virgil, Ovid, Cicero, and Caesar."

She knew who Ovid was, everyone in Constanta did. Caesar was a Roman emperor, and Virgil had written *The Aeneid*, but she had never heard of Cicero.

Who is Cicero?

"Marcus Tullius Cicero," the Reverend expounded. "Perhaps the greatest orator who ever lived. You and Tully will be spending a good deal of time together in the next few months. My prediction is that you will become the best of friends."

According to the schedule he and the Bey had devised, Reverend Muehler came to the house twice a week, on Mondays and Thursdays after breakfast. Although she was still wary of him, Eleonora enjoyed her lessons—the conjugation and declension, the steady order of rules piled on rules, the gravel scrape of the Reverend's voice—and she took to them with ease. She could recall the exact wording of a passage she had read a week before, she followed complex philosophical texts with dogged tenacity, and she saw connections even the Reverend had not considered. Of all her abilities, however, Eleonora's tutor was most impressed with her facility for learning languages. To her, learning a new language was little more than filling in a series of blanks. Within three weeks of their first lesson, she could read and write rudimentary Latin. Within two months, she was translating long passages of *The Aeneid* and composing her own rebuttals to Tully. Spurred on by these Latinate successes, the Reverend soon introduced her to ancient Greek, to Aristotle, the Ptolemies, Herodotus, Aeschylus, and St. Augustine.

The Reverend's lessons produced little change in Eleonora's external routine, but beneath the surface the waters were warming. She still spent most of her days reading in the armchair next to the bay window, alternating between *The Hourglass* and books assigned by the Reverend. Still, she refused to speak or leave the house. She found small pleasures, however, in the cantankerous argumentation of the ancients, and a pinch of magic in well-turned prose. *Gorgons and winged steeds flow in apace.* A line like that—from Plato's *Phaedrus*—would inevitably bring a smile to her lips. *Gorgons and winged steeds flow in apace.* She repeated the words over and over again to herself until they were right there with her, the gorgons, grim of aspect, glaring terribly, flowing in on winged steeds.

As much as she enjoyed her lessons, Eleonora still did not entirely trust the Reverend. There was no one incident that particularly stoked her misgivings. Rather, it was the mass of collected details. He often rescheduled their lessons, saying he had an important meeting that could not be moved. He asked strange questions about the Bey. And, more than once, she found him looking through the drawers of the Colonel's desk. The episode that permanently solidified Eleonora's mistrust occurred a few weeks after the Reverend began teaching her Greek. He was nearly an hour late that morning, and when he arrived he seemed distracted. He opened and shut the curtains twice before asking her to begin. Chewing on the tip of a pen, he paced back and forth while she read to herself, her finger following under the words. The swish and stir of his trousers marked the time like an anxious metronome.

Not long after, some cattle were stolen from Euboea by Autolycus, and Eurytus supposed—

Eleonora felt the light touch of the Reverend's hand on her shoulder and she stopped reading.

"What do you remember about Autolycus?"

As he shifted his stance, she felt the ruffling brush of his shirt sleeve against her arm. She squinted, holding her finger in place under the line.

He's in The Odyssey. *Odysseus's grandfather.*

Staring at the red paisley wallpaper in front of her, she recalled the relevant passage and wrote it out at the bottom of the page.

And indeed as soon as she began washing her master, she at once knew the scar as one that had been given him by a wild boar when he was hunting on Mount Parnassus with his excellent grandfather Autolycus—who was the most accomplished thief and perjurer in the whole world.

"Yes, exactly." The Reverend smiled and, lifting his hand off her shoulder, changed course. "If you don't mind, I have something new for us today."

Reverend Muehler sat down at the Colonel's desk and, reaching into his bag, removed a small silver tube. Studying the engravings along the top edge, he unlatched it and tapped out a rolled-up piece of paper. He flattened the note in the middle of the desk and secured it at either end with a paperweight. It was covered almost entirely with Greek letters, but the words were not Greek. He did not say where the document came from, nor why it was contained in such an ornate tube.

"As you can see," said the Reverend, "these letters don't make words. Not words we can understand, at least. But there's a pattern, a system. The purpose of the puzzle is to figure out the pattern. That is your lesson for today."

Holding her head in her palms, Eleonora stared at the letters. She concentrated as hard as she could, focusing her mind into a single point. This was what she did when she wanted to remember something: a quotation, a grammatical rule, a date, or a new word. She was very good at that, remembering things. Once she captured something in her mind, it never escaped. Figuring out this puzzle, however, was an entirely different undertaking, like learning a new language without a book, like seeing feathers as snow without being told. Exhaling, Eleonora sat up straight and let her mind relax. Instead of focusing on the letters, she let her concentration refract into thousands of tiny rays. She closed her eyes, unclenched her teeth, and let the letters move through the continuous field of light dancing on the insides of her eyelids. Each letter vibrated in its own self as well as the possibility of all other letters, in all the languages she knew. And then there it was: *Wednesday at noon. The back of Café Europa.*

She opened her eyes again, to the library and the Reverend with his silver tube. He raised his eyebrows and she wrote out the solution.

Wednesday at noon. The back of Café Europa.

"How did you come to that?"

Is that the correct answer?

"Yes," said the Reverend, chewing his bottom lip. "I believe it is. But more important is how you came to it."

You take the number associated with each of the Greek letters. Alpha is one; beta is two; gamma is three; delta is four. Then you subtract two, then transpose the new number into the Arabic alphabet.

"Exactly!"

He paused for a moment to confirm her solution, then rolled up the note and slipped it back into the document holder. Standing, he said that he was sorry but they would have to cut their lesson short. He would make it up to her on Thursday, he said, and left.

The Reverend's lessons provided Eleonora with a loose scaffolding for her days, though in total the lessons and the work he assigned did not comprise more than a dozen or so hours per week. Aside from the lessons, Eleonora was free to spend her time as she chose. Most days she chose to sit quietly in her room with a book. With the arrival of summer, however, the languid lengthening of days and the steady return of migratory birds along the Bosporus, she became more and more curious about her surroundings. Although she had no desire to leave the Bey's house, the smell of budding apricots increased the boldness of her forays through its corridors and empty rooms. One Wednesday afternoon near the beginning of June, she was struck by a sudden desire to explore the women's wing, which, according to the Bey, had not been used for many years. Marking her place in Pliny's *Naturalis Historia*, she made her way downstairs and took a left at the bottom of the staircase. At the end of the main hall—past the library, the drawing room, and a music room she had discovered a few weeks earlier—Eleonora found herself at the entrance to the women's quarters, a tall and narrow door engraved with interlocking hexagons.

The door opened onto a dim foyer embalmed with cobwebs and dust. A towering gauzy room scattered with unused furniture and the tattered remains of pink satin pillows, the antechamber of the women's quarters had a dusty, forgotten air that overcame her even as she stood in the doorway. Sneezing, she took a step into the room and closed the door behind her. Again she sneezed. Haunted by a half dozen or so furniture-size lumps covered with white canvas sheets, the room had two proper doors, one behind her and one directly in front of her. Aside from these portals, Eleonora also noticed a narrow staircase running crisscross up the back wall. It led, as far as she could tell, to a small doorway floating just beneath the ceiling. She had no idea where the door might lead, what she might discover behind it—but wasn't that the purpose of exploring?

Inhaling the stale air, Eleonora crossed the foyer and mounted the wooden stairs creaking with each step. She gripped the handrail for support. At the top of the stairs she tried the door handle and it gave easily into a dark corridor running flush against the inside of the wall. From where she stood, Eleonora could make out little more than a veil of dust and a family of mice scurrying across the baseboards. She wiped her forehead and took a few cautious steps into the corridor. In the distance, she could make out a mottled patch of light. With her arms in front of her face, she headed toward the light, ducking under beams and stopping every few steps to brush the cobwebs out of her hair.

The light, she discovered, was streaming into the corridor through a latticework screen much like those on the windows of the Bey's carriage. She put her face to the screen. There, laid out below her like a theater stage, were the bookshelves, globes, and reading tables of the library. As she later learned, such corridors were common in Stamboul. Designed so that the ladies of the house could observe social gatherings without compromising their honor, they were built into most of the grand old mansions along the Bosporus. However, when Eleonora first discovered the corridor, it was as if she had found the trapdoor to another world, her own private box from which she could observe every room in the house.

She might have turned back if she had not just then felt a current of cool air cutting through the darkness. Running her knuckles along the bare wooden planks that lined the walls of the corridors, she continued on, toward the source of the breeze. She passed above the dining room and the antechamber, where she spotted Mrs. Damakan dusting the banister of the staircase. Eleonora paused and watched the old handmaid make her way up the stairs, then back down. Wiping her hands every so often on the front of her smock, Mrs. Damakan finished the banister, then made her way counterclockwise around the perimeter of the room, the economy of her movements at once graceful and efficient. Even after Mrs. Damakan left the antechamber, Eleonora continued to watch her absence, now amid the settling dust. Then she moved on, toward the source of the current. At the corner of the house, beside where she figured her own bedroom must be, the corridor turned sharply and broke off in the direction of the kitchen. Leading down from this junction was a narrow wooden staircase. Eleonora could not be entirely sure, but it seemed as if the breeze was coming from the bottom of these stairs.

She took hold of the banister with her free hand and made her way carefully down the stairs to a room with a small iron door bolted into the wall. Not much taller than herself and only about twice as wide, the door was rusted orange around the bolts and frosted with a layer of dust. It was rather warm to the touch and looked as if it hadn't been opened in a long while. The source of the breeze, she saw, was a crack between the frame of the door and the wood of the house—a result, she supposed, of the house settling into its foundation. There was a small sliver of daylight streaming through the crack, and the smell of hay pervaded the space around it. Glancing back over her shoulder, Eleonora knocked at the center of the door. It made a deep, hollow sound, like a large bell. She put her ear to it, but aside from the echo of her own knock, she couldn't hear anything. Eleonora stood for a long while with her hand on the door handle before deciding not to venture through, into what she imagined was the Bey's stables. That was enough exploring for one day, she told herself as she scurried back up the stairs and retraced her steps along the corridor. Indeed, it was more than enough for one day.

Chapter Thirteen

Summer slipped into Stamboul under the cover of a midday shower. It took up residence near the foundations of the Galata Bridge and drifted through the city like a stray dog. Ducking in and out of alleyways, the new season made itself felt in the tenacity of fruit flies buzzing about a pyramid of figs, in the increasingly confident tone of the muezzin, and the growing petulance of shopkeepers in the produce market. Summer could be found in the sticky smell of cherry sherbet, in roast squab, and in rotting loquats. Like a freshly tanned hide pulled tighter and tighter, each day was imperceptibly longer than the previous, each morning earlier, and the sun stronger. Trees budded, bloomed, and gave fruit, while the straits were busy with migratory birds. Wave upon wave of hawk, stork, swallow, and cormorant flocked up the Bosporus on their way to old breeding grounds in Europe.

Gazing out on those languid straits, Eleonora watched a cast of white-collared falcons ride unseen gusts of warm air like bumps in the road. She saw a swoop of black kites steer between the domes of the Süleymaniye Mosque and a siege of snake-necked purple herons spread their wings wide as the caïques below. That morning, in the back recesses of the Bey's library, she had discovered a calfskin-bound copy of William Swainson's *On the Natural History and Classification of Birds*. Matching his lithographs to what she saw out the window, she was able to identify the falcons, the kites, and the herons as well as a convocation of white-tailed eagles and a lone peregrine falcon with a seabird in its talons.

As the sun softened and dipped into the trees behind Üsküdar, Eleonora saw a flash of amethyst at the corner of her eye, and a purple hoopoe with a crown of white-striped feathers landed on her windowsill. The bird cocked its head to the left as if indicating a point of interest, and she watched her flock come into view around the bend of the Golden Horn. As they steered toward her, looping and darting through the orange-gray sky, Eleonora felt something give inside her, like an ice floe breaking up. When she opened the window, the scout flew off to join its brethren.

Pushing a strand of hair from her eyes, she rested her elbows on the windowsill and watched the dusk unfold beneath her. That evening, the city felt charged with the energy of a new purpose. Instead of flagging with the sun, as it usually did, the boat traffic seemed to rise, and the passengers appeared anxious to get where they were going. She noticed a team of men stringing what looked like lanterns between the minarets of the New Mosque. And a series of barges docked along the Beşiktaş Pier. By the time the bottom of the sun touched the horizon, the city was empty. The Bosporus was shorn of boat traffic and the roads empty of carriage. The hawkers were quiet; the only sound she heard was the steady bleating of a lamb tied up outside the Beşiktaş Mosque. Then, as the last light of day escaped beneath the curve of the horizon, just as the sun disappeared, a cannon blast rang out from the vicinity of Topkapi Palace. Eleonora fell to the floor in fright and, struggling under her desk, covered her head with her hands. If there were more cannon shots, if there was a war, she wanted to be as safe as possible.

She was in this same position when Monsieur Karom came to her door with dinner.

"Is everything all right?" he asked, placing her tray on the bedside table.

Eleonora reached above her and fished a piece of paper out of the top drawer.

The cannon.

Monsieur Karom stifled a smile.

"The cannon shot," he said, helping her up, "marks the end of the fasting period. Today is the first day of Ramadan. You knew that, didn't you?"

Eleonora shook her head. She knew about Ramadan, the fasting during the day and the sumptuous meals at night, but she had never heard of using a cannon to mark the end of the fasting period. What Muslims there were left in Constanta employed a pious man to tromp through the town beating a large drum.

"Yes," said Monsieur Karom. He leaned out the open window and peered down at the barges. "You will have a perfect view of the fireworks."

Eleonora ate her lentil soup alone at her desk, watching stars light up the empty darkness like so many wordless candles. Stamboul was silent for the length of her dinner. Then, as she was finishing her date pastry, the city burst to life. The lanterns strung between the minarets of the New Mosque were lit, spelling out the words HAPPY RAMADAN. Sherbet vendors and fortune-tellers set up stalls along the water. Tents of swirling red and blue fabric sprung up in the courtyard of every neighborhood mosque. The streets filled with young children and their parents, cousins, great-uncles, and older boys in ragged packs pushing through the crowd. The first firework went up with the sound of a yowling cat and exploded in a burst of green. Then there was another, this one white, and the crowd let out a cheer. Launched from the barges beneath Eleonora's window, shoots of red, blue, green, and white illuminated the Ramadan night sky with smoky phosphorescence, continuing with the festivities until dawn.

Whether it was the sight of her flock that evening, the beginning of summer, Ramadan, or something else entirely, Eleonora didn't know. All she knew was that she felt different now. Standing in front of her closet that next morning, she touched a bare floorboard with the tip of her big toe and shivered. She had woken up late, and sleep lingered still at the corners of her eyes, but however sleepy she was, she could not deny that something inside her had shifted, the ice sea was breaking up. She stood considering her closet for a long while—a pale garden of silk, lace, and chiffon, seeded at the far left with a boy's wool suit—before choosing an elegant light purple dress from her second visit to Mme. Poiret. Slipping the dress over her head, she stepped into a matching pair of shoes and turned to look at herself in the mirror. Without Mrs. Damakan's assistance, she couldn't properly fasten the back of the dress, but she went downstairs regardless. There was something she intended to ask Moncef Bey and she wanted to do it now, before she lost her nerve.

"Good morning, Miss Cohen."

The Bey had already begun his breakfast, and was spreading cherry preserves on a piece of bread.

Good morning, she wrote on a scrap of paper. She paused for a moment and looked up at him, then continued with her question. *Moncef Bey, may I come with you today? Out to Pera? I promise I won't be a bother.*

He tightened his gaze and rested the jammy knife on the edge of his plate.

"Of course," he said. "You are always welcome to join me. And you are never a bother. I only worry you will be bored."

I won't be bored. Not at all. And I will be as quiet as a mouse.

The Bey took up his knife again. Spreading the remaining preserves on the edge of the bread, he broke off a piece of crumbly white cheese.

"All right then," he said. "But you must promise to keep quiet as a mouse."

She nodded her agreement and the Bey turned to Monsieur Karom.

"Tell the stable boys to prepare the carriage. Miss Cohen will be joining me."

"Yes, sir," the butler replied, bowing out of the room.

Before either of them could reconsider, Eleonora found herself seated in the Bey's carriage, watching the world pass through the latticework screen. As the last yellow of his house receded behind the Beşiktaş Mosque, she felt a cord inside her tug and snap. She had left. She was outside, a cool touch of wind on her forearm and the sharp, salty smell of the Bosporus in her nose. Purple wildflowers lined the edge of the road and the clouds overhead were white as spun sugar. She folded her hands in her lap, following along with the mosques and municipal buildings, mansions, fountains, plane trees, and fishermen. They passed a donkey pulling a cart laden with mounds of bright orange loquat, a string of Ramadan tents, and the remnants of the festivities from the night before. Eleonora looked down at her hands, her own open palms. She cupped her face and inhaled their soft soapiness.

"We must disembark here," said the Bey as the carriage rolled to a stop. "Beyond this, the streets are too steep."

The Galata funicular station was just a few steps from where the carriage stopped. Shaded by a gilded grotto of pink and yellow tile, European ladies, their porters, and an assortment of uniformed men stood in groups of two or three. Glancing occasionally at the dark cavern from which their train was supposed to emerge, the passengers spoke in hushed tones and watched each other with suspicion. After a few minutes, a gas light appeared at the top edge of the tunnel. With a pneumatic screech, the red-lacquer trolley stuttered to a halt in front of them. They boarded the front car and, although there was little to see through the darkness, Eleonora rode the whole way with her nose against the glass, straining to make out what lay ahead.

"Here we are," the Bey announced when the funicular stopped and they filed out of the station.

Pera was just as Eleonora had remembered it. The arcades were draped with painted cloth banners. Store windows jostled to advertise the new summer stock. And posh ladies glided up the boulevard in their dainty cream-colored dresses. She felt as if she were surfacing finally after a long dive, emerging from the silent, watery depths of herself into a hot and salty world. As she stood at the base of La Grande Rue de Pera, taking it all in, Eleonora felt the weight of a new sadness crushing down on her. She had stood in this very place with her father just a few months ago. He had taken her hand and walked with her up the boulevard. The tears welled up in her eyes as she recalled his smell, the feeling of his palm against the back of her neck. She and the Bey stood for a moment in silence. When it passed, Eleonora wiped her tears away. The Bey offered her two fingers. She reached up to take them, and they walked together up the boulevard toward the Café Europa.

Holding the red double doors for her, the Bey led Eleonora through the clattering, smoke-filled main room of the café, out the back door, and down a steep wooden staircase into a cobbled patch of foliage he called the back garden. As they descended, Eleonora noticed shreds of green-and-white fabric waving from the handrail, perhaps the scattered remnants of a Ramadan celebration. A pair of wizened old men in fezzes smoked narghiles under an almond tree, and directly beneath the staircase, a bespectacled young European man read the paper while his companion took notes in a small book. The Bey chose a table near the back of the garden, next to an empty birdbath, and they gave their orders to the waiter: two teas and a croissant. When the waiter left, the young man who had been taking notes approached their table with a backgammon board under his arm. He was a slight, nervous man dressed in a short blue frock coat, light gray pants, and a velvet smoking cap embroidered with tiny flowers. Eleonora couldn't quite place his accent, but it hinted toward the Caucasus. After exchanging a brief stream of greetings with the Bey, he pulled up a chair and began setting up the board. As he did, a stark-white cat with one blue eye and one yellow eye jumped into his lap. He stroked it absently with one hand, and with the other continued setting up the game.

Glancing into the cat's eerily unmatched eyes, Eleonora sat on her hands, the cold black metal of the chair indenting itself into her palms. This was not how she had expected the Café Europa to look, this sleepy tableaux of iron furniture and vines. She wasn't sure exactly what she had imagined, but it was not this. In any case, it was nice to be outside. There was so much she had forgotten. The warmth of the sun on her neck, the smell of grapes. As she took in her surroundings, the call to prayer echoed out across the city like a low, wispy cloud, and a member of her flock landed at the edge of the table. It stayed for a moment, twitched its head at the cat, and flew off, but neither the Bey nor his opponent noticed.

"Three-four," said the young man and bumped one of the Bey's pieces off the board.

The Bey scooped up the dice and blew into the cavity of his palm. He needed a five or a one to bring the bumped piece back into the game.

"The Viceroy," said the Bey's opponent, referring apparently to a previous strand of conversation. "He is not without options."

"Indeed," said the Bey. He rolled, a three-five, and moved the bumped piece back onto the board. "But perhaps the best option is to wait."

"One can only wait for so long."

For a few rolls, the two men played in silence. The Bey was winning. His pieces were unexposed and moving steadily toward home. Leaning in, Eleonora let herself fall into the rhythm of the game, the clatter of pieces and the click of the dice. She burrowed into it as she might a dense philosophical argument, letting the walls of the simple wood board close around her. A breeze rustled through the vines and she could feel the warmth of the chair against her shoulders.

"I see you are not fasting for Ramadan," said the young man, indicating the tea and croissant.

The Bey stirred his tea and sipped it.

"No," he said. "I abandoned that practice many years ago. Though I would prefer you not mention my lack of observance to any of our colleagues. Fasting for Ramadan is like tithing. No one truly does it, but society depends on the illusion that we all do."

"Surely the lumpen classes fast."

"They might," said the Bey pensively, rubbing the dice together. "But I can guarantee no one you know does."

"And your young friend?"

Eleonora was raising a piece of croissant to her lips.

"What about her?"

"Is she not Muslim?"

"No," said the Bey. "She is a Jewess."

He paused, weighing whether this explanation would suffice. When he saw that it would not, he continued.

"She is the daughter of my former business partner, Yakob Cohen. You remember the boat accident a few months ago?"

"The one the Tsar is upset about?"

The Bey nodded. He did not, apparently, need to elaborate beyond this. Their conversation continued, thrusting and parrying obliquely around the cause of the boat accident, for a few more rolls. When they had reached a stalemate, the young man turned to face Eleonora directly.

"What is your name?"

She glanced around for a piece of paper, but there was none on the table.

"Miss Cohen has not spoken since the crash," the Bey explained. "She communicates through writing."

"She can write?"

"Yes," said the Bey and, with evident pride, began naming the languages she could write in: "Latin, Greek, French, Turkish—"

"Is that so?" said the young man and, pulling the notebook out of his pocket, handed it with a pen to Eleonora. "Write something."

She took the notebook and opened it to a blank page.

What would you like me to write?

"Anything you like," he said. "A passage from Virgil, perhaps. Do you know *The Aeneid*?"

She nodded and began from the beginning.

Arms and the man I sing, who, forced by fate, / And haughty Juno's unrelenting hate, / Expelled and exiled, left the Trojan shore.

Eleonora handed the notebook to the young man for his inspection. As she did, she noticed the Reverend's name, James

Muehler, written in small letters and underlined at the top of the facing page.

"Very good," he said, glancing at what she had written. "Very impressive."

He turned to the Bey.

"How old did you say she was?"

"Eight," said the Bey. "Nearly nine."

The young man shook his head in disbelief.

"You will never cease to amaze me, Moncef Bey."

He then stood from the table, setting the cat at Eleonora's feet. Their game was not yet over, but neither of them seemed to care.

"Our friend," said the young man, doffing his smoking cap. "He will meet you tomorrow afternoon at noon in Le Petit Champs du Mort."

The Bey nodded and handed an envelope across the table. Without another word, the young man slipped it into his pocket and left the garden.

After he left, Eleonora finished her tea and played a few games of backgammon with Moncef Bey. She didn't ask anything about this strange young man. She didn't ask why the Reverend's name was in his notebook. She didn't ask whom the Bey was going to meet tomorrow in Le Petit Champs du Mort. She didn't ask anything, though she wondered many things. In particular, she wondered whether there was any connection between the young man and the note the Reverend had shown her, the Greek letters that spelled *Wednesday at noon. The back of Café Europa.* It was not Wednesday, but they were indeed at the back of Café Europa. Perhaps there was a connection. As much as she understood about the world, as much as she knew, there were still many things she didn't understand.

Eleonora reached down to stroke the cat, which was pacing at her feet, and she looked into its eyes. It was aloof, as cats usually are, but there was something strange about its manner, the way it jumped into her lap and purred with such purpose. It was almost as if the cat were urging her to stop asking questions, to stop wondering, and lose herself in its blank white fur.

Chapter Fourteen

The Commander of the Faithful, His Excellency Sultan Abdulhamid II put down his book and stared out the green tiled doorway of his mother's quarters. Her courtyard was much quieter than normal. A young odalisque was practicing the kemenche in a niche between two columns, and water gurgled up through the mouth of the marble fountain in the middle of the courtyard. As the Sultan watched water spill over the side of the top basin, a purple-and-white hoopoe landed on its rim, took a mouthful of water, and flew off. It had the same coloration as the bird he had spotted a few months earlier. Or perhaps it was the very same bird. In any case, it was quite an unusual color.

Glancing at his mother, the Sultan tried to read a few more pages of his book, an English mystery novel called *The Woman in White*, but the grumbling of his stomach ruined his concentration. It was only the second day of Ramadan and already he was wracked with an unbearable hunger. Abdulhamid chuckled at the irony. Here he was, Caliph of Islam, Servant to the Holy Cities, and yet his stomach growled during Ramadan just like anyone else's. Indeed, it is true what is written in the Sura of Maryam, *To Us shall return all that he talks of and he shall appear before Us bare and alone.*

The Sultan laid his book down again and watched his mother practice her calligraphy. Pen pinched between thumb and forefinger, she sat at a low walnut table, her shoulders stiff and legs crossed underneath. She had taken up calligraphy upon her arrival in the court of his father, Sultan Ahmed IV. While the other girls lounged about plucking the oud and gossiping, she sat alone in her private chambers, practicing an endless series of loops and dots in the hopes of improving herself and enhancing her standing. She didn't need to impress anyone now, of course. She was the Sultan's mother. When she spoke, the harem girls scattered like deer. It was incredible to think that someone of her birth, a lowly Circasian peasant, taken from her family and brought to the palace at the age of twelve, could rise through force of will and beauty to become one of the most important personages in the empire. She had been able to efface the coarseness of her upbringing almost completely, but Abdulhamid could still recognize his lowly ancestors in certain of his mother's personality traits—her irritability, for instance. He could tell from her posture that she was still upset with him, and he knew from long experience that he would have to make a concession if he wanted peace.

"If it means that much to you," he said, breaking a long silence, "I will cancel the meeting."

His mother finished the word she was working on before she raised her head.

"It doesn't mean anything to me, Your Excellency. I couldn't care less whom you invite to the palace. I am only worried about the impression your meetings might have on others. Once rumors get started, they are very difficult to stop. You remember, of course, the difficulties of your uncle Cehangir."

The Sultan nodded gravely, as he always did when his uncle's name was spoken. A voracious glutton, libertine, and the source of much malicious gossip, Cehangir had died at the dinner table with a piece of lamb lodged in his esophagus.

"Mother, I agree that rumors are dangerous, but meeting with a palm reader is not the same as eating an entire sheep."

"It's not just the palm reader," his mother said. "It's the snake charmers, the Sufi mystics, the dog with two tails, the talking parrot. People are saying you would rather meet with a beggar than the Ambassador of Genoa."

"That is not what happened."

She lifted the piece of paper and inspected the accuracy of her hand.

"Mother, you know that's not what happened."

"It's not important what happened," she said, putting the paper down. "I'm telling you what people are saying."

Abdulhamid stood and came around to inspect her finished work. She had rendered Al-Mutannabi's famously acerbic line— *Kings who are rabbits, sleeping with open eyes*—in a subtly squared North African Kufic script. Her workmanship was flawless as ever.

"Very nice, Mother."

"Thank you, Your Excellency. It is for you."

He lifted his mouth into a sour smile. *Kings who are rabbits, sleeping with open eyes.* It was not a delicate jab. Al-Mutannabi was known for sly and insulting verses that spared no one, not even his patrons.

"Your allusion is not lost on me."

"Your Excellency," she said, standing. "There is one more thing I would like to ask before I take your leave."

He nodded for her to continue.

"I have been thinking recently about that horrible boat accident."

Abdulhamid nodded. The accident had taken on new significance in the past weeks. The Tsar's private investigation into the matter had concluded that the crash was likely caused by sabotage. Although his report didn't name a saboteur, the Tsar was demanding financial restitution from Stamboul—for neglecting to properly protect the Russian subjects under its dominion—in the shape of fifty thousand pounds. And he was threatening to take action if his grievances were not redressed. The Sultan would gladly have paid twice that amount in private. However, someone had leaked the Tsar's demand to the newspapers. If he paid the restitution now, in public, he would look weak. And everyone would be lining up for a handout. If he didn't pay, the Tsar would have another excuse to rattle his sabers.

"It was a horrible tragedy," he said. "A tragic loss of life. But what can we do now? What more could we have done? I sent personal condolences to the victims' families, and to their respective governments. Jamaludin Pasha attended the funeral of the American Vice Consul and the French Ambassador. We even made provisions for an American naval detachment to enter the Bosporus in order to convey the Vice Consul's body back to New York. The Russians were offered this same opportunity for their general, but they declined."

"Of course it's a tragedy," his mother said. "And of course you did everything you could have done. I am asking if you think it was an accident."

There were a number of conspiracy theories circling about the palace. He had just listened to the Grand Vizier's theory—it was a British conspiracy to scare off the Americans and distract attention from Prussia—and he was in no mood to sit through his mother's. He had to admit, the evidence in favor of sabotage was overwhelming, but he did not want to contradict his own official report, which cited equipment malfunction as the cause of the crash. Conceding as much, even to his own mother, would only further bolster the Tsar's argument and weaken his own hand.

"Yes," he said, doing little to hide his annoyance. "I do think it was an accident. What else could it have been?"

"I believe," she said, looking over her shoulder, "that it was sabotage, sabotage planned and carried out by the American Consul himself."

The Sultan snorted in disbelief. He was used to his mother's conspiracy theories, but this was truly preposterous.

"Why would the Americans sink their own ship? Why would they kill their own Vice Consul?"

"Not the Americans," she said, grinning coyly. "The American Consul."

"But—"

"As you know, the American Consul is not only an American. He is also a member of the Hebrew faith."

Abdulhamid blinked. His mother's distrust of Jews was no secret. Given her feelings on the topic in general, Abdulhamid was inclined to dismiss the theory out of hand. As theories went, however, it had a certain amount of elegance.

"Think about it," she said and, setting her calligraphy on the table, she left.

Abdulhamid stood in the doorway of his mother's private quarters, watching an endless stream of water spill out the top of the fountain. It was a compelling theory, though it lacked a motive. As he tried to puzzle out how the attack might have advanced the cause of the Americans, or the Jews, Abdulhamid's stomach growled again and a pain stabbed at his kidney. Clutching his side, he felt another wave of pain roll through his gut, and tried to recall the conditions under which it was permissible to break the Ramadan fast. He was not infirm or traveling or pregnant, but what if the fasting impeded his ability to render judgment? What if it compromised his ability to perform his duties? It was obligatory to break the Ramadan fast if doing so would save a life. Surely there were lives in the balance of the momentous decisions he made every day. With this justification in hand, he glanced at the empty courtyard and stole into the kitchen next door.

The room was bare, its pots and pans stored in their cupboards and the chopping blocks scrubbed clean. The Iftar meal was prepared in the central palace kitchen, which left auxiliary kitchens like his mother's unused for the month. Surely, however, there must be some food in the larder. Maybe not a chicken, but a few scraps of bread, a dried apricot, or a date, something that would allow him to perform his duties properly until dusk. Glancing out again at the empty courtyard, he opened the larder doors and pawed through spices, a tin of sardines, and a stale piece of flatbread. He was on the verge of eating the bread with sardines when he discovered, at the very back of the larder, a box of baklava. Glistening with syrup, the pastries were dusted with bright green ground pistachios. His mother had a penchant for sweets. It would be no surprise if she had hidden the box specifically for consumption during Ramadan. She was not a young woman, and had been afflicted by the sugar disease for some time now. In either case, she would never know that it was him who had found it. Glancing over his shoulder, he popped one of the pieces into his mouth and swallowed it with only two chews. The next piece he took his time with, savoring the sweet, flaky crunch of the dough and that peculiar tang of ground pistachios.

Licking the tips of his fingers, Abdulhamid snuck back into his mother's quarters, where he found the Grand Vizier, Jamaludin Pasha, bent over the calligraphy. They regarded each other for a moment in silence, each fully aware of what the other was doing.

"Your Excellency," said the Grand Vizier. "I was just looking for you."

"It's a beautiful piece of workmanship," said the Sultan, indicating the calligraphy. "Is it not?"

"Yes, Your Excellency. Your mother has always had a wonderful Kufic script. One would almost think she was born in Fez."

He paused to scrutinize the line more carefully.

"Though I might have chosen another verse."

Abdulhamid did not take Jamaludin Pasha's invitation to carp on his mother, and so he continued with his original tack. The Grand Vizier adjusted his stance and held his wrists behind his back.

"We received reports this morning that the Sanjak Bey of Novi Pazar successfully put down another tax rebellion. Unfortunately, the village he made an example of was primarily composed of Orthodox Christians. You can imagine, Your Excellency, what the Russians will make of this. Just three days ago, their Ambassador told Hisham Pasha that the Tsar is determined to defend the Orthodox subjects of our empire as if they were his own."

"This is rather unfortunate timing," the Sultan said, popping his thumbnail off the edge of the doorway. "Is there anything we can do to mollify the Tsar?"

"We could pay the restitution they have demanded," said Jamaludin Pasha. "But I doubt whether even that will pacify them now. I imagine they will be quite upset. And the European newspapers, if they hear of what happened in Novi Pazar, it will be another Bulgarian Horror."

The Sultan was silent for a moment and his stomach growled audibly.

"Let us see how the Tsar responds," he said finally and changed the subject. "Now tell me some good news. How are our spies progressing?"

Covert operations were the personal prefecture of Jamaludin Pasha, and he could always be counted on to tout his successes in that realm.

"Here we do have some good news," said the Grand Vizier. "Just last week our men broke up a revolutionary meeting in Beyoğlu."

The Sultan nodded without much interest. Jamaludin Pasha's men broke up at least two of these supposed revolutionary meetings every week. For the most part, the agitators turned out to be little more than spoiled intellectuals drinking tea and orating for each other.

"It might also be of some interest," the Grand Vizier continued, "that the code, the code that led our men to this meeting, was cracked by a young girl, an orphan of eight years old."

"A young girl?"

"A Miss Eleonora Cohen," Jamaludin Pasha said. "The daughter of a Jewish textile merchant from Constanta. Apparently, she is something of a savant. In any case, her father died in the boat accident and she is living now with Moncef Barcous Bey."

"Moncef Bey?" the Sultan repeated. "Was this one of his meetings?"

"It was." Jamaludin Pasha smiled. "Coincidentally. Or perhaps not. The raid, unfortunately, did not yield any new information about him, or his goals. Moncef Bey insisted they want only to read Rousseau, and that the code was just a game. In any case, we have made note of the entire incident in his file."

The Sultan did not particularly want to have a conversation about Jamaludin Pasha's overzealous surveillance techniques, so he changed the subject.

"How did the girl crack the code if she is living with him?"

"Ah," said the Grand Vizier, flattening his mustache. "One of our men is her tutor. He brought the code to their lessons and said it was a puzzle."

The Sultan was silent for a moment.

"What more do we know about this girl? What is her name again?"

"Eleonora Cohen. I have told you all we know about her. If you like, I will attempt to uncover more information. It shouldn't be too difficult."

"Yes," said the Sultan. "I would like that."

Chapter Fifteen

As Ramadan dragged itself through the hot, ever-thinning days of early summer, Stamboul baked into a hard crust of acceptance. Steamers slowed through the straits and hugged its shady banks, the muezzin's voice scratched with lack of water, and Eleonora sat at the windowsill, fanning herself with a book. The tension of each new day simmered, rose, and was released with the cannon shot at sundown. Even those who did not fast—the Armenians, the Greeks, the Europeans, and the Jews—all felt the same wave of relief at the end of the day when the streets filled with ice cream vendors, fortune-tellers, and dusty red tents. Each night lanterns were hung between the minarets of the New Mosque, wishing everyone a happy Ramadan. And the fireworks continued apace, though in a somewhat diminished capacity. Most evenings, the Bey broke his fast outside the house, with friends, colleagues, or distant cousins. He offered more than once to bring Eleonora along with him, but she declined. The thought of all those people, all that food and noise, was just too much. She was content with the quiet routine of her lessons, her reading, and meals alone in her room. All this changed, however, one Tuesday in the third week of Ramadan. That afternoon, Reverend Muehler arrived at the Bey's house a few minutes late. He seemed more animated than usual, his face apple-red and covered with downy stubble.

"Well, hello there," he said, ruffling her hair. "If it isn't the famous young Miss Cohen."

He laughed at some private joke and set a stack of books on the corner of the Colonel's desk.

"I thought we might do something a bit different today."

He motioned for her to sit and produced a well-worn dark green book. Eleonora took it into her hands and examined the spine. It was *The Metamorphoses* by Ovid.

"You know my opinion of novels and love poetry," the Reverend said. "The sweet, witty soul of Ovid, however, is far beyond reproach. And, if I am not mistaken, I believe he spent the last years of his life in Constanta."

Still cradling the book, Eleonora opened it to the first page. It was inscribed, in a confident, tilting hand, *To the mellifluous and honey-tongued Jimmy, May 1865, New Haven.*

"Yes," he said, taking the book from her and flipping through it. "A gift from my undergraduate days."

That afternoon, the Reverend interrupted her silent reading only when he wanted to repeat a line aloud, to hear it roll off his tongue. Pacing back and forth behind her, he followed her index finger under the words, humming absently to himself as she read. Toward the beginning of the story of Calisto, the swish of his trousers went silent. Thinking that perhaps he had a question for her, Eleonora reviewed the previous few lines—*Her vest was gathered up, her hair was tied; / Now in her hand a slender spear she bore, / Now a light quiver on her shoulders wore*—and looked back over her shoulder. The Reverend was lost in thought. His arms were crossed over his chest, his eyes closed and lips slightly parted. After a moment, he opened his eyes and saw that she was looking at him.

"By all means," he said. "Please, continue."

Although his behavior was unusual, Eleonora thought nothing of it, and she had no reason to suspect anything was amiss when the Reverend said he would be staying on after their lesson to write down some thoughts. He often stayed on after their lessons for a few minutes. On these occasions, Eleonora usually read in one of the armchairs on the other side of the room, but that afternoon, because the library was exceedingly stuffy, she decided instead to explore the corridors above the women's quarters. Owing to their darkness, the corridors stayed much cooler than the rest of the Bey's house, and she often spent the hottest part of the day wandering through them.

Even after nearly a dozen visits, Eleonora's heart still flapped and fluttered in her throat as she shuffled along the corridors' splintered floors. She held the hem of her dress and hunched slightly, the ceiling above her growing steadily lower as she progressed, or so it seemed. In those dark, moldering passageways, dank with the soiled smell of rotting wood, she could not see much farther than her hand in front of her and the walls tapering inward as they rose. She had intended to revisit the small iron door she had discovered on her first visit to the corridors, but seeing the scattered patch of light above the library, she paused. Bending to her knees, Eleonora gripped her fingers through the holes in the latticework screen and looked down on the room she had just left.

Reverend Muehler was seated still at the Colonel's desk. From this vantage point, she could see the red of the sun on the back of his neck and a small patch of baldness sprouting up about his crown. She couldn't tell at first what he was doing, but as she leaned forward, she saw that he had opened one of the desk drawers and was furtively rummaging through it. After a short while, he apparently found what he was looking for and slipped it into his briefcase. Eleonora craned her neck to see better. As she did, she was suddenly overcome by an enormous, watery sneeze.

The Reverend looked up and scanned the room. A long silence passed.

"Hello?" he called out. "Miss Cohen?"

Eleonora could hear her blood beating in her ears, could feel her breath caught at the base of her throat. She wanted to run, to leave the scene as quickly as possible, but she knew it was best to stay silent and still. Breathing now through an open mouth, she watched the Reverend stand, call her name once more, and walk around the room, peeking under chairs and tables. When he saw that the room was empty, he grabbed his briefcase and left. Eleonora remained rooted to that same spot for a long while before retracing her steps down the corridor and out of the women's quarters.

For the rest of that afternoon and all through dinner, Eleonora revisited this incident in her memory, the open drawer, the briefcase, the sound of her own name. There were a number of plausible explanations for what she had seen—Reverend Muehler could have been asked to retrieve a document for the Bey, he might have been looking for a lost pen or a blank piece of paper—but no matter how many possibilities she was able to conjure, she had a difficult time convincing herself of any but the most obvious explanation. The Reverend had stolen from the Bey. From an ethical point of view, the real question was not what had happened but whether she would tell anyone what she had seen. Plato would seem to think she should. *Truth is the beginning of every good to the gods, and of every good to man.* Then again, there was Tertullian. *Truth engenders hatred of truth. As soon as it appears it is the enemy.* She stewed over the question all through dinner, the fireworks, and into her dreams.

When she came downstairs that next morning for breakfast the problem was still with her. As usual, she and the Bey did not communicate much beyond the requisite salutations and ci-vilities. Monsieur Karom brought her food as usual, and she ate as usual. Still, she could feel it, that question hanging over the room like the silent taxidermied head of a rhinoceros. She hadn't lied. She hadn't betrayed anyone's trust; still, she felt she had done something wrong. Or rather, she had not yet done the right thing. Was there a difference between these two sins? They ate in silence, Eleonora staring down at sliced strawberries bleeding red onto her plate. She needed to say something, to do what was right, but she didn't want to bear false witness against the Rev-erend. She pricked a strawberry slice onto her fork and chewed until it dissolved in her mouth.

"Miss Cohen," said the Bey as he stood from the table. "I won't be home until later tonight. I have been invited to the house of Haci Bekir."

Her memory of Haci Bekir, his venal improbity and temper, decided the question once and for all. She removed a piece of paper and a pen from her frock pocket.

Do you have a moment? There is something I would like to ask.

"Of course," said the Bey, still standing. "What is on your mind?"

Yesterday, she began after a long hesitation, *I was in the wom-en's corridors.*

She looked up at him, gauging his response. As far as she knew, the Bey had no idea about her explorations. Whether or not he did, he was not in the least taken aback by her revelation.

I found them by accident. I go up there sometimes when I want to be alone. I am sorry if I wasn't supposed to be there.

"I understand," he said. "Is that all you wanted to say?"

Eleonora glanced at Monsieur Karom, who was standing with his hands behind his back next to the buffet.

I was up in the corridors. And I saw the Reverend. It was after my lesson and he had stayed on in the library to write down a few of his thoughts. I didn't mean to be watching him, but when I looked down I saw him going through one of the drawers of the Colonel's desk.

The Bey tightened his mouth.

"Is that all?"

I can't be sure, because of the angle, but I think I saw him take something out of the drawer and put it in his briefcase.

"What was it?" the Bey asked, animated in a way she had never before seen. "A pen, a letter, a piece of paper?"

Eleonora felt the first tingling pangs of regret in the tips of her toes. She could see a mountain of unintended consequences at her feet, a mountain crumbling beneath her. For a moment, she wanted to take it all back, but she couldn't. Now that it had been released into the world, she had to tell the Bey everything.

It looked like a piece of paper. Or maybe a few pieces of paper, a small stack.

Without another word, the Bey strode down the main hall to the library. Eleonora followed a few steps behind.

"Which drawer was it?" he said when they arrived, sitting down at the Colonel's desk. "Do you remember?"

She pointed at the upper left drawer and the Bey rifled through it. When he didn't find what he was looking for, he removed the drawer's contents entirely. Placing the papers on the desk, he looked through them one by one. When he reached the bottom of the pile, he let his head sink into his hands.

"I should never have trusted him," he said. "The Rector of Robert's College offering to tutor a young girl."

Eleonora stood at the desk while the Bey mumbled into the cave of his arms. She felt a falling sensation, the world disintegrating by her own volition. Suddenly, the Bey looked up and, grasping her by the shoulders, looked hard into her eyes.

"Are you absolutely sure you saw him take a piece of paper from this drawer?"

She nodded, avoiding the harsh glow of his eyes.

"This is a very serious matter. If what you said is true, we cannot have him in the house anymore, under any circumstances. Your lessons will have to end and we will have to cut all ties with him."

The Bey paused and released his grip, seeming to collect himself.

"At the same time, you must take care not to bear false witness. It is, according to Muhammad at least, among the four greatest sins."

Yes. I am sure.

"Then there is only one course we can take."

If I may ask, she wrote tentatively. *What was the piece of paper?*

The Bey closed his eyes and took a few long breaths before he removed a blank sheet of stationery and a pen from the top drawer of the desk.

"What the Reverend took was of no great importance," he said. "What matters is that we cannot trust him."

With Eleonora looking over his shoulder, the Bey composed a short letter.

Dear Reverend James Muehler,

  I regret to inform you that we can no longer continue
the lessons between yourself and Miss Eleonora Cohen.
Due to circumstances beyond our control, which
unfortunately we are not able to discuss, we are forced to

terminate the relationship immediately. Miss Cohen has
enjoyed your lessons immensely and she wishes you all
the best in the future, as do I. We both sincerely hope this
decision will not cause you any undue inconvenience or
injury.

Sincerely,
Moncef Barcous Bey

The Bey read over the letter and looked to Eleonora for approval before he folded it and placed it in an envelope. Just like
that, her lessons were over. She had done the right thing, she
knew she had, but it didn't feel right. It didn't feel right at all. After attempting to read in the library for a few hours, Eleonora ate
lunch, wandered back upstairs to her room, and slipped into bed,
thinking about General Krzab's words to his wife on the nature
of truth: *A slippery fish, flashing scales in the water and a noble
fighter on the line, but dull as lead at the bottom of the boat.* It was
true. As much as she admired the idea of truth from a distance,
its practice left something to be desired.

Eleonora awoke that next morning to the click of the door
and the soft music of Mrs. Damakan humming a familiar melody. Her dreams scurried into the far corners of the room,
under furniture and into the cracks between the floorboards.
Rubbing her eyes, she slipped out of bed and followed Mrs.
Damakan to the bathroom. The air was heavy with condensa-
tion and the smell of soap. The morning pressed its face to the
small window above the sink like a beggar. Eleonora could feel
her skin gather into goose bumps as she slipped into the bath.
A shiver jumped across her back and she traced an S on the
surface of a square blue tile.

Lifting her arms to the edge of the tub, she leaned her head back and let Mrs. Damakan work her hair into a soapy froth. What she would do now, she had no idea. Without her lessons, the future stretched out like an endless expanse of waves, weeks and months rising and falling in an undifferentiated ocean of time. She didn't regret what she had done—she had done the right thing—but she mourned the loss of her lessons and feared that perhaps her accusation was false. Perhaps she had imagined the Reverend opening that drawer. Perhaps he was just curious. Relaxing into the motion of the lather, she let her shoulders slump forward and wrapped her arms around her knees. In the murky translucence of the bath, she could see the outlines of her reflection, her flesh scrubbed pink and a tower of soapy white hair as tall as an Austrian cake. She thought of lily pads as she touched her chin to the surface of the water.

"Eleonora."

Mrs. Damakan pronounced her name with care, as if it were an inscription etched into the back of an amulet. Moistening her lips, the handmaid brought her stool around to the front of the tub. Her kerchief was pushed back much farther than normal, revealing a stringy white field of hair woven through with strands of black.

"You did what was right," she said. "You did the right thing."

How the old handmaid knew what had happened, Eleonora didn't know. This pronouncement, however, that she had done the right thing, was spoken with such assurance that it washed away her doubts, at least for the time being.

"You did the right thing," Mrs. Damakan repeated and Eleonora knew it was true. She had done the right thing.

After rinsing Eleonora's hair, the old handmaid stood, pulled the plug, and quickly gathered up her things, leaving Eleonora alone to watch the remains of her bathwater swirl and cough down the drain. She opened her mouth, as if to speak, then caught herself. When the last of the cloudy gray water disappeared, a shiver ran from her shoulders to her knees, and the entire length of her skin bristled.

Chapter Sixteen

❖

The termination of Eleonora's lessons did not change much the structure of her daily routine. She still woke at the same hour, bathed, and went downstairs to breakfast with the Bey. Her afternoons, she still spent primarily in her armchair or at the Colonel's desk, twisting a strand of hair around her finger as she read. The Bey's library was large enough to keep her busy for at least a few more years, but without Reverend Muehler behind her, without the constant prodding and pacing of her tutor, she found it difficult to marshal her concentration. As she read, trudging through the annals of ancient history and oration, exhuming the petty rivalries and disputations of centuries past, her thoughts often wandered from the text at hand. Even lighter reading, like the stash of mystery novels she found alongside *The Complete Works of Honoré de Balzac*, had trouble holding her attention.

Although the question of Reverend Muehler was, for all intents and purposes, settled, Eleonora returned to it again and again. Gazing at the wallpaper in front of her, she lingered on her memory of the incident: the open drawer, the Reverend calling her name before he left the room. Her own role in the affair, she knew, was beyond reproach. There was no doubt she had seen the Reverend rummaging through the Colonel's desk; there was no doubt he had put a piece or a stack of papers in his briefcase; and there was no doubt she had done the right thing in telling the Bey. It was not a complicated situation, she told herself. Reverend

Muehler had stolen something and, as a result, the Bey did not want him in the house. Still, something about the matter bothered her. She didn't understand why the Reverend would want to steal anything from the Bey in the first place, nor why the Bey had reacted so strongly. Perhaps it was the influence of the mystery novels she had been reading; perhaps it was her natural sense of curiosity. Regardless of where it came from, Eleonora could not rid herself of the notion that the matter of Reverend Muehler was connected somehow to that strange young man at the Café Europa, and possibly also to the encrypted note the Reverend had shown her just a few weeks before his dismissal. How they were related, she didn't know.

It was during this period, between the termination of her lessons and the end of Ramadan, that the Bey began to propose various excursions around town. If they were discussing Homer, he might mention that the ruins of Troy had recently been discovered less than a day's ride from Stamboul. If she asked him a question about the architect Sinan, he might praise the interior of Sultan Ahmed Mosque. More than once he mentioned the wonderful view of the city from the top of Rumelihisarı, adding that it was by far the best picnic spot in Stamboul. Not wanting to pressure her into anything, however, Moncef Bey never suggested any of these excursions outright, and Eleonora never outright rejected them. Hinting and demurring, they returned again and again to the same positions, like a king and rook in eternal check. The Bey praised the beauty of the day and Eleonora nodded, her thoughts elsewhere.

One afternoon, toward the end of the month of Ramadan, Eleonora was sitting at the Colonel's desk in the library, reading Aristophanes. It had rained the night before, a short summer thunderstorm. As a consequence of this, Mrs. Damakan had pushed the curtains open and a late-afternoon light suffused the room, giving the furniture and the pages of her book a melancholy tint they weren't accustomed to.

What cares have not gnawed at my heart? And how few have been the pleasures in my life! Four, to be exact, while my troubles have been as countless as the grains of sand on the shore!

Eleonora exhaled and looked up at the stretch of wallpaper in front of her. It was the same design as always, a dark red paisley with gold stripes. As she stared, however, she noticed for the first time that a battery of tiny gold swords was scattered throughout the paisley. She leaned her chair back on two legs, so as to better observe the expanse of wallpaper, and her knee grazed the side of the desk. She looked down and her eyes came to rest on the curved brass handle of the left drawer. Rubbing her knee, Eleonora wondered, as she often did, what the Reverend had been looking for and whether he had found it. That afternoon, for reasons she could not explain even to herself, she did more than wonder. Scooting her chair back from the desk, she looped two fingers through the handle of the drawer and pulled. She had expected it to be locked, but it gave easily, and there, like a nest of birds hidden at the back of a clerestory, was a stack of letters tied neatly with a string.

Glancing at the door to the hallway, she unloosed the string and peeled off the top letter. It was a thick, square envelope, an invitation addressed to Mr. Moncef Barcous. The return address was embossed on the back flap: *American Consulate, Beyoğlu*. Underneath these words was a picture of an eagle with the world in its talons. She lifted the flap and, pushing together the edges of the envelope, let the invitation slip out. *The presence of the bearer is requested at a costume ball at the American Consulate*. At the bottom of the invitation was a date in October of 1883, almost two

years previous. Laying the invitation aside, Eleonora lifted out
the entire stack of letters. It was a hodgepodge of personal correspondence, a few invitations, and two pieces of what appeared to
be official communication from the palace, nothing of particular
interest. She was on the verge of going back to Aristophanes,
when she found, at the bottom of the pile, a letter quite unlike
the rest.

Covered with oily fingerprints and dust, it gave off an air of
provinciality. There was no stamp or return address, and the
only clue as to its destination were the words *Moncef Barcous
Bey, care of Mrs. Damakan*. Eleonora held the letter to her nose
and inhaled the remnant of a familiar smell, a country road buried somewhere deep in her memory. This was clearly not what
the Reverend had been looking for, but its smell struck a chord
inside her, as did the small, uncertain hand on the front of the envelope. Replacing the rest of the stack, she closed the drawer, sat
up straight, and pulled her chair closer to the desk. She slipped
the letter out of its envelope and let it fall onto the blotter. It was
yellow at the edges and folded into a square, two sheets covered
front and back with an anxious scrawl.

"Miss Cohen."

Before he said her name, Eleonora heard Moncef Bey clear
his throat. And in the shape of that sound she knew immediately
that he had been watching her for some time. He crossed the
room and leaned against the edge of the Colonel's desk. He saw
the letter. He was looking at it directly. Beyond his gaze, however, he did not acknowledge its presence.

"What is that you are reading?" he asked, motioning toward
the book.

She turned the spine to face him.

"Aristophanes," he read.

In the absence of anything else to do with her hands, she straightened the book and moved it to the middle of the desk.

"I have been thinking," said the Bey, "that it would be nice to take a trip to Rumelihisarı."

Eleonora nodded, unsure where he was going with this line of conversation but glad it had nothing to do with the letter on the blotter.

"The wildflowers are blooming," he continued. "I have no other appointments this afternoon. It's a short ride and we could bring a picnic dinner with us."

Eleonora glanced about the library, with its stuffy red velvet curtains, its globes, its carpets, and shelves upon shelves of books. How many hours had she spent in this room? How many pages had she read? The Bey clearly wanted very much to go with her to Rumelihisarı. She owed him that at least, didn't she?

"What do you think?" he asked. "Would you like to go to Rumelihisarı today?"

Yes. A picnic would be nice.

She replaced the Aristophanes book on its shelf, and within the hour they were off, riding along the western shore of the Bosporus toward the narrow mouth of the straits. It was indeed a glorious day. The late-afternoon sun was waning, a brown-and-white rabbit hopped alongside the road, and, with her face to the latticework, Eleonora could see flashes of her flock overhead. As the Bey had promised, the ride was rather short.

"This," he said as they rumbled to a stop, "is Rumelihisarı. It was from this tower, more than four hundred years ago, that Fatih Sultan Mehmet laid siege to Stamboul and took the city from the Byzantines."

A squat stone tower rising rather haphazardly from a pile of rubble and grass, Rumelihisarı did not at first glance seem like much of anything. As they disembarked, paid the guard, and climbed the curving steps to its crenellated crown, however, Eleonora saw that the tower itself did not matter. What gave Rumelihisarı its significance was its position at the mouth of the Bosporus, and the vantage point such a location afforded. At that time of year, the watch of Rumelihisarı was blanketed with light blue wildflowers, and tufts of grass sprouted up through cracks in the stone. The heat of the day had dissipated and a shallow breeze blew in from the sea. As the Bey arranged their picnic— cold meat, bread, cheese, and olives—hoopoes swept down from the minaret of a neighborhood mosque and stretched across the straits. A swath of purple against a bright orange sky, it contracted, then expanded, like an ethereal lung. She wasn't sure what it was trying to say, but Eleonora had the distinct sense that her flock was speaking to her. After a few passes across the water, the birds dispersed into a grove of pine trees behind Üsküdar.

Eleonora inhaled and let the city wash over her. Instead of the framed and lifeless landscape she saw from her bay window, this city was alive, teeming with people, with shouting, music, and the smell of baking bread. There was the turtle dome of the New Mosque, the needle minarets of Sultan Ahmed. There was the Bey's yellow-and-white house. And there, at the confluence of the waters, was the Sultan's palace, the jewel at the tip of the Golden Horn, with its gleaming white marble walls, crystalline towers, and gardens of wisteria. She bit the inside of her cheek as the last breath of the sun held itself just above the curve of the hill and painted the walls of the palace pale orange fading into pink. As the last light of the sun disappeared, a cannon shot rang out from across the water.

"A number of years ago," said the Bey as he motioned for her to sit down and partake of the picnic, "I was given the honor of visiting the palace."

He prepared a plate for her and handed it across the picnic blanket.

"You may know that, though, after the letters you read today."

He paused and placed an olive in his mouth.

"When I first offered to take you in, Miss Cohen, I can't say I was motivated by anything more than duty, and my fidelity to the memory of your father. The past months, however, while difficult in many ways, have proven to be some of the most gratifying this old bachelor can remember. Which is to say," he continued, "I don't at all appreciate you looking through my correspondence, but I understand the impulse. I understand you might have a number of questions about the letters and the matter with Reverend Muehler. Before you ask them, however, I would like to try to explain my end of things as best I can."

He took a bite of the sandwich he had made for himself and swallowed.

"You have read Jean-Jacques Rousseau?"

She nodded.

"As a young man," the Bey began to explain, "I was quite taken with Rousseau's ideas: the social contract, civil society, the general will of the people, and so on. You might say his ideas were a kind of revelation to me. And I was not alone. At that time there were a number of young men like myself—sons of businessmen, bureaucrats, military officers, and tax farmers— who took to Rousseau's ideas with full force. I started a reading group, which met once a month and was quite popular. I also wrote a number of forceful essays in the newspaper, advocating for the rights of man."

The Bey caught her eyes, to make sure she was following.

"It was as a direct result of Rousseau and my advocacy for his ideas that I was sent to Constanta. At the time I was a member of parliament and my father was a very important businessman, one of the largest suppliers of textiles to the military. So instead of putting me in prison, as he no doubt would have liked to do, the Sultan honored me with a diplomatic post at the edge of the empire."

Eleonora nodded, indicating that she understood.

"It was in Constanta that I met your father and there that I established many of my most important business connections. But as much as I enjoyed my time there, Stamboul is my home. And so, when the political climate calmed down, I returned. I returned on the condition that I never participate in politics again. And I have not. I still hold my views, but my methods have changed. Since I returned, the Grand Vizier has kept a close watch on my movements. His suspicions are unfounded, I can assure you of that. I do not nor have I ever advocated for a constitutional revolution. But I understand why he would want to keep a close eye on me, with my past and all the clamoring about the boat accident. I must say, I never suspected the Reverend. I don't know why I did not. In retrospect it makes all the sense in the world. I don't know if he is working for the palace, for the Americans, or both, but in any case there is no way we could continue with your lessons. You understand, don't you?"

Eleonora swallowed and looked up at the Bey. She understood what he was telling her. Still, her mind was buzzing with questions like a band of insects trapped in a jar of preserves.

"All this is to say," he concluded, "I've had a good life, a charmed life, but lonely, devoid of a female touch, and without children—until now, of course. You know I take my responsibilities as your guardian very seriously. To that end, I must ask that you not poke through my documents. It is in your own best interest that I ask this of you. I will give them to you one day, but not now."

Chapter Seventeen

As the Reverend approached the Gate of Greeting, he removed
a handkerchief from his jacket pocket and wiped the sweat off
his forehead. It was his first visit to the palace, and, in spite of his
best efforts otherwise, he couldn't help but marvel. Flanked on
either side by a pair of massive stone turrets, the sheer immen-
sity of the gate, and the delicacy of the carvings that adorned
it, conveyed both hospitality and impregnable hostility. Which
made sense, he supposed. Although he presumed that he himself
was in the good graces of the palace, one never knew when one's
welcome would wear out. The Reverend folded his handkerchief
in quarters and returned it to his jacket pocket. As he did, one of
the purple-coated palace guards approached him and presented
arms.

"The Gate of Greeting is closed to visitors," he grumbled,
oblivious, apparently, to the irony of this sentiment.

When the Reverend mentioned the name of Jamaludin Pasha, however, the guard dropped his bayonet and stood aside. A
foreigner meeting with the Grand Vizier was not a person one
wanted to offend, it seemed. The guard motioned to another,
stationed at the base of the ramparts, and Reverend Muehler was
escorted through a series of thick wooden doors to the inner
sanctum of the palace's second courtyard.

Once he was within the bulwarks of the palace, the rush and
tumble of Stamboul fell away. He could still feel the presence

of the city, like the moon hanging in its pale sky, but the concerns of the palace were of another, more delicate sphere. Reverend Muehler took in the cool trickle of water on marble, a bird setting up roost for the night, and the faint smell of hibiscus flowers in bloom. Foot traffic in the second courtyard was sparse as diplomats, chefs, and musicians headed home for the night, back to their families, the cafés, or some other late-night amusement. The guard who had led him through the gates said a few words to a herald, who then conducted him up one of the many leafy paths radiating from the Gate of Greeting. Up until this point, the Reverend's meetings with the Grand Vizier had taken place at the end of each month, in a clandestine location such as a graveyard or an empty bathhouse. He had no idea why Jamaludin Pasha would want him to come to the palace in person. Perhaps he had obtained word about his dismissal from the Bey's service. Perhaps the higher-ups at the department had crossed him. Perhaps it was about his recent interactions with the Russians. Or maybe it was nothing; maybe the Grand Vizier was just too lazy to leave the palace. With a nod, the herald unwound another tense knot of guards and led Reverend Muehler into a marble hallway lined with antique weaponry. This was, according to the herald, the Great Hall of the Council of Viziers. Jamaludin Pasha's audience chamber was located at the end of the hall to the left.

"You will know when you see it," the herald said before scurrying off around some corner.

And indeed he did. Swathed in red and green tiles, the audience chamber was no larger than a classroom at Robert's College, but its ceiling rose as high as a church. Against the far wall was a square mahogany divan and, reclining in the middle of it, the Grand Vizier. A nervous man in a white silk robe and green turban, he had the aspect of a well-fed rodent and eyes the color of unripe grapes. When Reverend Muehler entered the room, he rose slightly by way of greeting.

"Hello, my friend. I trust you found your way without much difficulty."

"Yes, thank you," said the Reverend. "Your heralds were very helpful."

The Grand Vizier clasped his hands together and wrinkled the base of his nose, as if considering the vicissitudes of this response. He concentrated fully on his guest but did not offer him a seat. In fact, the Reverend noticed, there were no seats to offer. Whether this was a conscious snub, he did not know, nor did he much care.

"Would you like a glass of tea?" Jamaludin Pasha asked. "Or coffee?"

"No, thank you."

"The coffee in the palace kitchen is the finest in the world," the Grand Vizier pressed. "I can assure you, you will not regret it."

"Yes," said the Reverend, adjusting his collar. "I can only imagine. But I think I will refrain nonetheless. I have trouble sleeping, you know. If I drink coffee too late I will never be able to get to bed. I hope you aren't offended."

"Not at all."

Tapping the side of his nose, the Grand Vizier said a few words to one of the guards, who disappeared through a door hidden in the back wall. They were both silent until the guard returned a few moments later, balancing a single tulip-shaped glass of tea on a silver tray.

"Now," said Jamaludin Pasha, stirring in a spoonful of sugar. "I assume you have seen the news about our situation with the Russians?"

"Yes," the Reverend said. "I read a piece about it yesterday in the paper."

"As I am sure you can imagine, we are troubled by the insinuations in the Tsar's report. On balance, however, this is not a particularly consequential matter and we would like to be done with it as soon as possible."

The Reverend mumbled his agreement.

"Of course, we cannot accede to the Tsar's demands as they stand."

"Of course not," said the Reverend.

"His threats are empty," said the Grand Vizier, raising the twinge of a question.

"They would seem to be."

"We would like to know this for certain. I assume you don't have any information that might help us assess the possibility of reprisal should we refuse to meet his demands for restitution."

"No," said the Reverend. "Unfortunately, I do not."

"No connections to the Russians we might exploit for further information?"

The Reverend shifted and crossed his hands in front of him. Jamaludin Pasha clearly knew about his recent association with the Russians. The last thing he wanted, however, was to negotiate between these two intractable empires. He had enough trouble juggling his current obligations. Add another ball and he would drop them all.

"None that would be of any use to the palace."

Jamaludin Pasha smiled and stroked the tip of his nose.

"Very well," he said. "Tell me, how are things otherwise?"

"Quite well," the Reverend replied. "Robert's is Robert's. My article on the religious rites of the Yazidis is coming along well and a new volume of my translations should be coming out soon."

Nodding, though mostly to himself, Jamaludin Pasha stared down into the folds of his robe. He pursed his lips, as if considering a perplexing moral question, then looked up again at Reverend Muehler.

"I am assuming you have no new information for me, beyond your academic pursuits."

"No," the Reverend said. "I do not."

"What about Moncef Barcous Bey?"

The Reverend uncrossed his hands and held them at his side.

"Yes, well, there has been an unfortunate turn of events regarding Moncef Bey."

"What would that be?"

"Moncef Bey and Miss Cohen decided recently that they no longer require my services as a tutor."

"And why was that?"

The Reverend paused to collect his thoughts.

"Circumstances beyond their control, that was how they put it."

"You have no idea what those circumstances may be? You didn't press him for more information?"

"They informed me of their decision in a letter, which stated in no uncertain terms that they were unable to discuss the circumstances leading to their decision. I assumed it was a financial question."

The Grand Vizier pressed the bridge of his nose between his thumbs.

"Can you think of any other reason why you might have been dismissed? Is it possible that Moncef Bey might have suspected your intentions?"

"That was what I imagined at first," said the Reverend.

He thought back to the incident that afternoon in the library. Any number of people could have seen him taking those papers from the desk—Miss Cohen, Monsieur Karom, Mrs. Damakan—but even if someone had seen him, even if he knew for certain that he had been dismissed for spying, he wasn't going to tell the Grand Vizier.

"After careful consideration of my activities," the Reverend continued, "I have concluded that there is no reason to believe Moncef Bey had any suspicions."

"None that you can think of?"

"No," the Reverend said after a pause long enough to suggest serious consideration. "None that I can think of."

"Well," said Jamaludin Pasha. "That is most regrettable. Fortunately, we have other people watching Moncef Bey, other people very close to him."

He paused to take a sip of his tea, allowing the Reverend to wonder who these other informants were.

"Now tell me, what do you know about the student?"

"Miss Cohen?"

"Yes, Miss Cohen. You mentioned before that she is a savant of sorts?"

The Reverend unclenched his sweaty hands, glad to be done with the previous line of questioning.

"Miss Cohen has a phenomenal aptitude for languages, a nearly perfect memory, and an understanding of history and philosophy far, far beyond her years. It's really quite extraordinary. Just a few weeks ago she recited the entire first book of *The Iliad* from memory. I mentioned, I believe, that I am planning to write a paper about her."

"Yes, I believe you did."

"It will be more difficult now that our lessons have been terminated, but I am confident I have enough information to proceed."

The Grand Vizier took another sip of tea.

"Can you think of any way we might use Miss Cohen in the palace?"

Reverend Muehler shifted his stance, looking down at the floor to think. He did not want to embroil Eleonora in palace politics, but he needed first and foremost to preserve his own well-being. The Reverend had seen what happened to spies who lost their usefulness, and he had far too many skeletons to risk drawing Jamaludin Pasha into his closet.

"You might," he began, without knowing how he would end the sentence. "You might be able to put her to use in the Bureau of Translation."

"We already have more interpreters than we know what to do with."

"Perhaps," said the Reverend. "Do you have any cryptographers?"

"We do."

"Are there any encryptions they are unable to break?"

The Grand Vizier leaned back into the cushions of the divan, as if to better consider the proposal.

"There are a few that have given us trouble."

"With a bit of training, Miss Cohen could be a master cryptographer. To her, breaking a code would be as easy as learning a new language."

"Interesting," said Jamaludin Pasha and wrote a few words in the small black notebook he always kept in his pocket. "What about her relations? I know she lives with Moncef Bey. But does she have any familial connections in Constanta?"

"Her father is deceased," said Reverend Muehler. "I believe I heard mention once of an aunt or a stepmother, but she seems rather peripheral."

"Is there anything else we should know about her?" the Grand Vizier asked. "What are her political sympathies?"

"As far as I know, she doesn't have any," said the Reverend. "She is only a child, after all."

"Yes, I suppose so."

"There is one more thing you might want to know about Miss Cohen," the Reverend said. "She tends to keep her thoughts, and any feelings she might have, to herself; it's a trait which is only exacerbated by her refusal to speak."

Jamaludin Pasha raised his eyebrows, encouraging the Reverend to continue.

"She has not spoken since her father died, in the crash."

Moving his lips slightly, Jamaludin Pasha wrote a few more notes in his book, then stood. The interview, apparently, was over. He produced a pouch from the pocket of his robe and handed it to the guard closest to him, who crossed the room and gave it to the Reverend.

"I hope this will compensate you for your trouble," said the Grand Vizier. "It should more than supplement the income lost by your lessons."

The small leather pouch felt much heavier than usual.

"Thank you, Jamaludin Pasha. It was my pleasure."

"If you hear anything more from Moncef Bey or Miss Cohen," the Grand Vizier continued, "please do notify us immediately. Otherwise, we will contact you when we are in need of your services."

As the import of these words sunk in, the Reverend was escorted out the door and down the Great Hall of the Council of

Viziers to a hidden exit that deposited him just outside the palace walls. Ducking behind the dark facade of a shuttered fishmonger, he opened the pouch and counted fifteen pounds—three times his normal rate. Apparently, he had given Jamaludin Pasha something of interest.

Chapter Eighteen

In the dream, she's rowing. The clouds are dusty purple, and behind them stars flicker like jellyfish. There is a crowd of people lined up along the shore. They're trying to tell her something, but she doesn't look back. If she looks back, it will only slow her down and she's slow enough already. She has a message for the person in the tower. The message is written on the piece of paper in her hand and she is rowing.

Haydarpasa Station is a giant sleeping on the edge of the horizon, a Cyclops in the opening of his cave. Pulling itself up to its full height, it yawns. Those tracks are veins, connecting the fingers to the heart. Those trains are arms. The clock is its eye. Behind the station is an island with a boxy white tower like a jail. That is where she is taking her message. The moon winks. She understands.

Kiz Kulesi, she thinks. Maiden's Tower. The name sticks in her mind like taffy. She tries to remember the story of the tower. There was a girl and her father, who was the Sultan. There was a curse, an asp, and a basket of grapes. The girl was locked in the tower. Aphrodite may have been involved. Or was that another story? Does it even matter? Now that she is rowing through the stiff-peaked straits and waves spackled with jellyfish, does the story matter?

The strange thing is that she can't remember the message. She can't remember what she is supposed to say to the person in the tower, or why. But she knows that it is important. She knows the message is written on the piece of paper in her hand. She rows past Haydarpasa Station and a fish jumps out of the water, whipping drops from its tail. Then there's another fish, then another. Then the water is alive, teeming with fish. They splash her, flopping like rubber erasers, but she rows past. She rows as hard as she can past the train station, through the fish and the slow water.

Her boat runs aground with a crunch. The tower sways, pale and sticky, a drunk stabbing the night with his cane. When she hears the crunch of her boat running aground, she sees the birds. It's her flock, hundreds of purple-and-white hoopoes swirling like violins. They are swallowing the stars. They're saying something. They're trying to tell her something. But even if she could hear, even if she could understand, she doesn't want to know. That is not what she came for. She has come with a message for the person in the tower.

She opens the door to the tower and the staircase is filled with birds. It is damp and flapping with purple, an anxious spiral chattering with voices. She lifts the hood of her coat and shakes her hair out. They're all talking at once, they're all trying to tell her something. Are they saying it or singing it? She can't tell. She is pushing up the stairs, through the birds, toward the room at the top of the tower.

At the end of the stairs, she stops. The birds are gone. Now there is a crowd, a forest of legs and trunks. They are gathered around the room at the top of the tower, waiting for the message to arrive. She shows them the message. She waves the piece of paper in front of them and tells them that she is the one with the message. Here it is, she yells. Here is the message you're waiting for. I am the messenger! But no one is listening. And even if they were listening, it wouldn't matter. Because the piece of paper in her hand is blank.

When she awoke, Eleonora was sweating along the ridge of her forehead, and her pillowcase was wet with saliva. Morning spread over the city like a sheet of gauze, its pink-orange fingertips smothering tufts of fog and sleeping night watchmen. Rolling onto her back, Eleonora gazed up at the lace canopy over her bed. Her dreams were usually little more than incoherent strips of memory—the smell of bleach, an injured deer, a view of a distant port—nothing like this. This dream was something entirely different. Like Penelope's vision of the geese, Pip's dream of himself as Hamlet, or Jacob wrestling with angels, this dream was real, something she could hold on to. She could feel that it meant something. What, she had no idea.

Unable to fall back to sleep, Eleonora slid out of bed and pulled on her dressing gown. Feeling the weft of the carpet with her bare feet, she shuffled across her room to the bay window and watched the city come to life. Compared to its image in her dream, Kiz Kulesi looked ponderous and sad. A boxy stone tower topped with a watch room and a thin copper spire, the building had been used variously as a prison, a lighthouse, and a customs station. It was empty now, as far as she knew, the tiny island uninhabited but for birds. There was a pair of black storks poking their beaks in the shallow water around the island, and a lone goldfinch on the sill of the watch room. Watching the finch hop from one end of the sill to the other, Eleonora thought she saw a flash of purple inside the tower. She squinted against the sun, leaned forward, and opened the window a crack to dispel the glare, but all she could see was the finch. If that had been a member of her flock inside the tower, it was gone now.

As the goldfinch took flight, Eleonora noticed a carriage pull up the front drive of the Bey's house. This was unusual. The Bey rarely had visitors at home and never so early in the morning. Tightening the belt of her dressing gown, she watched the ornate purple-and-gold coach slow to a stop at the edge of the water. Once the horses were settled, the carriage door opened from the inside. Without so much as a glance to either side, a man in a purple uniform walked straight up to the front door of the house and knocked. Overcome by curiosity, Eleonora pulled on a proper dress and rushed out to the landing above the antechamber. Peering through the bars of the railing, she watched Monsieur Karom open the door in his usual haughty manner. When he saw who it was, however, he took a step back and knelt down on one knee.

Eleonora could not hear what they were saying, but when Monsieur Karom stood again he looked back over his shoulder in the direction of her room. Seeing her there on the landing, he called up.

"Miss Cohen. Could you please come down for a moment? There is someone here who would like to speak with you."

As she descended, Eleonora got her first real glimpse of the man in the purple uniform. He was standing at attention, his chest stiff, hat cocked, and purple satin coat pierced with crystal buttons. There was a hint of lavender in the air around him and he held in his left hand a silver tube the size of a cucumber. In order not to stare, she kept her eyes on the carpet as she crossed the anteroom. When she reached the door, Monsieur Karom began with a formal introduction.

"May I present Miss Eleonora Cohen, daughter of Yakob Cohen, formerly of Constanta and late of Stamboul, the current charge of Moncef Barcous Bey."

Straightening his back even further, the visitor cleared his throat.

"Miss Cohen," he said. "The Servant to the Holy Cities, Caliph of Islam, Commander of the Faithful, and Supreme Padishah of various realms, His Excellency Sultan Abdulhamid II, requests an audience with you at the palace."

He held out the silver tube and she took it.

"We will send a carriage tomorrow morning at this time," he continued. "I trust that is convenient."

Eleonora looked down at the exquisite object she had been given. She held the tube, engraved with an overlapping floral pattern and topped by a hinged ivory cap, in both hands like a sword. It was similar in workmanship and design to the document holder from which the Reverend had produced his puzzle. She could hear a torrent of blood rushing through her temples and the anteroom felt as if it were closing in on itself.

"Yes, of course," she heard Monsieur Karom say.

With a single motion, he took the document holder from Eleonora's hand, removed the invitation inside, and returned the empty holder to the herald.

"We are honored," he said, scanning the invitation. "Miss Cohen is honored by His Excellency's attention."

The afternoon passed in an anxious haze of disbelief. How the Sultan knew who she was and why he wanted to meet her, of all the thousands of people in Stamboul, of all the millions of people in the Ottoman Empire, Eleonora had no intimation whatsoever. The air in her room that afternoon was thick with questions that could not possibly be answered, at least not by her. Pacing from dresser to bed to desk, paging blankly through her book, sitting in the armchair next to the bay window with her hands crossed in her lap, she tried her best to absorb this news. Tomorrow she was going to meet the Sultan. The sovereign of millions, the ruler of lands from Selonika to Basra, he who could meet with anyone he wanted, had requested an audience with her, Eleonora Cohen.

Dinner was served early that evening. She sat in her normal seat and Moncef Bey sat in his. Monsieur Karom served a plate of stewed beef with broad beans. She thought she was not hungry, but as she cut a piece of meat and raised it to her mouth, her stomach growled audibly.

"It is an honor," said the Bey, unfolding his napkin in his lap. "You have been given a distinct honor."

Eleonora nodded as she chewed. If she understood anything about the invitation, it was this.

"I myself have been invited to the palace twice, but never for a formal audience with His Excellency."

The Bey cut off a piece of beef and speared it with his fork.

"I do wonder, however, what His Excellency's motivations might be. He is known to have a strong interest in—"

He paused, searching for the right word.

"The extraordinary—fortune-tellers, talking birds, and the like. At first I suspected this might be the motivation behind his invitation, that he had heard about your abilities of memory, which are quite extraordinary, and wanted to discuss them with you."

Eleonora swallowed and laid her silverware on the edges of her plate, waiting for the Bey to continue his thought.

"I wonder, though, whether there might be other motivations as well," he said. "Perhaps he is curious about our relationship. Perhaps he wants to know if you have seen anything suspicious in the house."

Eleonora had not considered this possibility. In fact, she had not considered the Sultan's motivations at all.

"You know I have nothing to hide," the Bey continued, extending his arms as if inviting anyone to search him. "We discussed this the other day at Rumelihisarı. I just want to be sure, for both of our sakes, that you are careful about what you tell the Sultan tomorrow. I am not, in any way, suggesting you should deceive anyone, least of all His Excellency or the Grand Vizier. Just be cautious and be sure to consider how your words might affect others."

She nodded. She understood.

"You see, of course, how our fortunes are interconnected."

Eleonora picked up her fork and lifted a single dull green bean to her mouth. She saw very clearly how her fortunes were connected to those of the Bey. He, his handmaid, and his butler were the closest thing she had to family. He was, as Miss Ionescu said of her father, *the stone castle overlooking my orchards, the rain that nourishes them, and the team of horses to which my plow is attached.* The last thing Eleonora wanted was to do anything that would adversely affect his fortunes. She found it somewhat curious that the Bey would be so adamant in pressing this point, but it was understandable that, as a former victim of undue political persecution, he would be anxious about the Sultan's motivations.

After dinner, Eleonora excused herself and went upstairs to her bedroom. It was still very early and she was not tired in the least, but she wanted to be alone with her thoughts. She had already decided which dress she was going to wear, but she was still unsure on the question of jewelry. Pulling out the top drawer of the dressing table, she looked through her small collection of bracelets and necklaces. Here was the pear-shaped emerald pendant the Bey had bought for her on her third day in Stamboul.

Here were the bangles from that cramped gold dealer in the textile market. As she slipped the bangles over her hand, Eleonora's gaze fell on the wooden bookmark she had taken with her from Constanta, her mother's bookmark, with which she had jimmied the lock of her father's trunk. She picked it off the dresser, held it like a magnifying glass, and considered her reflection through the negative spaces in the wood. She opened her mouth and inspected the iridescent reddish-yellow space where her tongue rested. Tomorrow she would have an audience with the Sultan.

Eleonora knew from Machiavelli that she should not offer advice unless the Sultan asked her. If he did ask, however, she would tell him the truth as best she could. As for how she should comport herself, she had no idea. None of the characters in *The Hourglass* had ever been granted an audience with their king, though Miss Holvert had been invited on a riding party with a Hapsburg Prince. That episode, of course, had ended disastrously—*the only remnants of the day a box of dried wildflowers, tears, and a stack of unposted letters*—though it was useful as a counterexample. She should not expect too much of the Sultan's attention during their meeting. It was likely that he would be distracted by other concerns.

She did not know how long she had been standing in front of the mirror when the door opened and Mrs. Damakan stepped into the room. She had neither towels nor sheets, nor any other pretense for visiting. Eleonora laid the bookmark on top of the dressing table and closed the drawer.

"You are going to the palace tomorrow," said Mrs. Damakan, placing a light hand on Eleonora's shoulder. "It is an honor."

Eleonora looked up at the old handmaid and caught a mischievous spark at the corner of her eyes.

"It is an honor," Mrs. Damakan repeated. "But I think you are nervous."

"I don't know—"

The words slipped out so easily, Eleonora hardly noticed what she had done until it was done. She had not thought about speaking, or not speaking, for some time now. Her silence was a comfortable habit—the listening, the nodding, the writing out of any responses that were absolutely necessary—but it had long ago lost its power. She realized this now, now that she had discarded the cloak of voicelessness, letting it pool at her feet. The spell was her own to break; it had been all along. Mrs. Damakan nodded, waiting for her to continue her sentence.

"I don't know what I should say," Eleonora whispered. After so many months of silence, her voice was soft, and scratched in her throat.

Mrs. Damakan let her hand slide down to Eleonora's arm, and squeezed it gently.

"How can you know the answer if you haven't heard the question?" she said. "Trust yourself. You know even more than you think."

The old handmaid leaned forward and kissed Eleonora on the forehead. Then she turned and waddled out of the room.

Chapter Nineteen

Trimmed with gold and black rubber, the imperial carriage sat at the edge of the water, its doors, roof, and under-gear shining the brilliant purple of an unripe eggplant. Eleonora held her dress above the cobblestones as she followed the herald across the drive. She wore a pale blue silk gown with black patent-leather shoes, her hair arranged in a wispy spray. The entire morning had been spent preparing, bathing, choosing her jewelry, and sitting still while Mrs. Damakan pinned up her hair. It was only now, however, that the reality of the situation fell upon her. She, Eleonora Cohen, was going to the palace for an audience with the Sultan. If there ever had been, there was no turning back now.

Halfway across the drive, Eleonora could see the horses' skin gleaming with the dull radiance of meerschaum and their eyes like sad, black marbles. As she approached the great beasts, they stiffened their posture and, like soldiers presenting arms for review, each raised its left foreleg. She nodded, acknowledging their tribute, and the lead horse flared its nostrils, a signal that the rest of the team could relax. The coachman held the door for her and she stepped up into the carriage. As she did, a seagull cried out from the roof of the Bey's house and took off flapping across the Bosporus, its yellow-orange beak pointed toward the palace.

The interior of the carriage was upholstered in dark purple velvet with ivory fixtures and a seam of gold around the baseboard. Eleonora smoothed down the back of her dress and seated herself across from the herald, facing backward. Horses clomping along the shoreline, she watched the Bey's house slide out of view, shrinking smaller and smaller in the back window until finally it disappeared behind a curve in the road. She looked down at her shoes, into the shiny black patent leather pinching her toes together, and she inhaled deeply to calm herself.

"You have been granted an enormous privilege."

Eleonora looked up at the herald. His nose was framed between sunken eyes and he had a large mole just above his left nostril. She had thought at first he was the same man who had called on her the day before, but now she was unsure. In any case, he expected a response.

"Yes," she said. She spoke quietly, as she was still getting used to the feeling of a voice vibrating in her throat. "I am very honored."

"It is a great honor to be given an audience with the Sultan."

"I am greatly honored."

Rattling across the wooden planks of the Galata Bridge, they turned left at the Egyptian Bazaar, dispersing a crowd of pigeons set up under the exterior arches of the New Mosque. From across the water, Eleonora could see the Galata Tower leaning over the city like a stern finger. There was Beşiktaş, sprawled out languid along the shore: the pier, the Beşiktaş Mosque, and the waterfront houses, in the middle of which she could easily pick out the yellow facade of the Bey's. She leaned closer to the carriage window, until the tip of her nose touched the glass. There, on the second floor, third from the left, was the bay window behind which she had spent so many afternoons, reading, watching the ships pass, and imagining the lives of the people across the water. Whether anyone on this side of the straits—a fish monger, a servant buying turmeric in the spice bazaar, or a faithful shop-keeper performing ablutions at the public fountain outside the New Mosque—had ever glanced up and speculated about her own life, Eleonora could never know.

"Are you at all familiar with the protocols of the court?"

"No," she said, raising her chin.

The herald made a small sound at the back of his throat and his face took on the glaze of great solemnity.

"In the Sultan's court there are certain rules one must follow. Entire books have been written on the subject. Unfortunately, we do not have time for that now."

Eleonora nodded.

"The three most important rules to remember are as follows: First, you must bow as soon as you enter the audience chamber. When you bow, touch your forehead to the ground."

She touched her forehead with her thumb to show she under-stood.

"Second, you must always address the Sultan, if you address him at all, as His Excellency."

"His Excellency," she repeated.

"Your Excellency," the herald corrected. "If you address the Sultan, call him 'Your Excellency.' If you were talking about him to a third party, which you should not do, you would say 'His Excellency.'"

"Your Excellency."

"Third, you must remember always to face the Sultan. No matter who is speaking to you, do not turn your back to the Sultan."

Eleonora repeated the three rules to herself.

"Those are the three pillars of court protocol. There are many more rules. You must never contradict the Sultan, for example.

You must never interrupt His Excellency when he is speaking. And you must never offer him advice, unless advice has been explicitly requested. However, we do not have time for these rules."

By then, the carriage had turned onto a steep, curving street, edged in by shops and choked with a dusty stream of supplicants. The horses slowed as they passed through the multitudes—the crisp white head garb of the Bedouin, Caucasian knives hooked through brightly embroidered sashes, and geometric tattoos on the chins and foreheads of Berber women—all clamoring up the hill toward the palace. The Gate of Greeting was a sight unto itself. Topped with a shingled green roof like a wave, it was protected by six guards, two to unlock the gate and four to hold back the pilgrims. At the front of the crowd, Eleonora noticed an ancient peasant wearing a tattered red fez. Clutching a sheep under one arm, he was waving his staff in the air and repeating a single word over and over again, as if repetition might somehow rectify whatever wrong had been done.

"What does he want?" Eleonora asked as they stepped down from the carriage.

The herald looked at her for a moment with a blank face. When he realized who she was referring to, he snorted contemptuously.

"There is no end to what people want from His Excellency."

She might have pursued the conversation further, but at that moment the inner gates were opened and a guard ushered them into the palace proper. Redolent of jasmine, the palace gardens were arranged in gently sloping concentric circles, each planted with a different variety of fruit tree. The herald led Eleonora up a wide path lined with topiary, past pashas and janissaries gliding silent as snakes through water. He walked quickly, leaving no time for her to admire the great blue-and-white-tiled fountain at the center of the gardens or to linger on the buildings peeking through the leaves. He stopped finally at the far end of the gardens, in front of a gate nearly as large as the one they had just passed through. It was guarded by four men in uniforms the same bright purple color as the imperial carriage. They were, without a doubt, the largest men Eleonora had ever seen, each as tall as a horse and leg muscles bulging through their uniforms.

"This banner," said the herald, pointing to a somewhat frayed piece of green cloth on a block of sandstone next to the gate, "is the flag of the Prophet Muhammad, peace be upon him."

Eleonora leaned closer to the flag, which was embroidered in silver calligraphy. *In the name of God, the merciful and magnificent.*

"It marks the entrance to the private chambers of His Excellency. I cannot pass beyond this point."

He made a motion to one of the guards, then bade his farewell and hurried down a side path. Eleonora stood for a few moments next to the banner of the Prophet before she spoke.

"Excuse me," she asked in the general direction of the guards. "Should I stand here, or is there somewhere else I should wait?"

Staring straight ahead, at some undefined point in the middle distance, the guards remained silent. Still quite unsure in her voice, Eleonora thought it was possible that she had not spoken clearly enough.

"Is this where I should wait?" she repeated, much louder this time.

Still, the guards did not acknowledge her presence. It was as if she hadn't spoken at all.

"Excuse me."

She took a step forward and waved her hand in front of the

guard closest to her. He had dark blue eyes like tiny jewels, and a thick scar split his cheek from temple to mouth. Lowering his gaze, he looked at her, then placed his hands over his ears and shook his head. He was deaf, it seemed. Pointing to a bench at the other side of the gate, the guard resumed his post.

Eleonora didn't feel like sitting. She was far too nervous to sit. Nevertheless, she followed the guard's finger to the marble bench, turned, and looked out over the garden she had just come through. It was then that she noticed a small contingency of her flock perched on the uppermost level of the main fountain. There they were, four purple-and-white hoopoes, watching over her on this most momentous of days. Their presence alone gave her new confidence. And when she was shown through the gate to the Sultan's audience chamber, she knew they were waiting for her just outside the door.

The walls of the audience chamber were decorated with green and red and blue carved plaster. Bundles of light fell from a latticework screen just below a peacock-colored ceiling and the room smelled faintly of lilac. It was much smaller than she had expected, about the same size as her bedroom in the Bey's house. A tidy row of Viziers and their heralds lined the wall to her right. To her left, Jamaludin Pasha, the Grand Vizier, was seated in an oversized wooden chair. And at the center of the back wall, reclining on a massive crimson divan, was the Sultan himself, His Excellency Abdulhamid II. Physically, the Sultan was a slight man, with dark bushy eyebrows, a crisp mustache, and lips like a doubled cherry. Eleonora felt her skin pucker. Here was the Sultan of the Ottoman Empire, the Caliph of Islam. Here was one of the most powerful men in the world. And yet, he was a man like all the rest.

She bowed on one knee, as the herald had instructed her, and pressed her forehead to the cool marble floor. When she stood again, the Grand Vizier smiled and shifted in his seat. He adjusted the band of his turban, then removed a small notebook from the folds of his caftan.

"Miss Cohen. As you can imagine, we have quite a large amount of business to attend to every day. Nevertheless, His Excellency was quite intrigued by what he heard about you, your studies, the story of your life—"

"Indeed."

Eleonora could barely hear what the Sultan had said, but when he spoke the room fell silent. She bowed again and a flush crept up through her body. He was speaking to her, she told herself. She could feel the sweat forming on her palms.

"Would you mind," the Sultan began, "if I asked you a few questions? We have heard a number of amazing things about you. But it is difficult sometimes to know what is true and what is not true."

"Yes," Eleonora said. Her voice croaked. "Thank you, Your Excellency."

"Is it true that you can read in five languages?"

Eleonora counted in her head. She didn't want to contradict the Sultan, but the truth was that she could read in seven languages: Romanian, Greek, Latin, Turkish, French, English, and Arabic.

"If you please, Your Excellency. That is not true."

The Grand Vizier jotted something in his notebook.

"How many languages can you read in?"

"Seven, Your Excellency."

"And is it true," the Sultan continued, with a sly smile, "that you have read all the books in the library of your guardian, our friend Moncef Barcous Bey?"

"Your Excellency, I have read many of the books in the library, but I have not read them all."

The Sultan nodded.

"And which, of the ones you have read, is your favorite?"

"*The Hourglass*, Your Excellency."

She glanced at the Grand Vizier, who was recording her answers in his notebook.

"*The Hourglass,*" Abdulhamid mused. "I do not think I have ever come across that book."

"It is quite wonderful, Your Excellency."

He turned to the Grand Vizier.

"Have you read *The Hourglass*?"

"No, Your Excellency, I have not."

Then the Sultan turned to the line of Viziers on his left.

"Have any of you read *The Hourglass*?"

There was a shower of nervous murmuring before one of the Viziers spoke.

"Your Excellency, I don't believe this book has been translated into Turkish."

"Well, then we will have to have it translated—"

Just then, a herald entered the room and whispered something in Jamaludin Pasha's ear. He nodded and the herald left as silently as he had come.

"I myself," the Sultan continued, "am quite partial to stories of mystery and suspense. The authors are British in the main. Edgar Allan Poe and Wilkie Collins are the best, though there are some French writers I admire as well."

He paused and regarded the ceiling.

"Then, of course, one is also drawn to the great Arab and Persian poets."

Before Eleonora could respond, a new herald came into the room and handed a telegram to the Grand Vizier.

"Your Excellency," Jamaludin Pasha said, after reading the telegram. "I am very sorry to disturb our conversation with Miss Cohen, but a matter of the utmost urgency has just come to my attention."

One of the guards stepped forward to lead Eleonora out of the room, but the Sultan lifted his hand and stopped him.

"She can stay," he said. "This will not take more than a few moments, I presume, and I would not like to leave our guest waiting outside."

"Yes, Your Excellency," said Jamaludin Pasha. "Of course."

He pressed the telegram flat against his notebook and read it again to himself before summarizing its contents for the court.

"The German Imperial Admiralty informs us that the *Mesudiye* continues to be harassed by Russian torpedo boats, even after withdrawing toward Sinop. They say they have made numerous attempts to contact Russian naval commanders in both Sevastopol and St. Petersburg, with no success. It appears from the Russians' silence that this is an official act of belligerence."

Abdulhamid sighed and squeezed the bridge of his nose.

"The telegram is from General von Caprivi himself. He says he understands the delicacy of the situation, and that he respects our sovereignty in the utmost. However, he reiterates his recommendation to respond with force."

"And what would you recommend?" the Sultan asked.

"I would recommend giving the *Mesudiye*'s captain carte blanche to respond as he sees fit. These new Russian torpedo boats have some armor, but they can't possibly stand up to the firepower of an ironclad."

"Are there no other options?"

"None that I can see. I understand that you are reticent of Russian torpedoes, Your Excellency, but these boats are clearly within Ottoman waters. If we do not respond to belligerence in sovereign waters, we will further erode our standing in the Black Sea. To do nothing would admit fear, to St. Petersburg as well as to Berlin."

After considering the Grand Vizier's advice for a moment, the Sultan turned to the line of Viziers on his left.

"Do you all agree with Jamaludin Pasha?"

There was a chorus of nodding and mumbled assent. Clenching his eyebrows, Abdulhamid thumbed the hem of his caftan. He seemed to lose himself in the pattern of the fabric. Then he looked up at Eleonora.

"What do you think?" he asked. "What would you recommend?"

"Me?"

"Yes," he said. "As a former resident of the Black Sea provinces and a student of history. What would you recommend?"

The Grand Vizier coughed hard into his hand and wrote a few words in his notebook.

"I can't say," Eleonora began. "I can't say I fully understand the situation."

The herald had said she could give the Sultan advice if advice was explicitly requested, and His Excellency had clearly requested her advice. Still, she didn't know anything about politics, except for what she had read in books. Biting the inside of her cheek, Eleonora thought through all the books she had ever read, trying to recall an analogous situation.

"Perhaps," she said finally, "Your Excellency, perhaps this

situation is somewhat similar to that of Bithynia after the rise of King Mithridates."

"Go on," said the Sultan.

"According to Appian, Bithynia and Rome were both threatened by King Mithridates. However, the threat to Bithynia was more immediate. Knowing this, Rome was able to incite them to battle against Mithridates. The Bithynians lost the battle, and took heavy losses, but their loss gave the Romans time to gather their forces."

The Sultan thought for a moment before he spoke.

"By firing on the Russian torpedo boats, we would be instigating a battle that is more in the Germans' interest—"

"Your Excellency," the Grand Vizier interrupted. "A matter of great importance and secrecy has just come to my attention. Could I have a word with you in private?"

Chapter Twenty

When the audience chamber was empty, Jamaludin Pasha rose from his chair and approached the Sultan's divan.

"What is on your mind, Jamaludin Pasha?"

"Your Excellency," he said. "If you don't mind me speaking frankly."

"Not at all."

"I hope you will excuse my interruption of your audience with Miss Cohen. But I must say, Your Excellency, I do not think it entirely wise for you to be taking advice from a child."

Abdulhamid stroked the hairs at the back of his neck.

"And why is that?"

"First of all, and most important, Miss Cohen does not understand our political situation, nor our relationship with the Russians, nor our relationship with the Germans. She herself admitted as much. Second, it is unseemly for a monarch to request advice from a child, no matter what the circumstances. And third, we know nothing of her political inclinations. She could right now be passing information to Moncef Bey or Reverend Muehler. She could be a spy herself, for the Russians, the Romanians, the French—"

"Thank you," said the Sultan. "Thank you for your perspective on this matter. As always, I appreciate your advice, but in this case I must disagree."

Jamaludin Pasha looked down again at the telegram.

"Miss Cohen," the Sultan continued, "heard nothing today that she would not be able to learn from the newspapers tomorrow. And she has proven through the sagacity of her advice that she understands the political situation quite well. As for the wisdom of taking advice from a child, I am personally of the inclination that sound advice is sound no matter where it comes from. I would think that you should appreciate this position as well as anyone."

"I do, Your Excellency."

"Furthermore, it just so happens that Miss Cohen perfectly articulated my own thinking on the matter. If she were a beggar, if she were a monkey, if she were the very Tsar of Russia, I would take her advice just the same."

"Your Excellency," the Grand Vizier began. "Apart from the issue of where the advice comes from, I must counsel strongly against a strategy of nonengagement."

He paused to gauge the Sultan's reaction before expanding on this point.

"By not firing at least a warning shot, we will cede de facto control of the Black Sea to the Russians. Additionally, I fear General von Caprivi will regard our inaction as a direct affront to our alliance with the Kaiser."

"What, my friend, is the use of an alliance if it compels you to act against your own best interests?"

"As you know, Your Excellency, the Germans are among our most important allies. They possess the second most powerful navy in the world and they have vowed to protect our interests anywhere they are threatened."

"Why don't they protect us from the Russians now?"

Without waiting for an answer, Abdulhamid issued his final command.

"Tell the captain of the *Mesudiye* that he is under strict orders not to fire unless fired upon, and that he should avoid direct engagement as best he can."

The Grand Vizier was silent for a long while before he responded.

"Your Excellency, I understand that the memory of the *Intikbah* might compel one to shy away from firing on a Russian torpedo boat—"

"The *Intikbah*," Abdulhamid said, standing from his divan, "has nothing to do with my decision."

Without another word, the Sultan left the audience chamber. Blinking against the harsh white light of the sun, he paced along the garden path of the Enderun, from the Library of Ahmet III to the Pages' Quarters and back. Regardless of his feelings on naval engagement, it was clear that the Russians were trying to incite a response, which they could then use as a pretext for a wider battle. It was also clear, in spite of anything Jamaludin Pasha said to the contrary, that the Germans would benefit enormously from an Ottoman-Russian skirmish in the Black Sea. For now at least, nonengagement was the best response, no matter what General von Caprivi recommended. Abdulhamid did not relish backing down from a fight, not at all, but as Darius I so wisely said, "There is no need for force where subtlety will serve."

Even if he wanted to respond with force, Abdulhamid knew the empire was too weak to withstand a prolonged war with the Russians. He could barely staff the palace, let alone the provincial governments. The minorities were clamoring for greater representation, in some cases demanding self-rule. And his army, once the terror of Vienna and Budapest, was being retrained by European generals. Even with the translation college, the modernization of the officers' corps, and the railroad, even with all the constitutional changes he had implemented, the empire was on the brink of disaster. Every day, Abdulhamid could feel the shackles tightening around him. If he could drag the empire out from under the thumb of the Great Powers, satisfy its debtors, reverse the capitulations, and dismiss the foreign military advisors, then he might be able to reassert naval dominance in the Black Sea. At this point, however, he needed to be cautious.

Pausing at the sundial next to the Pages' Quarters, Abdulhamid ran his fingers along the grooves that represented the hours of the day. The shadow of the sun bent over his knuckles and continued on its way. As powerful as he was, he knew there were many things that were out of his control. One had to work as best as one could within the bounds of history. If only Jamaludin Pasha understood this. If only his advisors were more like Miss Cohen, untainted by convention and unafraid to speak their minds. He paused to consider a purple-and-white hoopoe perched on the curled roof of the audience chamber. It jerked its head to the left, then flew off across the water. That was it. Rapping the gnomon of the sundial with his knuckle, the Sultan made straight for the Library of Ahmet III.

When he entered, the librarian nearly fell off his ladder with shock.

"Your Excellency," he said after descending carefully and bowing. "What a pleasant surprise. How can I be of service?"

"I have a request," the Sultan said. "A request that needs to be carried out in the strictest of confidence."

"Of course, Your Excellency. Anything you need."

"First, I need you to gather all the decrees and correspondence related to our relationship with the Great Powers, specifically the Russians and Germans. Then, have copies of these materials made and have them brought to Miss Eleonora Cohen, at the residence of Moncef Barcous Bey."

The Sultan paused to let his librarian write down these details.

"Come to me when you are done assembling the materials and I will give you a note to include as cover. Is that clear?"

"Yes, Your Excellency. My only concern is that the volume of material you are requesting might exceed the capacity of a single carriage."

"Make a limit of six crates and prioritize the most relevant documents."

"Yes, Your Excellency. Right away."

His orders given to the librarian and the Grand Vizier, Abdulhamid set off that next morning at dawn on his annual birding excursion to Lake Manyas. Summer was not the ideal time of year for bird-watching in the region, but Dr. Benedict, the eminent British ornithologist who had been invited to lead the trip, had a very busy schedule and the Sultan intended to make the most of their time. The journey across the Sea of Marmara took most of the first day and that evening they camped near a Cossack fishing village on the northern side of the lake. The next morning they rode around to the southern shore and raised a more permanent camp, a few kilometers from a village of Tartar refugees. Both the Cossacks and the Tartars sent gifts in honor of the Sultan's visit. For the most part, however, Abdulhamid and his party did not concern themselves with the human residents of the region. And aside from a somewhat restless first night's sleep, the standoff in the Black Sea did not weigh too heavily on the Sultan's thoughts. After setting up camp, he and his party spent most of their time with their field glasses at their eyes.

Although the spring migration had ended a few weeks earlier, they were able to observe a number of species in the process of nesting and breeding. As the waters of the lake receded, warblers, egrets, and swans made their nests in the vast swath of exposed reeds and wildflowers. Leading the Sultan's party along the shore, Dr. Benedict pointed out the nest of a penduline tit, an elaborate pear-shaped contraption hung from the branches of a pine tree. Woven from discarded spiderwebs, animal hair, and plants, the nest had a false entrance and a trap door to confuse potential predators. Over the course of the trip, the Sultan saw more than fifty species of bird: white frosted geese, golden orioles, night herons, glossy ibises, a mass of spoonbills, and three pairs of bright orange-billed Dalmatian pelicans. It was the penduline tit, however, with its convoluted, piecemeal nest, that most captured his imagination.

On the fifth and final night of the expedition, just before dusk, the Sultan was in his tent, contemplating the empire's political situation as it compared to the nest of the penduline tit, when a wild boar charged the camp. Before any of the dragomans could think to react, Dr. Benedict shot the boar dead with his handgun. Although he did not partake of the swine himself, Abdulhamid ordered the animal skinned and roasted in honor of Dr. Benedict, his knowledge, and his heroism. It was a wonderful finale to the trip. In addition to the boar, the Sultan's party was treated to stuffed quinces, roast lamb, and a hearty barley soup.

When Abdulhamid returned to the palace late that next evening, he could tell immediately something was amiss. Because it was exceedingly late, however, he went straight to bed. When he awoke, he saw that his instincts had been correct. The proof of this was his mother, sitting patiently in a chair next to the door of his sleeping chamber.

"Good morning, Mother."

"I hear your excursion was a success," she said, rising to bow.

"Yes." He smiled. "Very much so. I saw three pairs of Dalmatian pelicans and the nest of a penduline tit."

"A penduline tit," she repeated. "Excellent."

"But I can't imagine you have been sitting by my bed all morning in order to ask me how my trip went."

"No, Your Excellency. I must admit, I have not."

"What is troubling you, Mother?"

"I don't want to spoil your first morning back with my concerns."

"If you are concerned," he said, sitting up in bed, "I am concerned."

She took her seat again and turned it toward him.

"I heard a rumor yesterday that troubled me deeply, a rumor that troubled me so much I felt compelled to wake my favorite and firstborn son from his sleep."

"Tell me, Mother."

"People are saying that you asked that Cohen girl for her advice regarding a delicate military situation, and that you are planning to send her confidential materials, for her perusal."

His silence confirmed that the rumor was correct.

"Where you get your advice is of no consequence to me," she continued. "I know I raised you well enough to tell sound advice from unsound. What I care about is your reputation. Inside the palace, people are already beginning to talk about the situation in disparaging terms."

"Let them talk," he said. "They will always talk."

"And to give this girl access to the internal deliberations of

the palace, to give potentially sensitive information to a child—
a Jewess—whom we know nothing about, frankly that worries
me as well."

The Sultan rolled onto his back. The information had spread
rather quickly, even for the standard of the palace.

"Who told you this?"

"Jamaludin Pasha."

"And where did he hear it from?"

"I had assumed you told him yourself."

"No," said the Sultan, rolling onto his side. "I did not."

Getting out of bed and taking leave of his mother, Abdulhamid told the closest herald that he wanted to eat his breakfast
in the Library of Ahmet III. This was a highly unusual request,
but the herald barely blinked before bowing and scurrying off to
inform the kitchen staff. Meanwhile, the Sultan made his way to
the library. As he had hoped, it was empty. The only movement
was in a shaft of dust particles, the only sound the constant twit-
tering of silverfish. Abdulhamid seated himself at the librarian's
desk, waited, and a few moments later his breakfast was served
to him there. While he ate, he paged through a large blue ledger
in the middle of the desk. It was a record of all the books that had
been requested and removed from the library in the last month.
He could see that much of the official deliberations and correspondence regarding the empire's relationship with Berlin and
St. Petersburg had been requested. However, there was nothing
in the ledger to indicate that he, the Sultan, had requested these
documents. So the librarian had covered himself in this respect,
at least. The Sultan closed the ledger. As he finished his tea, the
librarian himself entered the room.

"Your Excellency," he said, his face as pale as a silverfish. "To
what do I owe the honor of your visit?"

"Merely checking on the request I made last week."

The librarian was calmed by this explanation, though not entirely.

"It is nearly finished, Your Excellency. I hope to bring you the results tomorrow morning. Six crates full of letters and official decrees."

"Very well," Abdulhamid said, glancing at the closed ledger. "I also have one further question."

"Yes, of course, Your Excellency."

"Did I not tell you that the request was confidential?"

"Yes, Your Excellency, you did."

"Why, then, did my mother wake me this morning with the information that the project has become common knowledge?"

His ankles quavering, the librarian prostrated himself in front of the Sultan and his empty breakfast dishes.

"I did not say a word to anyone. I swear, Your Excellency."

The Sultan considered the librarian's back for a moment before motioning for him to stand.

"You are a pious man, are you not?"

"I am, Your Excellency. I do my best."

"Then bring me a Koran."

The librarian did as he was told, and Abdulhamid opened it to the first sura.

"Will you swear on the Koran, the memory of the Prophet Muhammad, peace be upon him, and the rightly guided caliphs, that you did not speak to anyone, anyone at all, of this matter?"

The librarian put his hand on the Koran.

"Perhaps," he said, his nostrils wide with fear, "it is possible, Your Excellency, that I did not convey the confidential nature of the request to the palace archivist, or to the copyists who have been assisting me. If that is the case, I take full responsibility for the matter. And I am happy to offer my resignation if you see fit."

"Beyond the palace archivist and the copyists, did you tell anyone else of the request?"

"No, Your Excellency, as you wish I swear on the Holy Koran and the memory of the Prophet Muhammad, may peace be upon him. I did not."

"Very well then," said the Sultan and he stood from the desk. "Bring the crates to my chambers as soon as they are complete."

As Abdulhamid left the room, the librarian crumpled to his knees and laid his forehead against the floor.

Chapter Twenty-One

Eleonora sat alone at the head of the Bey's shiny dining-room table, considering the residual crumbs of her breakfast. It had been more than a week since her audience with the Sultan, but the memory of it was with her still, floating at the edge of her recollection like a hot-air balloon. She stirred the last, lukewarm sip of tea with her smallest finger and touched it to her lips. The morning after the audience, she and the Bey had discussed her experience at some length. She described to him the palace garden, the guards, the Viziers and their heralds, the impasse in the Black Sea, and her advice to the Sultan. The Bey listened to her descriptions with pride and keen interest, particularly after it became clear that the Sultan had acted on her advice. His primary concern, however, was whether the Sultan or the Grand Vizier had asked her any questions about himself, his routine, or anything else to that effect. When Eleonora assured him they had not, his face relaxed. And eventually the questions tapered off. She wiped the corner of her mouth with a napkin. Thumbing a herd of crumbs around the edge of her plate, she attempted to recall some of the smaller details about the palace: the gentle curve of the audience chamber's roof, the smell of lilac and lavender, the interlocking silver triangles embroidered on the collar of the Grand Vizier's caftan, and the patterns of light that fell through the branches of the walnut trees around the great fountain.

She was lost in these memories when she heard a knock at

the front door and the confident clomp of footsteps entering the house. The footsteps, she saw, belonged to a troop of palace porters. From behind the doorjamb, she watched them stream through the front door like a procession of purple beetles, each with a wooden crate as large as a steamer trunk. The great carpet of the anteroom had been rolled back and the crates were stacked two by two by two in the space between the visiting table and the front door. Monsieur Karom and a palace herald watched in silence as the procession unfolded. When the final crate was put into place, the herald produced a silver document holder from behind his back.

"This is for Miss Cohen."

"I will see that it gets to her," said Monsieur Karom.

The herald glanced at his outstretched glove.

"His Excellency has requested that the letter be given directly to Miss Cohen, and no one else."

Eleonora stepped out from behind the doorjamb.

"If you please."

The entire assembly turned to watch her pad across the room in her slippers and housedress. When she reached the herald, he lowered his head, as if he were unsure whether to bow.

"I should mention," he said as he unlatched the silver tube and unfurled a heavy sheet of paper, "that the note was written by the hand of His Excellency himself."

Eleonora held the letter at both ends. It was written in French, in an elegant and confident hand.

Dear Miss Cohen,

Before delving into the matter of the crates, I would first like to express my sincere pleasure at the opportunity to make your acquaintance the other day. One can tell from first glance that you are truly an uncommon person, with regard to your intelligence as well as your character. I trust you enjoyed your visit to the palace and sincerely hope we will be able to meet again in the future.

As for the crates, which are no doubt already stacked up along the wall of the Bey's anteroom, you will find inside them ten years of official reports, treaties, financial statements, and diplomatic correspondence, relating specifically to the question of our relationship with the Russian and German Empires, as well as the other Great Powers, France, Britain, and the Hapsburg Empire. Please review these documents with care. In two weeks' time I will send for you again so we can discuss their contents. I probably do not need to tell you that said documents are strictly confidential and that you should not share their contents with anyone, under any circumstance.

I eagerly await our next meeting.

Sincerely,

Abdulhamid II

Ultimately, the crates found their way to the library, and were lined up neatly under a bank of windows facing the Beşiktaş Harbor. On the other side of the glass, an unseasonably harsh wind blew off the water, lashing tree branches and tossing sea birds into somersaults. Inside, however, was quiet. Thick veins of cigar smoke were striated with the musty smell of old book leather and cognac, while fringes of the heavy curtain brushed against the tops of the crates. Pushing up the lid of the crate stamped with the number one, Eleonora leaned over its mouth and fingered through it. She plucked out a miscellaneous bundle of letters tied with a silk cord and unloosed it. The top letter was enclosed within a large square envelope. Addressed to Major General Nikolay Karakozov, it was smudged at the corner with what appeared to be strawberry jam. There was no return address. Eleonora pushed together the edges of the envelope and let the missive slip out. It was a handwritten invitation to a party celebrating the newly renovated residence of the French Ambassador. Finding nothing of immediate interest in this particular bundle, she replaced it at the back of the crate and carried the first two files to the Colonel's desk.

Crate number one was a mishmash of correspondence between Stamboul and St. Petersburg: personal notes, invitations, veiled threats, unveiled threats, remonstrations, apologies, and a few pleas for asylum. For the most part, the correspondence was in French, with Turkish and Russian words mixed in when appropriate. The import of the letters was generally quite clear, though the Russian Consul at times referred to agreements, conversations, and officials with which she was not familiar. Other than a short break for lunch, Eleonora read straight through the day. By the time Monsieur Karom knocked to announce dinner, she had read through nearly half of crate number one. Although there were still a number of large gaps in her understanding, she apprehended now the basic outline of the relationship between the Russians and the Ottomans.

Every day for two weeks, Eleonora immersed herself in the world of the crates, in the delicate ephemera of diplomacy, mutual acrimony, and unsteady alliances. As she read, her understanding of the current geopolitical situation expanded. The War of 1878 and the subsequent Treaty of Berlin had forced the Ottomans to relinquish their hold on much of southwestern Europe. The Crimean ports were handed back to the Russians,

Bosnia was given over to the Hapsburgs, and more than a few new nations were birthed, including the kingdoms of Bulgaria and Romania. Meanwhile, France and Britain sat perched at the edge of the carnage, biding their time like crows on fence posts.

Caught as they were between Moscow and Vienna, London and Paris, the Ottomans had turned to Berlin. At the behest of the Grand Vizier, German admirals were brought on as military advisors, the Kaiser was welcomed to Stamboul with an imperial parade, and the empire took onto its books an enormous loan from Deutsche Bank, intended in large part to finance the Stamboul-Baghdad link of the Berlin-Baghdad railroad. Such an artery, the Kaiser wrote in one of a few personal letters to Sultan Abdulhamid II, would bolster both empires and would serve to reinforce the relationship between them for years to come. The Kaiser signed his letter with an official stamp and the strangely informal valediction: *With Regards in Alliance, Willy.*

Those first twelve nights, Eleonora slept soundly, her mind whirring through connections and possibilities. The last night, however, the night before she was set to visit the Sultan, she could not bring herself to sleep. The sky was a bottomless silky black, sprinkled with stars like spilled sugar and quiet but for a few lonely stray cats prowling the waterfront. A loose association of ships slipped through the straits and the moon was pregnant with reflected glow. Eleonora rolled onto her stomach and pulled the blanket tight around her shoulders. She had read about insomnia, in Aristotle's treatise *On Sleep and Dreams* and in *The Hourglass.* In these books, the word conjured romantic scenes such as that famous depiction of a sleepless young Colonel Raicu haunting the garden of his recently deceased father's house, a cup of warm milk in his hand and the rise of a still unraveling sonata at his lips. Insomnia itself, however, was an entirely different and unpleasant experience. She could feel an alloy of fatigue and dread at the base of her neck like a five-kilogram weight. She wanted to sleep, desperately, but as much as she did, her mind would not cease and her limbs stirred with an anxious anticipation of morning.

She had gone through the crates, all six of them, through hundreds of pages of saber-rattling and cautious rapprochement. Still, she had no idea what to think, what to say when the Sultan asked for her advice. Bound up inexorably by geography, the Russian and Ottoman empires had been locked in the same bloody stalemate for centuries, grappling over the same relatively unimportant swaths of territory, building up their armies, and placating the Great Powers. She had no idea what to say. Even if she did know what to say, how could she, Eleonora Cohen, possibly have any influence over such enormous, intractable forces?

Three times that night, the fog horn sounded, guiding sleepless freighters through the straits and rustling the residents of Stamboul in their beds. Just after dawn, the fourth blast roused Eleonora from a sleep she had fallen into moments before. She knew she would not be able to return to the land of sleep. It was hours still before breakfast, but the kitchen fire was lit. Bread peddlers cawed up and down the street like gulls separated from their flocks. And the prowling felines of the night before skulked in fetid alleyways with their plunder. Eventually, Eleonora reasoned that if she could not sleep, she might as well take one last look at the crates.

She was not particularly surprised to find the Bey in the library, though his appearance did somewhat shock her. He was asleep in his armchair next to the fire, his suit rumpled and his eyes drooping like lazy dogs. There was an empty tea glass on the table next to him, as well as a kerosene lamp and a bundle of letters. The crates, it seemed, were undisturbed, resting silently beneath their curtains. Eleonora shut the door behind her and, seating herself in the chair across from him, pulled her knees to her chest. As she watched him sleep, embers creaked in the fireplace and a dim halo of sunlight stole through the drapes. Finally, the Bey stirred and opened his eyes.

"Miss Cohen."

His voice trailed off as he glanced about the room.

"It is morning?"

"Yes sir, almost."

He stood and straightened his suit, pulling down on both legs and running his hand along the length of each sleeve.

"I couldn't sleep," he said, glancing at the tableaux on the table beside him.

Eleonora tucked her legs beneath her housedress.

"Neither could I."

In the silence that followed, the Bey removed his pince-nez from an inside coat pocket and glanced about for a handkerchief. Finding none, he wiped the glasses on the corner of his shirt. Then, he removed two letters from the top of the pile next to him and held them out to Eleonora. She took them from him.

"I wanted to wait until you were older," he said. "But the time has come."

"Thank you," she whispered, though she knew not what for.

"I will leave you with your thoughts," he said and, taking the rest of the bundle with him, left the room.

Rearranging herself in the seat of the armchair, Eleonora leaned over the letters the Bey had given her. The top letter was the same one she had found a few months previous in the Colonel's desk. Covered with fingerprints and dust, it bore no stamp, nor postmark, nor return address, only the words *Moncef Bar-cous Bey, care of Mrs. Damakan* written across the front. She held it to her nose and inhaled. The paper was yellow at the edges and folded into a square, two sheets covered front and back with a small, anxious script. Already the ink was beginning to brown, but she could read it with no trouble in the rising light of the morning.

My Dear Moncef Bey,

    I sincerely hope this letter finds you in good health and happiness, though I must admit I harbor some doubts as to whether it will reach you at all. I do not in the least distrust my messenger's fidelity nor her ardent desire to deliver this missive. It is, in fact, at her urging that I write. However, a woman traveling such distances, alone and through the heat of battle, with such a messenger, one cannot help but retain some reservations. Nevertheless, I have faith; there is no other choice. The telegraph wires are still down and the postal service has been discontinued.

    As you know, Constanta fell nearly two weeks ago to the Tsar's royal cavalry. In the interim, I have witnessed such horrors I never before could have imagined: pillage, arson, vandalism, and the repeated brutal outrage of our city's female population. There is no time to describe these events, though they will be stamped on my mind for eternity. It will suffice, I think, to say that the reputation of the Cossack is no hyperbole. He is boorish and rude, violent, merciless, and drunk. The Ottoman troops, unfortunately, are not much better. Those few hundred cowards stationed in Constanta fled the night before the attack, leaving the city without defense. But I will not detain you with details. Undoubtedly, you have already heard many such accounts, and I have only a limited space to impress upon you a matter, which, as you will see, is of the utmost importance. Let me come to it directly.

In the midst of this rampage, my dear wife Leah went into the labor of childbirth. Shortly after delivering a baby girl, she succumbed to excessive bleeding. The blow of her death has all but overshadowed any joy I may have taken from the birth of my first child. Only now, weeks after the events described, do I have enough strength to write a letter of any length. It does no good, I know, to envisage counterfactuals, but I cannot help imagining what might have been if the birth were attended by our town physician, Dr. Husic. Instead of Dr. Husic, who was busy tending to the wounded, Eleonora's birth was overseen by a pair of Tartar midwives who appeared quite miraculously on our doorstep just as Leah's labor began.

They were drawn to our house, they told me, by an ancient prophecy, heralded by a confluence of signs— birds, a circle of horses, the moon phase, something of that nature. I must admit, I do not understand the nature of these signs, nor do I place much confidence in them. However, I do know that these two women, one of whom is the carrier of this message, have been of invaluable assistance to me. I know not what I would have done without them. They have agreed to stay on with me, helping to manage the household, until they leave for Stamboul. As I mentioned in my telegram of a week ago, both of them will be in search of work when they arrive in Stamboul and I strongly recommend them both for any household employment you may require.

As this letter draws to a close, I must also make a small request of my own. Being that my daughter came into this world with only one parent and very little in the way of extended family, I feel compelled to arrange a formal contingency should anything happen to me. As I have expressed previously, I consider you among the most honorable, honest, and staunchly moral men I know, and I would be honored to place my daughter in your care should anything happen to me. I hope that you will consider this request apart from the circumstances in which it is delivered. And I sincerely hope we will see each other soon, in happier times.

Until then I remain,

> Your loyal friend,
> Yakob Cohen

When she finished reading the letter, Eleonora folded it along its creases and placed it back in the envelope. Retying her housedress, she looked up at the ash-gray embers of the previous night's fire. A dozen thoughts whisked through her head and departed before she could detain them. There was so much to consider: the violence of her birth, the prophecy, the horses and the birds. Her father didn't seem to place much confidence in Mrs. Damakan's signs, and Eleonora trusted her father above all else. Still, there it was, right there on the page, a destiny already written, an ancient fate the nature of which she didn't know. She had so many questions, about herself, her father, her flock, Mrs. Damakan, and the Bey; about her birth, the midwives, the prophecy, and why no one had ever told her any of this. She was so absorbed by these questions, she nearly forgot about the second letter. Addressed also to Moncef Barcous Bey and stamped with a date in the middle of February, it was much shorter than the first letter. She slid the paper out of its envelope and read over it quickly.

Moncef Barcous Bey,

Thank you for your heartfelt condolences. They are accepted and appreciated. Yakob told me many times how much he loved and respected you. I can see now why he held these feelings so strongly. He also mentioned once that he requested you to act as Eleonora's guardian should anything happen to him. Although I am, you are correct, her aunt as well as her stepmother, I unfortunately must request that you discharge the aforementioned duty. It pains me to ask this of you, but I am not currently in a position to care for Eleonora. As for the monetary concerns your previous telegram implied, please feel free to avail yourself of any money Yakob may have made while in Stamboul. That should be more than enough to provide for Eleonora's expenses.

Thank you for your understanding,
Ruxandra Cohen

Eleonora stood and placed both letters on the table in front of her. She felt the prickly sting of acid in her throat, followed by an aftertaste of numbness. Ruxandra had indeed replied to the Bey's telegrams. This knowledge was oddly comforting. Even if the content of the letter stung, even if the letter proved beyond a doubt that Ruxandra had callously abandoned her, the release of hope was itself a relief. Eleonora could not say she was angry with the Bey for concealing the letter from her. It made perfect sense that he would want to spare her the injury of such a note so soon after her father's death. In any case, these were not the questions that most concerned her at the moment. Her mind was still swimming with horses, birds, and ancient prophecies. And there was only one person who could answer her questions.

With the turn of a knob, Eleonora slipped out of the library and into the hallway. Doing her best to quiet her thoughts, to concentrate on the task at hand, she paused and put a hand to her chest. Her heartbeat thumped through the thin material of her dressing gown. She inhaled, emptied her mind, and, one step at a time, made her way along the perimeter of the dining room, under the brief light of the chandelier, and through the kitchen door. Uncarpeted and drafty, the kitchen smelled of cooking oil and onions. Apart from a succession of pans hung above the stove, there was no decoration to speak of. At the far end of the room were three doors fixed with heavy iron hardware. The left-hand door, she knew, led outside to a small courtyard. The right-hand door led to the pantry. And the middle door, a few fingers taller than the rest, led to the servants' quarters.

The door opened easily onto a steep wooden staircase dissolving into a fog of dim candlelight. Eleonora mounted the first stair with a creak, and the door swung shut behind her. She put her hand on the worn iron rail and climbed, one step at a time, to a hall at the top. The candlelight, she could see now, trickled out from beneath one of the two doors. She hoped dearly that this was Mrs. Damakan's room. If it were Monsieur Karom's, she would say that she was looking for someone to help her with a woman's concern. She wasn't sure exactly what that was, but she knew that it would get her to Mrs. Damakan without any further questions. Eleonora took a few muffled breaths in front of the door before she knocked, ever so quietly. A long moment passed, then she heard a cough and a shuffle. The door opened. It was Mrs. Damakan.

"My dear," she exclaimed, laying a hand on Eleonora's shoulder. "What are you doing here?"

Eleonora tried to respond, but she was overcome. It began with a few muffled sniffs, a soft choke, and a welling of tears. Then, she felt a loosening in her stomach and it rose up inside her, from the very bottom of her gut, up through her lungs, and into her throat, like a pale-eyed sea creature finally surfacing after decades of haunting the deep. When she opened her mouth, her small body shuddered. The pressure of the past two weeks, the prophecy, the Sultan, and all her questions, all this came tumbling out. Eleonora pressed her face into the old handmaid's lap and cried. She cried for her father, for her mother, and for Constanta, for Mrs. Damakan, her niece, and all the suffering she knew nothing about, but most of all, she cried for herself, for the improbability of her own existence and the raw uncertainty of her place in the world.

When she was spent, Eleonora sat for a long while on the edge of the bed, engrossed in the bare candle flickering on the desk in front of her. Mrs. Damakan held her, stroking her hair and whispering in a language she didn't understand. Eventually, Eleonora sat up and apologized under her breath.

"I'm sorry," she said, wiping her tears on her sleeve. "I hope I'm not bothering you."

"Not at all."

Eleonora looked down at her hands, nestled among the folds of her dressing gown. Just the presence of Mrs. Damakan calmed her.

"You are a very special child," the old handmaid said, stroking Eleonora's hair. "You know that, don't you?"

Eleonora mumbled a yes.

"You know you are special, but I think that you aren't sure how."

She nodded. That was, indeed, the crux of it.

"For thousands of years," Mrs. Damakan continued, "my people have carried with us a prophecy—given by our last great king in the last hour of his deathwatch—the promise that a young girl would come, to push against the tides of history and put the world right again on its axis. There would be signs at her birth. A sea of horses, a conference of birds, the North Star in alignment with the moon, and two of our own. From these signs, he said, we would know she was truly the one."

Mrs. Damakan looked at Eleonora with a mixture of fear and reverence, her face shadowed deeply by the sputter of the candle.

"You are that one."

Eleonora broke Mrs. Damakan's gaze and looked down at the pool of her tears. Whether she believed them or not, these words, spoken with such unwavering conviction, shivered her to the marrow.

"What about the Sultan and the crates?" she persisted. "What am I supposed to do tomorrow? I don't know what to say. How can I be this person if I don't even know what I am supposed to say?"

Mrs. Damakan swallowed and closed her eyes.

"Trust yourself. Listen to your stomach. This is all we have."

Chapter Twenty-Two

⬧

While Mrs. Damakan fastened the hooks up the back of her dress, climbing one by one like the rungs of an unsteady ladder, Eleonora took a moment to observe herself in the dressing-table mirror. Her exhaustion showed as clear as a map. Her eyes wilted at the corners, her cheeks were pale as china, and, as much as she tried to quiet them, her hands quivered faintly at her sides. She had not eaten anything at breakfast that morning, and the base of her stomach felt slick as an empty bathtub. Neither she nor Mrs. Damakan mentioned the exchange that had transpired just a few hours earlier, but the memory of it hung over them. The very fact of her father's letter, a physical proof of his absence, would have been enough to unnerve her. On top of that, she had to assimilate also his violent account of her birth; this prophecy, however true it may be; and the letter from Ruxandra. All this as she prepared to meet the Sultan. Regarding herself in the mirror, she could feel tremors of anticipation in the soles of her feet, and her nerves like so many tentacles reaching out to touch the world around them. She didn't want to go to the palace, not now, not in this state, but one could not refuse the Sultan. And even if one could, it was too late. As Mrs. Damakan threaded the last hook into its corresponding eyelet, an imperial carriage pulled up to the Bey's house. Moments later, there was a knock at the front door.

Eleonora and the Sultan's herald rode in silence past yawning boatmen and night watchmen tending the sickly embers of their braziers. They rode past a knot of gossipy young madrassa students outside the Egyptian Bazaar, through a smattering of supplicants, and up to the Gate of Greeting. As the inner gates of the palace were opened, the Sultan's herald touched her knee.

"Take care," he said, pulling down on his lower eyelid to reveal the veiny rim of its socket. "You are all we have."

Without another word, without even a glance back over his shoulder, the herald led Eleonora through the palace gardens and deposited her in front of the prophet's banner. She was shown into the audience chamber immediately. Bowing, she noticed that the room was nearly empty. Besides the Sultan, herself, and a few guards, only two other people were present. One she recognized as the Grand Vizier. The second was an older woman she had never before seen.

"Good morning, Miss Cohen."

When the Sultan spoke, everyone in the room stopped what they were doing and turned toward him.

"Good morning, Your Excellency."

"I trust that your ride to the palace was pleasant."

"Yes," Eleonora said. "Very much so."

"I'm glad to hear that."

Gesturing to the Grand Vizier, he continued.

"You have met Jamaludin Pasha?"

"Yes, Your Excellency."

Eleonora and the Grand Vizier had not been formally introduced, but she recognized him from her previous audience.

"I do think, however, that I should need to introduce you to my mother," the Sultan said, nodding to the older woman on his left. "The Valide Sultan. She was quite taken by my description of our first audience and wanted the chance to meet you in person."

The Sultan's mother was an elegant and graceful creature, her neck hung with jewels and skin swimming in woozy bursts of perfume.

"It is a pleasure to meet you," Eleonora said, bowing again, though not as deeply as she had upon entering the room.

"The pleasure is all mine, my dear."

"Before we begin with our official business," said the Sultan, folding his hands under his chin, "I thought it might interest you to hear that our translators finally finished rendering the first volume of *The Hourglass* into Turkish. I only just began it a few days ago, but already I can see why you enjoyed it so much."

Eleonora nodded. Unsteady from the rush of the bow, her head flooded with scenes from *The Hourglass*: Miss Holvert hiding, curled up in the cellar of her cousin's farmhouse; Lieutenant Brashov riding through towns ablaze with torches and heavy artillery; Judge Raicu laughing uncontrollably in his own crowded courtroom. All this galloped through her head, but she could not think of how to respond to the Sultan. All she could come up with was a line from the fourth volume: *The string of fate pulled him through muck and brambles, hardship, tragedy, and countless sleepless nights. At times it seemed a pointless struggle, but when he arrived finally at the end of the line, then he understood that it was all necessary.* Was her entire life up until this point nothing more than preparation for this one moment? She blinked and steadied herself.

"Yes, Your Excellency."

"There is one more thing I wanted to mention," the Sultan said, reclining on his elbow. "Before we begin with our official business. As you may know, I have for many years been an amateur bird-watcher. Stamboul is a crossroads of sorts for migratory birds, and the palace provides an ideal vantage point from which to observe their movements. In the past few months, I have noticed more than once a rather curious flock of purple hoopoes roosted around Moncef Bey's house. I wouldn't trouble you with my observations, but such birds are not common to the region and, furthermore, the literature indicates that they are primarily solitary creatures. I ask you for your thoughts in part because the flock seems somewhat attached to you."

He paused, allowing her to respond.

"That's my flock," Eleonora said. "They were with me when I was born and they followed me here from Constanta."

According to her father's letter and Mrs. Damakan, her flock was also connected, at least symbolically, to the prophecy. She thought it best not to divulge this connection, however, as she didn't fully understand it herself.

"Your flock," the Sultan repeated. "As simple as that."

Eleonora smiled in confirmation.

"In any case," Abdulhamid continued, changing the subject, "I understand that you were able to read through the documents I sent, and that you found them interesting."

"Yes, Your Excellency. I did."

"What was your impression of them?"

Eleonora shuffled her heel against the floor.

"I found them quite interesting," she said. "There were a few letters I did not entirely understand, but for the most part I found them very interesting."

"Which letters didn't you understand?"

"It's hard to say."

She addressed herself to the Grand Vizier, who had asked the question. Then, remembering the rules of protocol, she turned back to the Sultan.

"There was, for example, one letter from the Russian Consul to the palace, outlining the terms of a prisoner exchange, and then there was also an early draft of the Treaty of San Stefano. I don't think I entirely understand the political context of either situation."

"With so many documents," the Sultan reassured her, "and such a complicated set of politics, I did not expect you to understand every detail. Though surely I can furnish you with documents to provide context for these two situations."

He turned to Grand Vizier.

"Will you see that this gets done?"

"Yes, Your Excellency."

"Now," the Sultan continued, turning his attention back to Eleonora. "Although you have not had the opportunity to read through all the pertinent documents, I would enjoy hearing your impressions of the situation as a whole, as well as any advice you may have."

Eleonora clenched her fists, pushing her fingernails into her palms. The enormity of the Sultan's question enveloped her like a cloud of gnats. She opened her mouth to excuse herself, to tell them that she was very tired and, in all honesty, she didn't really have an impression of the situation as a whole. Before she could speak, however, the Sultan's mother broke in.

"You do know that your previous advice to His Excellency was enacted? And, so far at least, it has been successful."

"No," Eleonora said. "I did not."

"It was in all the local papers."

"I don't read the local papers."

"It was in the international press as well," the Grand Vizier persisted, jotting something in his notebook.

"I don't read any papers," said Eleonora. "If I was supposed to, I apologize. I thought I was just supposed to read what was in the crates."

The Grand Vizier put his notebook aside. He looked as if he were going to ask a question, but instead he just wrinkled his nose.

"Your strategy was quite successful," the Sultan said. "When they saw that we weren't going to engage, the Russians stopped bothering us and went back to Sevastopol. As for the Germans, they were rather upset at first, but in the end they almost seemed glad that we ignored their suggestion."

The Grand Vizier cleared his throat.

"Which is why I would very much like to hear your impressions of our political situation in general."

Eleonora wiped her palms down the back of her dress and swallowed. It was just as Mrs. Damakan had said. She had to trust herself. There was nothing else. Her mind swarmed with caliphs and muftis, long-dead kings and abandoned capitals. If only she could think of an appropriate analogy.

"The situation of the empire in general," she said, grabbing on to the first complete thought that came into her head, "is not dissimilar, I would think, to that of the Hyrcanians, as described by Xenophon in his *Cyropaedia*."

Eleonora paused to gauge the effect of this analogy. It seemed, however, that no one present was familiar with the Hyrcanians— or Xenophon, for that matter.

"The Hyrcanians were subjects of their more powerful neighbors, the Assyrians, and badly used by them in matters political as well as military. In the particular occasion Xenophon describes, the Hyrcanian cavalry was ordered to bring up the rear of an Assyrian column, so that if any danger should threaten from behind they would bear the brunt of it. But—"

Eleonora paused for a moment to wet her lips. As she did, her head swam. The sun shifted from behind a cloud and shone down into the room, illuminating the patch of marble on which she stood.

"As they," she said, trying to put her thoughts in order. "They—"

With that, Eleonora collapsed. First she sank to her knees. Then, with a violent shudder, she crumpled and fell to the floor. There, on the floor, in the middle of the Sultan's audience chamber, her seizures began in earnest, and her mind went blank. The last thing she remembered was the sound of the Sultan shouting for a doctor.

Although Eleonora had read the entire Koran—had memorized it, in fact—the revelations within had not particularly resonated with her. Unless called upon by circumstance, she rarely reflected much on its contents. It was strange then that the Sura of the Overwhelming Calamity was the first thing that came into her mind when she opened her eyes and, blinking, tried to make sense of her surroundings. *Therein is a fountain flowing / Therein are thrones raised high / And drinking-cups ready placed / And cushions set in a row / And carpets spread out.* Through an open doorway, she could see a vast courtyard peopled with beautiful young women, plucking at string instruments and murmuring to each other in quiet, giggling tones. Here was the fountain flowing, there the carpets spread out and cushions set in a row.

She was lying facedown on a high divan in the middle of a small room just off of the courtyard. Her head was supported by a den of velvet pillows and her feet were bare. There was a tingling numbness in her right hand, which, she soon realized, was trapped between her body and the cushion. With some difficulty,

Eleonora pulled the hand out from under herself and rolled onto her back. When she did, she saw that she was being watched over by the Sultan's mother. She tried to sit up, but when she raised her head, a sharp pain pierced through from one temple to the other. Just then, the end of the sura came to her and it seemed to make sense. *Therefore do remind. / For you are only a reminder / You are not a watcher over them.*

"You don't have to move. Just rest, lie here."

The Sultan's mother touched Eleonora's forehead with the back of her hand and raised a large chalice to her lips.

"Here," she said. "Drink this."

The contents were deep red and had the sweetish tang of pomegranate. When Eleonora was finished drinking, the Sultan's mother placed the half-empty cup on the floor.

"You were thirsty."

Eleonora nodded and brought her own tingling, sweaty hand to her forehead. She wanted to ask where they were, what had happened, and so on, but she was too tired to speak. She was too tired to think, really.

"The Sultan is very concerned with your well-being," said his mother. "Once it was determined that your condition was stable, he insisted that you be brought here, to his private quarters. It was thought that this would be the most comfortable place for you to recover."

Eleonora again tried to speak, but the words didn't come. They lost themselves on their way from her mind to her mouth, and by the time she realized they were gone, she had forgotten what she wanted to say.

"Take another sip of pomegranate juice. It will give you strength."

As she drank, Eleonora could feel the strength rushing back

to her, the sugar pumping through her bloodstream. With the strength, however, there was also a wobbly lightness of mind.

"What do you remember?" the Sultan's mother asked her, stroking the back of her hand. "Do you remember what you said to us?"

Eleonora raised her chin in order to shake her head.

"You don't remember anything you told us? About Reverend Muehler and the puzzle? About Moncef Bey and that strange young man at the Café Europa?"

"No," she whispered, forcing the word out. Besides the Hyrcanians, she remembered nothing. "What did I say?"

"It's not important," said the Sultan's mother. Standing, she brushed a strand of Eleonora's hair off her forehead. "It's for the best really that you don't remember."

Eleonora rested her head on the pillow and gazed out again onto the courtyard, with the young women and their string instruments, trying to recall what she had said. When she could not, she returned her thoughts to their current surroundings.

"Who are those women?" Eleonora asked. "Are they the Sultan's musicians?"

"You could say that," said Abdulhamid's mother, looking back over her shoulder to hide a smile. "Music is a common pursuit among those who live in the harem."

"They live here?" Eleonora asked. "All of them?"

"Yes," the Sultan's mother replied. "All of them live here."

"Where are their parents?"

The Sultan's mother paused, as if she had never really considered this question.

"They are mostly orphans," she said finally. "Those with parents were sent here to improve their status. I was once a young

odalisque myself, you know, in the court of Ahmed IV, Abdulhamid's father. It's a rather charmed life."

"Were you an orphan?"

"Yes," the woman said eventually. "I lost both my parents at a
young age, just like you."

Eleonora wanted to ask more questions, about the palace, and
the odalisques, and the music they were playing, but she was
enveloped at that moment by an irresistible fatigue.

Later that afternoon, Eleonora was transported back to the
Bey's house. She spent most of the following week in bed, resting.
Drapes pulled shut and covers cinched up around her chin, she
ate toast dipped in tea and drank such quantities of pomegranate
juice that her teeth took on a purple hue around the edges. She
was not sick, nor was she injured. As she explained to the Bey, to
Mrs. Damakan, and to the interminable stream of doctors sent
by the palace, she had merely lost her strength. It was, she told
them, as if she had been tapped somewhere close to the core of
her being and all the strength had drained out of her. The doctors had other, more scientific theories, ranging from epilepsy to
meningitis to sugar sickness, but none of them could say for sure.
And it didn't really matter. Whatever it was that afflicted her, she
was on the mend.

Meanwhile, Stamboul was humming with gossip. Even as
the imperial carriage brought Eleonora back across the Galata
Bridge, the story of her episode seeped out under the palace
gates and rolled down the hill toward the heart of the city. If
you listened carefully, you could almost hear it, that unmistak-
able sound of gossip. Like a swarm of locusts, it descended from
on high and, buzzing, progressed from house to house. Borne
lightly on the breath of its hosts, it mutated as it spread.

Eleonora had done nothing wrong, nothing untoward or immoral. As such, it was not a full-blown scandal. Still, one could not deny that it was an interesting story. Despite Stamboul being a city of 2 million souls, scores of neighborhoods, and dozens of languages, gossip traveled as quickly as through the square of a small village. By the time Eleonora climbed into her warm, white bed and slipped off to sleep, the rumor had already broken into two competing strains.

The first branch, which held that Eleonora was a seer or prophet of some sort, spread along the banks of the Bosporus, stopping in at the summer houses of the rich on its way to the Princes' Islands. The story stewed on the islands for a few days, paying visits at all the right galas and dinner parties, before making its way back to Stamboul proper on the backs of returning servants. The second branch, which purported that Eleonora was a British spy sent to disrupt the Ottoman-German alliance, made its way straight across the Galata Bridge and up the hill to Pera, where the foreign communities whispered it among themselves. Glancing over their shoulders occasionally to be sure that no other spies were listening, they relayed the story of the young orphan, a charge of Moncef Barcous Bey, who was agitating against the Kaiser.

Inside the palace, the first version dominated and was bolstered by firsthand accounts of Eleonora's dramatic seizure in the audience chamber. Certain factions in the government, however, including the Grand Vizier, held on to and repeated the second branch of the gossip, insistent that Eleonora was a foreign agent or at least a puppet exploited by Moncef Barcous Bey. What the Sultan himself thought was a mystery, though over the next few weeks it became clear that he had taken Eleonora's advice very much to heart.

Chapter Twenty-Three

A steady dribble and tap of rain persisted to the edge of morning, rinsing the dust off the red tile roofs of Robert's College and restoring some luster to its foliage. Even with the windows shut, the Reverend's study smelled of damp earth and pollen, the same smell as the dandelion field behind St. Ignatius. The Reverend bit the tip of his pen and clacked it between his teeth, allowing himself a brief reverie. The gutters babbled and the light that fell from the stained glass window above his desk had a rinsed-out quality, as if it, too, were submerged. As exquisite as the light was, however, one needed to concentrate on the task at hand. Laying his palms flat on either side of the letter in front of him, he read over what he had written so far.

My dear Donald,

I sincerely hope this letter finds you in good health and spirits, and that you will excuse the extended absence

Capping his pen, the Reverend rambled across his study to the fireplace. The correct word was "delay," not "absence," but he was in no mood to start the letter over again. When it came down to brass tacks, he didn't care what Donald Stork thought of his epistolary style—or much of anything else, for that matter. Why their correspondence had continued for so long was a question of obsequiousness and courtesy rather than friendship.

The Reverend was certainly not interested in Donald's exploits on Wall Street, nor did he care much about the parties he and his wife attended. To be fair, James could not imagine Donald had much interest in the intricacies of Stamboul society or the steady development of Robert's College. He probably would have found some curiosity in the city's covert underbelly, but even James knew better than to post such sensitive information in a letter. Leaning against the cool stone of the mantel, Reverend Muehler noticed his aspidistra was drooping. He reminded himself that he must talk to Mrs. Eskioğlu about the proper manner of looking after houseplants. Even as he made this mental note, he knew it would be lost in the shuffle of tasks that needed attending to before his dinner that evening with Fredrick.

Fredrick Sutton. Of all his friends from Yale College, Fredrick was among the last James would have expected to pay him a visit. Not that they hadn't been close. Both being sons of working families, he and Fredrick had always had a certain inescapable mixture of affinity and rivalry. The tides of life, however, had drawn them in nearly opposite directions: Reverend Muehler to the cloth and Fredrick to the grubby toil of journalism. In addition to this professional divergence, Fredrick had never been much of a letter-writer. They had exchanged postcards for a few years after graduation, but these updates soon wilted to nothing. He continued to hear Fredrick's news from other, more conscientious friends. He knew about the promotions, the affairs, the move to New York, but he had not received word from the man himself in at least two years. Until a month ago, that is, when he found a yellow telegram on his desk with the following message: *Coming to Stamboul on the second of August. Holland America lines. See you then my friend. Fredrick Sutton.*

In spite of the perfectly comfortable guest quarters available at Robert's College, Fredrick had insisted on staying at the Pera Palace. James was somewhat hurt by his friend's decision to stay at a hotel, but in the end it was probably for the best. He had a great deal of work to accomplish in the next two weeks, and the last thing he needed was a houseguest to entertain. Just that afternoon, he wanted to finish his letter to Donald Stork, prepare the outline of his report to the American Consul, and go over the final draft of his article on the varied manifestations of childhood genius. Before submerging himself again in his work, however, he thought it would be best to take a short walk, to clear his head.

Outside, the air was heavy with evaporation and the sun bled through a shelf of swiftly moving cirrus. The trees hung with soggy moss, and just outside his study a group of first-formers were playing some sort of circular game with a ball. The simplicity of childhood, he thought, could only be appreciated from a distance. He raised a hand to the students in greeting as he crossed the main yard to his favorite contemplation spot, a wooden bench overlooking the Bosporus. It appeared that the storm had cleared all the way to Princes' Islands, where a school of ships scuttled out from under a low curtain of thunder clouds. He shielded his eyes from what sun there was and squinted. Perhaps one of those was Fredrick's. One never knew. One never knew which ship was which until they came out from under the glare of the sun.

Following an hour or so of meandering contemplation, the Reverend rose with a clear head and a newfound determination to accomplish whatever needed accomplishing. He was walking along the narrow path between the chapel and his study, drafting the next section of his letter to Donald Stork, when a student waylaid him. A slight, squirlish child he had engaged months before to keep a watch on Eleonora's movements, the boy was panting and his collar was stained with perspiration. He took a moment to catch his breath.

"Have you heard?" he said. "Sir, have you heard the news?"

The Reverend nodded absently, giving the child leave to continue.

"Miss Cohen," the boy said. "She was at the Sultan's palace yesterday and she fainted. She was shaking on the ground and speaking in tongues."

"My child," said the Reverend, in his most admonishing voice. "Think about what you are saying. Shaking on the ground? Speaking in tongues? This is very difficult for me to believe. Tell me where you heard this."

"Everybody's talking about it, sir."

The Reverend crouched down to the boy's eye level and laid a hand gently on his shoulder.

"Who is everybody?"

"I heard it yesterday from my brother," said the child, wiping the perspiration from his upper lip. "Then we heard it again at the café. And my mother said she heard it from her friend whose husband's brother works in the palace."

"Is that all you heard, my child?"

The boy nodded.

"Are you sure?"

"Yes, sir."

"Thank you. You may go."

Reverend Muehler watched the boy run off along the path. This was certainly an interesting development. Rubbing his temples, he tried to imagine Miss Cohen shaking on the ground and speaking in tongues. It was an odd picture, but not altogether impossible. He had seen much stranger things, to be sure. And, now that he considered the possibility, the idea that she might be afflicted with a neurological disorder, epilepsy or perhaps encephalitis, made perfect sense. Such a condition would explain the shaking and the speaking in tongues. If researched further, it might also be able to explain her mnemonic abilities. That said, one had to take what one heard in this city with a spoonful of salt. The Reverend had learned this lesson the hard way, having more than once given spurious information to his handlers. He would need a towering spoonful of salt and independent verification before he could pass along this piece of intelligence. Tightening his belt, he looked around. He had forgotten exactly where it was he was going, which was just as well, as it was getting on along toward dinner.

After changing out of his habit, James took a carriage to Le Petit Champs du Mort and walked down the boulevard to the Pera Palace Hotel. A grand rococo structure in the French style, it was painted pale yellow and embellished with a number of somewhat eccentric oriental flourishes. He found Fredrick in the lobby, surrounded by a party of German travelers who, from the looks of them, had just returned from an afternoon excursion.

"Four feet long," said Fredrick, marking the distance with his hands. "And thick as my arm. It was the largest snake I've ever seen. And when I came upon him he was wrapped around a camel's neck like a collar."

"You've been to the Fortune-tellers' Quarter?" one of the travelers asked in a heavy British accent. "Our dragoman, Elias here, he took us yesterday."

"First place I went," said Fredrick and he winked at the old dragoman. "Right off the boat. I told the stevedores to take my trunks to the Pera, then point me to the Fortune-tellers' Quarter. My column on it should be in next Sunday's paper."

As the Germans nodded approvingly, Fredrick noticed James standing at the outskirts of the conversation.

"Jimmy," Fredrick cried and rose to embrace him. "It's been much, much too long, my friend."

The maître d' led them through the main dining room of the hotel to a table for two near the entrance of the smoking lounge. It was not the best table in the house by any means, but at an establishment like the Pera Palace, Reverend Muehler and his journalist friend were hardly very important personages. On his way through the dining room, the Reverend had spotted the Baron von Vetz, as well as the new American military attaché and a party of doctors from the Italian Hospital. In any case, the table's relative obscurity would suit their purposes well. They warmed quickly to each other as they caught up on the past three years and traded gossip about old friends from New Haven. Living in Albany, of course, Fredrick had more gossip to share—the Horners' separation, Darby's new book, and Jack's tussle with the governor—though the Reverend had a few juicy bits of his own. He had kept in close contact with a number of their fellow classmates and, as he had found, people were more apt to divulge their secrets to a distant confidant.

"This is perfect," said Fredrick when their first course arrived, a simple Turkish salad dressed with olive oil and lemon juice.

He leaned back to appraise the dining room with a mixture of arrogance and naiveté.

"It's the spitting image of a Rivera hotel, but there is a decidedly Oriental lilt too. It would be perfect for my series."

"Tell me again," said the Reverend, spearing a piece of cucumber with his fork. "What is this series?"

Fredrick cut a piece of tomato in half and inspected the interior meat, as if it might, in fact, be some strange Oriental vegetable masquerading as a tomato.

"Nothing of particular interest. 'Sketches from Abroad' is what the series is called. Essentially, the paper sends a reporter to Europe each year to write on a particular place, rough up some local color, and perhaps dabble in society."

"I see."

"It's a reward really, compensation for the damage done to my nose by the grindstone in Albany. Four years up there in the slush and tumble of the statehouse equals one month of this."

He gestured grandiloquently at his surroundings.

"I'm starting to think it might be a fair trade."

"Pera is just the beginning," said James. "Just a small nibble of Stamboul. The city is full of color if that's what you want."

"That is exactly why I requested to be sent here," said Fredrick. "They fought me on it at first. Didn't think the readers would want a sketch from Asia. So I told them, first of all, half the city is in Europe. And second, this is exactly what the readers want. They want dervishes and elephants. Just look at Kinglake. Look at the *Arabian Nights*. People want Oriental color."

The Reverend raised his glass in toast.

"To Oriental color. And old friends. Welcome to Stamboul."

They clinked and both finished their glasses. A moment later, the waiter arrived with the main course, chicken à la Pera. It was the chef's specialty: a quarter of a small hen simmered in an orange-olive reduction and topped with sour cherries.

"You have heard of the talking bear?" the Reverend asked after a few bites.

"Of course."

Reverend Muehler felt the sparks of their old rivalry rise up in him. Less than a full day in Stamboul, and here was Fredrick posturing as if he knew the city inside and out. He didn't know the half of it, not a quarter. For a brief moment, James considered divulging to Fredrick the details of his most recent covert activities, if only because he knew it would impress his friend. Soon, however, James thought better of the impulse. He was in a hard enough spot as it was. The last thing he needed was whispering among the foreign press.

"Quite a colorful city," James said, a bit louder than he had intended. "Stamboul is the capital of color, really. There's the Fortune-tellers' Quarter, which you have been to, the Slave Bazaar, the Snake Charmer of Üsküdar. And that's not even to mention more commonplace attractions like the Grand Bazaar, the Hagia Sophia, the ruins of Troy."

"Yes," said Fredrick. "We will need to go to Troy. That is one sketch my editors insisted on. It's not far from the city, is it?"

"Less than a day's ride."

As they finished their main course, a waiter passed by their table with a large bronze pot of Turkish coffee and poured them each a cup.

"It smells marvelous," said Fredrick, bringing the shot-size cup under his nose. "What is that spice?"

"Cardamom."

"Cardamom!" Fredrick said triumphantly. "I could write an entire sketch on Turkish coffee."

Reverend Muehler was silent for a moment. He wanted to astound his friend, to introduce him to part of the city he would never see otherwise.

"You know," he began, feeling the flush of his wine at the base of his neck, "the snake charmers and fortune-tellers are just for show. All that's just for foreigners. If you want some real color, I have a former student—"

"Not to be crass, Jimmy, but I don't think anyone cares much about your boys."

"She's a girl," said the Reverend, watching his friend over the rim of his aperitif. "Eight years old, and she's an advisor to the Sultan."

Fredrick narrowed his eyes.

"I tutored her for a few months, but after a while I had nothing left to teach her. The Sultan heard about her ability with languages and he invited her to the palace. As to what happened at the palace," the Reverend said, lowering his voice, "there are many stories. It's difficult to know which is true. This is a city of tall tales, you know, a city of rumors. But I heard from a fairly credible source that she was shaking on the ground and speaking in tongues."

Fredrick finished his coffee and placed the empty cup upside down, as if one of the waiters might tell his fortune. The Reverend could see his friend's mind whirring, then a smile broke over Fredrick's face.

"I already have the headline," he said, and he rapped the table with the tip of his spoon. "It's perfect."

Chapter Twenty-Four

✦

Although she woke each morning with noticeably more vigor than the previous, her appetite larger and strength flowing to her extremities, Eleonora's recovery was slower going than she might have wished. Per doctors' orders, she took meals in her room and left the bed only for visits to the bathroom or to sit in her favorite armchair next to the bay window. She spent most of her recovery ensconced in that chair, not reading, not thinking much, just watching the life of the city pass beneath her. She had forgotten how very pleasurable it was to observe the boat traffic along the Bosporus, the steady back-and-forth of steamers between the Marmara and Black Seas, crisscrossed by a web of caïques reaching from Beşiktaş to Eminönü, Üsküdar, Haydarpasa, and beyond. From her perch at the lip of the straits, Eleonora saw patterns she had never before noticed: the plodding progression of beggars from mosque to mosque, the southerly drift of jellyfish and debris, the thin shadows of minarets sweeping across the city like the hands of a great clock.

On the fifth morning after her episode, Eleonora ventured downstairs and took breakfast in the dining room with the Bey. When breakfast was finished, she retreated back upstairs to the stuffy lethargy of her room. The next two mornings were spent in this same manner. On the eighth morning, however, Eleonora decided, quite unexpectedly, that she would rather spend her day in the library. The thought of another hour in her bedroom was just too much to bear. And there was no reason why sitting in her room would be any different than sitting in the library. So it was that, instead of trudging upstairs to the bay window, Eleonora pushed herself off her chair and ambulated down the great hall to the library.

By the time she arrived at the end of her journey, Eleonora was exhausted and it was all she could do to collapse into the armchair next to the fireplace. When she caught her strength, she examined her surroundings. It appeared the Bey had spent much of the previous night in that very chair. Its seat was cratered from excessive use and the side table disordered with various personal effects, tea glasses, and cigar ends. Beneath the muddle of the night before lay the Sunday edition of a newspaper she had never before encountered. Tucking her legs under herself like a mantis, Eleonora lifted the *New York Sunday News* gently out from under a half-drunk glass of cognac. She unfolded the paper and began paging through it. There was an article about the rebuilding of Vancouver and a long piece reflecting on the accomplishments of the National Geographic Society in its first year, neither of which particularly held her interest. She was just about to put the paper down, in fact, when she happened upon that week's "Sketch from Abroad." The article in question took up most of the back page and was illustrated by an engraving of the Bosporus. Beneath the picture, the headline was printed in thirty-point font: THE ORACLE OF STAMBOUL.

Centuries ago at Delphi, in the age of Homer and Plato, young women augured the fortunes of all those citizens fortunate enough to find themselves in possession of a few coins and the strength to know the truth. Under the banner of two simple words—"Know Thyself"—these oracles foretold the destiny of kings, poets, philosophers, and merchants. The story of Alexander and the Pythian oracle is well known, as is that of Cicero, and Phillip II. One would think that much has changed since the days of Caesar. But in Stamboul, monarchs still confer with mystics. Your correspondent has heard on good report that the Grand Poobah of the Turks, Abdulhamid II, consulted a seer last week not dissimilar from those ancient oracles of Delphi, a precocious young Jewess by the name of Eleonora Cohen, who purportedly broke into a prophetic seizure at the foot of the sovereign during their meeting.

Reading her name in the newspaper, Eleonora had the rather strange feeling of being outside herself, of watching herself from above. It was as if her mind had snuck off to the corridors of the women's quarters while her body remained there in the armchair, reading. The sensation lasted for no longer than a moment, but when it ended, when she was back inside herself, she felt as if she had been given a new perspective on the world, and herself as she made her way through it.

"It is quite disconcerting," said the Bey as he closed the library door behind him, "to read about oneself in the newspaper."

Eleonora looked up. She had no idea how long the Bey had been standing there in the doorway, watching her. Although he was smiling, the rest of the Bey's face conveyed a heavy gravity of purpose. The angle of his eyebrows, the crispness of his hands folded at his waist, everything about his demeanor indicated that the matter they were about to discuss was of the greatest seriousness.

"I myself have had the good fortune that the articles written about me have been mostly true. Calumnious, but for the most part true."

Eleonora touched her clavicles with her fingertips and folded the newspaper in half. She did not want the Bey to think she was not giving him her full attention.

"Since your meeting with the Sultan," he said, seating himself in the chair across from her, "a collection of rumors has been spreading."

"What are they?" she asked.

"This article," the Bey said, picking the paper off her lap, "although erroneous on a number of points, is actually a fairly accurate cross-section of the rumors, at least as far as I have heard them."

"The rumors," Eleonora asked, not sure how, or even if, he wanted her to respond. "Are they true?"

The Bey lifted his left eyebrow. Flattening the newspaper, he laid it over the arm of his chair.

"That is precisely what I wish to speak with you about. In the past few days, I have noticed a number of incongruous, unfamiliar men lurking around the docks, the Beşiktaş Mosque, and the Café Europa. All this leads me to believe that our house and my person are under increased surveillance."

Eleonora's throat tightened and she felt the glow of shame rising to her cheeks. Moncef Bey had been so kind to her. He had protected her in her time of need, he had watched over her and provided for her, all without ever asking for anything in return. The last thing she wanted was to increase his troubles.

"I know your memory is still weak," the Bey continued. "But for your protection and well-being, as well as my own, I need for you to tell me everything you recall of what you said to the Sultan."

"If I could remember," she said, "I would tell you. But truly, I don't. All I remember is the Hyrcanians."

"The Hyrcanians?"

"I told the Sultan, or at least I began telling him, the story of the Hyrcanians and the Assyrians, from Xenophon."

"Xenophon," the Bey repeated, glancing in the direction of his books. "Well, whatever it was you said, you had a very significant effect on the Sultan's thinking. As such, there are a number of powerful forces interested in the matter."

The Bey then stood and walked across the room to a bookshelf full of histories. He was smiling still, but in the twitch of his mouth and the tension at the base of his back, Eleonora could see he was anxious. After paging through a copy of Xenophon's *Selected Works*, he returned to his chair.

"It is a rather apt analogy," he said, leaning into the leather. "The Hyrcanians and the Assyrians."

Eleonora did not respond. She did not know what to think. After a long silence, the Bey handed the newspaper back to her and stood again.

"Tell me one thing," he said, standing now over her chair. "Do you remember saying anything to the Sultan about Reverend Muehler or the meeting you witnessed at the Café Europa?"

Eleonora laid the paper across her lap and, in an attempt to relieve the tension building behind her eyes, she pressed the bridge of her nose between her thumb and forefinger. It was the least she could do, to remember, but that section of her mind was entirely blank.

"When I was recovering," she said finally, "in the Sultan's private chambers, his mother asked if I could remember anything I had said. When I told her I couldn't, she asked if I remembered anything I had said about Reverend Muehler and the puzzle, or your meeting with—"

She stopped and put her hand to her mouth, realizing what it was she had done. She had betrayed her greatest friend and protector. That the betrayal was unintentional meant little. Eleonora looked up at the Bey, who was standing still next to her chair. His lips were pursed to subdue a quiver.

"I didn't mean to," she said.

"I know you didn't."

He laid his hand on her shoulder, then continued.

"What concerns me is that the Grand Vizier might jump to unfounded conclusions. You see, the man you met at Café Europa is high on the list of suspects in the case of the boat accident. He and I have worked together in the past on issues of constitutional reform. It turns out, however, that he also has ties to a number of radical nationalist organizations. In any case, any connection between him and me would be rich fodder for the Grand Vizier's suspicions. Thus, the increase in surveillance."

Eleonora glanced down at the newspaper in her lap.

"They won't do anything to you?" she said, the tone of her voice rising to a question. "You haven't done anything wrong."

The Bey nodded, though he did not seem to fully agree.

"Unfortunately, that's not always how it works."

Later that evening, after a restless and question-addled nap, Eleonora received the first trickle of what would soon become a river of communications from admirers around the world. The Bey often received letters and telegrams after dinner, and so neither he nor Eleonora were particularly surprised when the doorbell rang and Monsieur Karom came into the dining room with two letters on a salver. However, instead of opening the envelopes and handing them to the Bey, as he normally did, the butler came around the other side of the table and placed the tray next to Eleonora. The envelope closest to her was of pearl-white stock. Her full name, Miss Eleonora Cohen, was written across the front. The second letter was written on somewhat coarser paper and was addressed to *The Oracle of Stamboul*.

"Would you like me to open them?" asked Monsieur Karom, standing at attention.

"Yes," she said. "Please."

He removed the letter opener from his breast pocket and, with a small flourish, tore the pearl-white envelope perfectly across its top. It was a motion Eleonora had seen him perform dozens of times, but as she watched him open this, the first letter she had ever received, her breath caught and stumbled.

"It's an invitation," she said after reading it through. "My presence is cordially requested for dinner at the British embassy."

"Curious," said the Bey, but he did not say why he thought it so.

The second letter was a request from a young woman whose father had died suddenly, before he could formally arrange a suitable match for her. She now had three suitors at her door, all of whom claimed her late father's blessing. It wasn't clear exactly what the young woman wanted from Eleonora, though she concluded the letter with the words "I am confident you will be able to help."

Over the next three days, Eleonora was inundated with invitations, calling cards, letters, and telegrams requesting her presence and guidance. Most of the communicants lived in Stamboul, though a few came from more distant reaches of the Ottoman realm, cities such as Selonika and Trabzon, places she had heard of and could place on a map, but knew little of besides. Later in the week, telegrams began arriving from as far afield as Copenhagen and Chicago. No matter where they came from, and no matter how tattered or fine the stationery, Eleonora answered these missives all the same. She declined politely the invitations to parties and dinners, explaining that she was still not in possession of complete health. And she tried her best to answer the requests for guidance with the soundest advice she could muster. Though the truth was, she was having a hard enough time finding answers to her own problems.

Chapter Twenty-Five

By the end of August, Eleonora had recovered entirely from her episode at the palace. In spite of this happy resolution, she could not escape the feeling that something inexorable in her life had shifted. It was like sitting down to a sumptuous meal of roast lamb, stuffed quinces, and barley salad, only to find the silverware missing. As she went through the familiar routine of life in the Bey's house, Eleonora could not help but feel the uncomfortable tightness of fate constricting about her, limiting the scope of her future like an ever-shrinking dress. She felt as if she were waiting for something to snap, to tear, to reveal a weakness in the fabric.

Even those relationships that mattered to her most did not feel steady. Although she had told the Bey everything she could remember about her second audience with the Sultan and her recovery afterward in the harem, although she had explained to him her views on the connection between the Hyrcanians and the Ottoman Empire, although he had forgiven her multiple times for her inadvertent betrayal, although they spoke more candidly and frequently now than they ever had before, Eleonora felt a piece of her relationship with the Bey was forever altered. Even when he spoke to her of trivial matters—the heat, the rising price of cotton, or the availability of cherries in the produce market—his forehead was tense and his eyebrows cocked into a question.

And it wasn't just the Bey. Monsieur Karom was far more

deferential than he had ever been. He bowed almost imperceptibly as he handed Eleonora her mail and held his breath when
he brushed her crumbs from the table. At bath time, Mrs. Damakan scrubbed her like a delicate piece of glassware she feared
damaging. And when the old handmaid buttoned up the backs
of her dresses, Eleonora could feel her fingers trembling. Even
Eleonora's flock had changed. They were more eager and determined now, as if they could sense the fulfillment of a promise
hidden somewhere beneath the blanket of hot air. Each morning, she watched them set out one by one from the ledge beneath
her window. And at the conclusion of the day, she followed their
return one by one in the same order they had departed. Where
their sorties led them, what they sought out there in the wilds of
the city, Eleonora could only guess.

It seemed sometimes that the entire world was off its axis.
Eleonora had taken occasionally to glancing through the Bey's
discarded copy of the *Stamboul Herald*. As she read through
the news of the previous day, she could not help but feel that
something essential had come unmoored. In a period of just two
weeks, she read of a tense standoff between the British Navy and
the emperor of China, a devastating earthquake in the southern
United States, a cholera outbreak in Spain, dozens of suicides
(including a sensational fake suicide jump from a bridge in New
York), more than a few stabbings, and a rash of brazen bank rob-
beries in Geneva. In addition to all this conflict and disease, the
Stamboul Herald also reported that His Excellency Sultan Abdulhamid II was in the process of disassembling the empire's
long-standing alliance with the Germans. The article included
no details beyond this, though it attributed the Sultan's motivation to the influences of his "youthful advisor."

The greatest shock, however, came in the form of a telegram, delivered late one morning at the height of summer. Eleonora was reading through the classifieds on the back page of the *Stamboul Herald* when Monsieur Karom came into the dining room with a pile of letters and telegrams. He placed the stack and his letter opener on the table next to her and bowed out of the room, knowing she preferred to open her letters herself. As was her custom, she went through the stack and examined each of the envelopes before setting in with the opener. Among the stack was a telegram from Paris, a somewhat shabby letter from Trabzon, and a few of her own letters that had been returned for one reason or another. Near the bottom, she came upon a curious telegram that she couldn't quite decipher at first. It had been sent through a British company called Imperial and International Communication Ltd. In spite of its origin, the message was not written in English, at least not that she could tell. Eleonora stared down at the purple muddle of characters, and blinked. She flattened the paper on the table, allowed her mind to relax, and focused as sharply as she could. Soon she worked out the puzzle. Though composed in Roman letters, the telegram was written in her mother tongue.

READ ABOUT YOU IN THE NEWSPAPER CONGRATULA-TIONS COMING TO STAMBOUL SOON WOULD LIKE TO SEE YOU THEN THINGS IN CONSTANTA ARE WELL—YOUR AUNT RUXANDRA

After reading over it twice, Eleonora lifted the piece of paper off the table. She stared down into the empty polish and watched her reflection shift through the texture of the wood. Her aunt Ruxandra. She bit her lip, crumpled the telegram into a small pale blue ball, and did her best to chase it from her mind. She knew, however, that this was not possible. No matter what she did, no matter if she burned it or swallowed it or ripped it into tiny pieces, she would not be able to rid herself of this message, nor the knowledge of how callously her aunt, her only remaining family, had abandoned her in her time of need. No matter what Eleonora did, her hands would smell of the ink and the words would be written on her mind in capital letters.

"Miss Cohen?"

Eleonora recognized Mrs. Damakan's voice, but she did not look up.

"Are you feeling unwell, Miss Cohen?"

She felt a shudder escape to her extremities. She was not feeling well, not at all. She shut her eyes and closed her fingers ever more tightly around the balled-up telegram, feeling its corners dig into her palm. As much as she wanted to show Mrs. Damakan the note, to seek her advice and her sympathy, Eleonora kept the telegram crumpled in her hand. To tell anyone, even Mrs. Damakan, about the telegram, to speak its name aloud would make it real in a way Eleonora could not yet stomach.

"It's the heat," she said, raising her head. "If you don't mind, I think a glass of water would do me well."

Mrs. Damakan was happy to oblige. When she returned with it, Eleonora drank the glass of water in two long gulps.

"Thank you," she exhaled. "I feel much better."

And it was true. She did feel much better. However, the telegram still remained.

"I think I could use a short walk," she said, taking care to conceal her clenched fist. "Just about the house."

Mrs. Damakan took the empty glass from the table.

"If you need anything—" she began.

"If I need anything, I will be sure to let you know."

As she turned to leave, Mrs. Damakan gave her a look of dejected resignation, a look such as an illiterate father might give a son who has rebuked him for his ignorance. Eleonora had not meant to be so sharp. She loved Mrs. Damakan like an aunt, like a mother.

"Thank you, Mrs. Damakan. It's just that I am feeling restless."

Eleonora wandered through the Bey's house with no particular destination in mind. She ambled down the great hall, under the sullen gaze of the Barcous clan, past the library and the drawing room. She had never felt quite so alone. For the first time, she truly understood what General Krzab meant when he complained of *the leaden weight of responsibility, that onerous plow the better part of humanity strives endlessly to yoke round its neck.*

Eleonora found herself eventually at the entrance to the women's quarters. She had not visited the corridors for quite some time, but she felt drawn to them now, to their dark and dusty solitude. Clearing her mind as best she could, she crossed the foyer and climbed the stairs to the corridors. She wandered to a particularly dark corner above the kitchen and lay down on her back. Resting her head against the wood, she steadied her breathing and stared up into darkness without end. She knew there was a ceiling there, but she could not make out its contours. Eventually, her hand relaxed and she let the telegram drop to the floor beside her. She put her mind to work in trying to decipher the situation she now found herself at the middle of, to piece together what she knew about Ruxandra, the Bey, her father, the Sultan, and Reverend Muehler, but no matter how hard she thought, the pieces wouldn't fit.

Chapter Twenty-Six

His Excellency Abdulhamid II spread a white cloth napkin across his lap and lowered his nose to the plate of cold roast chicken on the table in front of him. Although he understood well the importance of etiquette, of courtly pomp and protocol, the constant attention to procedure sometimes grew tiresome. Sometimes His Excellency wanted nothing more than to eat an entire plate of cold roast chicken with his hands, to tear it limb from limb. And that was precisely what he intended to do. He was the Sultan after all. Grinning to himself at the perfect luxury of such a crude meal, he ripped the poor bird's leg from its body and sunk his teeth through the flesh. The chicken had been roasted in the Aegean style and finished with a syrupy walnut paste. Even cold, its skin crackled. After sucking the leg bare, Abdulhamid used a piece of flat bread to pull the meat off the breasts and back and underside.

When he was finished with the chicken, its carcass lay ravaged on the plate like some wayward harlot. Wiping his hands, he laid his napkin over the empty bones and reclined into his chaise lounge with a glass of mint tea. He allowed himself a brief reverie of an untoward nature before taking up again the second volume of *The Hourglass*. It truly was a wonderful book, filled with twists and turns, romance, pride, and greed. The translation of such great literature was a service to his subjects and an honor to the Turkish language. It was also beneficial to

his own reading pleasure, but that was just a secondary consequence, a providential return on his munificence. Propping the
book up against his stomach, Abdulhamid quickly lost himself.
Engrossed as he was in the gruesome battle scene near the end
of the volume, during which Lieutenant Brashov learns of his
brother's supposed death, the Sultan did not hear the click of
the door opening.

"Your Excellency."

It was the Grand Vizier, brandishing a rolled-up newspaper
like a rapier.

"What is it?"

"Your Excellency. I know that you asked not to be disturbed.
But I think you would like to see this."

The Sultan righted himself and, pulling his napkin over an
exposed chicken bone, leaned across the table to take the unfurled newspaper from his advisor.

" 'The Oracle of Stamboul,' " he said, glancing at the headline. "What is this? An editorial calling for my resignation? Another cry for religious freedom?"

"Much worse, Your Excellency. If you don't mind me saying so."

The Sultan read through the first paragraph, which took him
some time as he was not especially practiced in English. Jamaludin Pasha coughed and clasped his hands in front of his body.

"I was particularly upset by the line about your mother," he
said, indicating from a distance. "In the middle of the fourth
paragraph."

The Sultan read aloud:

" 'And she is rumored by some to be in league with the Sultan's own mother.' "

He punctuated the end of the sentence with a loud staccato laugh.

"Miss Cohen in league with my mother. Against whom? To what end?"

Jamaludin Pasha, however, was not amused. And Abdulhamid knew that he would not be able to get back to his book until this matter was resolved. Taking on an air of gravity, the Sultan folded the newspaper and laid it next to the remains of the recently dismembered chicken.

"I see, of course, why you find this article troubling," he said. "It is an assault on my fitness to rule. Not to mention the piece about my mother. But what action can we take against a newspaper in New York?"

"We have tracked down the author of the piece. He is staying at the Pera Palace, room 307. If you wish, I can summon him to a meeting at the palace. We can give him a scare, something impressive to write his next installment about, then put him on the next ship back to New York."

"Yes," said the Sultan. "Very well."

"I might also suggest, Your Excellency, that it would be best if you did not meet again with Miss Cohen, in light of these rumors."

The Sultan closed his eyes and pressed the bridge of his nose between his thumb and index finger.

"I thought you might suggest that," he said. "Please leave the newspaper here. I will peruse it more closely and give you further directions this evening."

"There is one final piece of information, Your Excellency," said the Grand Vizier. "If you don't mind."

"No, by all means."

"I have contacted Miss Cohen's aunt, Ruxandra, who appears to be the only relative of any use. My intention was nothing more than to alert the aunt of her niece's whereabouts. In the course of our exchange, however, I felt compelled to offer the assistance of the palace should Miss Cohen decide she wants to leave the care of Moncef Bey and return to Constanta."

The Sultan murmured something to himself and rose from his seat, signifying that the meeting was over.

"As I said, I will give you further instructions this evening."

"Yes, Your Excellency," said the Grand Vizier, bowing out of the room.

When the door clicked shut, Abdulhamid sat down again and unfolded the newspaper. It was rather an amusing piece, he had to admit, though inaccurate on many accounts and filled with quite damning implications. One could only imagine the rumors such a story would engender, had already engendered. He had just come again to the section about Miss Cohen and his mother when the woman herself burst into his room. Whatever the original intention of her visit, it was derailed by the sight of the article in her son's hand.

"I do hope that whoever wrote that insinuating slander is going to be punished severely."

The Sultan folded the paper in half and straightened his back.

"A good day to you too, Mother."

"Excuse my impertinence, Your Excellency," she said, bowing. "It's just that—"

"Not to worry," he said. "I just now told Jamaludin Pasha to track down the author and punish him accordingly. We thought deportation would be sufficient."

"Deportation would be sufficient, I suppose, though it will not repair the damage done by this piece of refuse."

"The question then," said the Sultan, ruefully sipping the lukewarm sediment at the bottom of his tea glass, "the question to my mind is what action we should take to dispel these rumors."

"What has Jamaludin Pasha suggested?"

"He is agnostic on the matter."

"Agnostic?"

"Yes. He said he had no strong opinion."

This was a lie, of course. His mother knew better than anyone that the Grand Vizier was agnostic about nothing, but she could not directly contradict the Sultan. So she moved forward on a different tack.

"Beyond punishing the author and dealing with the rumors," she said, "there is also the matter of the girl herself. Something must be done about her. I see no need to punish her. She has done nothing wrong. But until something is done about her, we cannot begin to counteract the rumors."

"What approach would you suggest, Mother?"

She raised her hand to her neck and stroked its full length, as if considering the question for the first time.

"As I see it, there are two paths we could take. Neither is perfect, but both would serve our purposes well."

"Yes," said Abdulhamid, glancing at the swirl of tea leaves and mint at the bottom of his glass. "Go on."

"The first path," she said, "is deportation. Send her back to Romania and forget about her. The second path would be to invite her to live here in the palace. We could find a room for her somewhere on the edge of the harem, give her lessons in music and calligraphy. Both solutions have their problems, of course, but they both also have their benefits."

"Intriguing," the Sultan said, scratching the back of his head, just beneath his turban. "I can't say I have considered the second option, but it is rather intriguing, especially coming from you. Let me think on it."

Later that afternoon, a train of imperial carriages pulled up to the entrance of the Çemberlitas Baths, and the Sultan disembarked, wearing a light blue silk caftan piped with red and silver. He was followed into the baths by a retinue of barbers, masseuses, towel boys, and assorted other attendants. Six days a week, the complex teemed with the hairy backs of common men, grunting and slathering themselves with soap. On Saturdays, however, Çemberlitaş was closed to the public. On Saturdays, Abdulhamid could lie alone in the middle of the main room, watching strands of sunlight fall through the steam. Although the palace possessed a series of magnificent baths, of the finest design and craftsmanship, Çemberlitaş was without rival.

Undressing, the Sultan entered the condensation-heavy main room. A gently rising dodecahedron, the ceiling sloped through endlessly repeating tiles to a vaulted glimpse of sunlight. A dozen faucets were arranged around the perimeter of the room, all pointing toward the large, light gray marble slab at the center. It was like a mosque dedicated to the human body. Indeed, as he lay on his back at the center of the marble slab, the sunlight fell perfectly through the steam and he felt in the presence of something greater than himself. After a few minutes of solitude, Abdulhamid summoned his team of attendants, who set to work washing, stretching, and massaging the royal corpus. It was during these cleansing sessions that he did his best thinking. Succored in the presence of God, his senses obscured by steam and a team of hands scrubbing at the husk of his physical body, his mind was free to wander unfamiliar paths, to amble aimlessly along the highway of logic. It was here that he dreamed up the Hajj Railroad, here that he had resolved so many of the conflicts with the Public Debt Administration, here that he had decided finally how to deal with the Safavids.

On that particular day, the dilemma, of course, was what to do with Miss Cohen. He wasn't entirely convinced that anything needed to be done about the girl herself, but both his mother and the Grand Vizier had insisted. And he knew that in those rare moments when the two of them agreed, it was worthwhile at least to consider all the available options. The current situation, he could see now, was not tenable. Not that he suspected Moncef Bey of anything more than his reading groups. It was solely a matter of Miss Cohen and her growing reputation. His mother had put it quite well. There were two distinct choices. They could send Miss Cohen back to Constanta, a path that the Grand Vizier seemed to favor, or they could invite her to live in the palace, give her some music lessons or a job in the bureaucracy, and allow her to live out a life of sheltered obscurity. He couldn't imagine Jamaludin Pasha would be fond of such an arrangement. He was already quite upset about the disintegration of the German alliance, so much so that the Sultan wondered sometimes whether he could faithfully discharge his other duties. That, however, was a question for another day. Inhaling, the Sultan closed his eyes and, following the web of colors the light made on the insides of his eyelids, he focused his attention entirely on the matter of what to do with Eleonora Cohen. When he opened his eyes again, it was clear.

And so it was, amid the steam and ambergris of Çemberlitaş, that Abdulhamid decided to invite Eleonora to live at the palace, where she could serve as his personal advisor and answer queries to her heart's content. Of all the options available, it was the only one that made good sense. Naturally, her presence in the halls of power would constitute a threat to his other advisors, but they would learn to live with her, just as they had learned to live with each other, and if they couldn't, they would have to find a more suitable position. He was the Sultan and he could take advice from whomever he chose.

Chapter Twenty-Seven

❖

Eleonora's third visit to the palace was rather different than the previous two, in shape as well as purpose. When the imperial carriage pulled up to the front of the Bey's house, she was upstairs in her bedroom, dressing herself with the assistance of Mrs. Damakan and contemplating her plans for the day. It had been thundering for much of the morning, and there was a stack of letters on her desk that needed responding to, not to mention the telegram from her aunt Ruxandra, crumpled into a ball next to the stack. Although she was still not quite ready to return to her prior regimen, the thought of reading for pleasure was beginning to appeal to her in a way it hadn't since her episode. And she thought she might also like to spend some time exploring the Bey's house. Of course, the arrival of the imperial carriage scuttled these plans. Without a word, Mrs. Damakan buttoned up the back of Eleonora's dress and they hastened downstairs to the anteroom, where the Sultan's herald was waiting, his hands clasped at his belt and heel pattering restlessly against the floor.

"Miss Cohen," he said, bowing at the waist. "His Excellency has requested to see you as soon as you are able."

"Yes . . ." She hesitated. "Of course."

She turned to Mrs. Damakan, then back to the herald.

"May I have a moment to change?"

"You may," said the herald. "However, I should advise you

that His Excellency indicated he would like to see you as soon as you are able, without concern for clothing or condition."

Eleonora felt Mrs. Damakan push her gently from behind, and she was out the front door, following the herald across the walk. Without time for another thought, she was in the carriage and on her way. Instead of turning up the hill toward the Gate of Greeting, the carriage followed the curve of the Bosporus around the Golden Horn, past a green copper-topped public fountain, to the northeast corner of the palace. The gate protecting this entrance was much smaller than the Gate of Greeting, but still imposing in its own right. Carved from a single piece of basalt and adorned with star-shaped turquoise tiles, the mouth of the gate resembled an enormous whale opening its jaws to swallow them whole.

Upon disembarking from the carriage, she was approached by a languid young woman, much like those she had observed when she was recovering from her episode in the Sultan's private quarters. She was quite young, no more than seventeen, though very much a woman in her loose cotton frock. Without a word, she took Eleonora's hand in her own and kissed the tips of her fingers.

"The Sultan is waiting."

She had striking green eyes, mined with gold and resting in a heavy nest of lashes. Allowing some time for Eleonora to grow comfortable in her presence, the young woman then turned and led her into the palace proper. They traveled down one path and up another, turning right twice and left once before entering a vaulted hall that smelled of citrus and musk.

"I must leave you," she said, stopping in front of a tall door flanked by two palace guards. "The Sultan has requested to meet with you alone."

The guards stepped aside and Eleonora felt the scratchy taste of bile at the back of her throat. She held on to the young woman's hand.

"Excuse me," she said. "Can I ask you a question?"

The young woman regarded Eleonora with a combination of sympathy and affection, as if she were a baby sparrow found wandering alone in the woods.

"Do you know what he, His Excellency, wants to speak with me about?"

"No," the woman said. "I don't. But you can be confident that he will treat you well no matter what it is he wants."

Eleonora tried to think of another question, but none came. And so, the young woman turned to walk back down the hall.

The room Eleonora had been escorted to was known as the Iris Chamber, after a floral design etched into the plaster around its doorway. A small and relatively spartan room, its far wall was taken up mostly by a semicircular blue divan, on which the Sultan was reading. Apart from the divan and a hunchback wooden chair inlaid with mother-of-pearl, the Iris Chamber was furnished only with a writing desk and a painting of a fox hunt. Eleonora watched the Sultan read for some time before she spoke.

"Is that *The Hourglass*?"

"Yes," he said, laying his book facedown on the divan. "I cannot thank you enough for recommending it to me."

"Where are you?"

"The third volume. When you entered I had just come to the scene in which General Krzab calls the remaining members of his family together to berate them and to distribute the fortune he uncovered at the back of his mother's closet."

" 'Truth is a slippery fish,' " Eleonora said, quoting General Krzab's famous line a few pages earlier. "'Flashing scales in the water and a noble fighter on the line—'"

The Sultan smiled and finished the quotation.

"'—But dull as lead at the bottom of the boat.'"

As the Sultan spoke, Eleonora realized that she had committed an enormous breach of etiquette. Not only had she addressed him directly, without title or form, she had neglected also to bow upon entering the room. Covering her mouth, she humbled to her knees and touched her head to the floor.

"Please," said the Sultan.

She turned to look at him, her temple still pressed against the cool tile.

"There is no need. You may sit if you like," he said, motioning toward the deep wooden chair on his right.

She moved toward the chair cautiously, for fear of violating protocol again, and perched at the edge of its seat. Up close, she noticed, the Sultan's face was quite similar to that of the Bey, especially about the nose and upper lip. Unlike the Bey's leafy cigar smell, however, the Sultan's aroma was lavender and lilac, with a touch of orange.

"I wanted to speak with you in private," he began. "I have an important question I would like to ask and I want you to answer on your own, without the pressure of the court. Do you feel comfortable answering for yourself? Are you ready to make a very big decision that will affect the rest of your life?"

Eleonora looked down at her shoes, polished and swinging above the ground.

"Yes. I am."

"Naturally, the decision is entirely up to you, but I pray you keep in mind that the effects of your choice will impact the lives of many."

He paused to look at her. Her hands were folded in her lap and her face set in an expression of supreme serenity.

"What I want to ask you is whether you would like to live at the palace. You would stay here, in the seraglio—if you like, in this very room. Your days would be spent reading, playing the oud, learning calligraphy, whatever you please, really. Your every want would be provided for. There is nothing you would need to do in return, except occasionally to discuss an issue of state with me or with the Grand Vizier."

Eleonora unfolded her hands and pushed her fingers back through her hair. It was indeed an enormous question, and it took her somewhat by surprise. There were so many contingencies, so many consequences to consider. She tried to think it through, to work it out, but as she did, she was overcome by a swirling, heavy feeling not unlike the swoon before her episode. She blinked and came back to herself.

"What about the Bey?"

"The Bey? I can only assume that Moncef Bey will continue to live his life just as he did before you arrived."

"Would he be upset?"

The Sultan seemed somewhat perplexed.

"I can't say how he would react. I would remind you, however, that this is your decision alone. Although I agree we should consider those around us, it is important to remember your own self-interest."

She nodded.

"What will happen to me if I decide not to live at the palace?"

"Well," said the Sultan. "No one can know for sure. But that is a very good question. It shows you understand your situation well."

He paused, working his mouth about a lozenge of some sort.

"I trust you know that your aunt is on her way to Stamboul.

It is her intention, as I understand it, to bring you back to Constanta. Of course, if you chose to live at the palace we would make alternate arrangements for her."

As the Sultan spoke about life in the palace and the holdings of the imperial library, Eleonora let her gaze wander to the painting of the fox hunt. Horses and dogs dominated the frame, so much so that it took her a moment to spot the tiny curl of fox at the bottom right, hidden in the hollow of a tree. She realized she had been silent for some time when the Sultan stood.

"May I ask which option you are inclining toward?"

Eleonora was not inclined toward either of these options. What she wanted was to continue her life as it had been before, living quietly with Moncef Bey, Monsieur Karom, and Mrs. Damakan. She understood, however, that this was no longer an option, for a number of reasons. Naturally, one could not voice such thoughts.

"I am inclining toward the palace," she began. "But, if I may, I would like some time to make my decision."

"That is fair," said the Sultan, and he seated himself again on the divan. "It is a major decision and I wouldn't want you to rush into it. I will send a herald tomorrow morning. If you decide to live here, have your luggage ready. If not, I hope you will do me the courtesy of meeting with me again to discuss your choice."

"I will."

The Sultan stood again and saw her to the door. For a moment, standing there at the entrance to the Iris Chamber, they looked at each other: a small girl and a small man on the far side of middle age. Bending at the waist, Abdulhamid took her hand and kissed it.

On the carriage ride back from the palace, Eleonora saw Stamboul in a new light. The waterfront mansions, the old men fishing over the side of the Galata Bridge, the thrush of commerce in the markets, even the sea birds tooling overhead, everything was imbued with the scent of possibility. She thought of the line from Lieutenant Brashov's speech to his brother, just before his death: *With every choice, even the choice of inactivity, we must shut the door to a host of alternate futures. Each step we take along the path of fate represents a narrowing of potential, the death of a parallel world.* The path of fate was really more like a tunnel, and it was constricting about her with every step she took.

Eleonora was not in a particularly voluble mood when she returned home. She had a great deal to think through, and not much time. After she told the Bey about her visit to the palace and the Sultan's offer, they spent the afternoon ensconced in mutual silence, he paging through the newspapers of the week and she tending to unanswered letters. Among them was a letter from a child in Paris, who wanted to know which books she had studied exactly, and a long complaint from an Italian monk describing the political situation around Siena. She wrote a few responses before losing herself in contemplation of a distant bank of clouds. If only she could focus her mind on her own situation, solve it as she had solved the problems of the Sultan and all the people who wrote asking for her advice. Laying her pen down, Eleonora folded her hands in her lap and closed her eyes, concentrating her attention on the vicissitudes of the choice in front of her. If only she knew how it all fit together—the Reverend's puzzle, the young man at the Café Europa, the Bey, the Grand Vizier, the Sultan's mother—if only she could figure out what it all meant, she thought, she would be able to make the correct choice.

After a long while, she opened her eyes, no closer to the answer. She watched her flock returning home, one by one, each

bird from its own foray into the depths of the city. As the linden tree grew purple with their chattering, Eleonora realized her
very question was wrong. She thought of Miss Ionescu's maxim:
There is no sage wiser than the dictates of your own personal heart.
Then she recalled the lines that followed: *When you follow the ar-
dent instructions of your heart, when you follow not the easy path nor
the selfish path, but the path you knew all along was correct, you can
only but do what's right by the world.* The truth was, Eleonora realized, she didn't want any of it. She didn't want the Sultan's protection, nor did she want the Bey's. She didn't want Constanta
or Ruxandra. She didn't want Mrs. Damakan's prophecy and she
didn't want all these people asking her advice. What she wanted,
more than anything, was to be alone, without anyone's plans or
expectations, unencumbered and unattached.

After a mostly silent dinner of stewed beef and rice, Eleonora
excused herself and trudged upstairs to bed. Setting her candle
on the bedside table, she crossed to the bay window. She rested
her elbows on the windowsill and gazed out across at the white
walls of the palace. The straits sparkled like rock candy, reflecting a fresh string of lights hung between the minarets of the New
Mosque. She could see the outlines of ships cutting through the
water like so many ghosts, and, in the far distance, she heard the
wail of a train brake as it pulled into Sircesi Station. This sound
carried with it the outline of a thought, alighting delicately on
the windowsill like a sea bird from across the ocean. It appeared
at first glance to be just the solution she was looking for, but before she could fully think it through, there was a knock at the
door.

"Come in."

In the light of the doorway, where he remained, the Bey's features took on a spectral cast.

"I hope I did not wake you," he said, though it was obvious he had not.

"No," she said, turning fully now to face him. "Not at all."

"I wanted to tell you that I will do my best to support you, to advocate for your best interests, regardless of what you decide."

He was silent for a moment and the candlelight played nervously on his face. Then, reaching into his coat, he removed a small pouch.

"Your father," he said, holding the pouch in his upturned palm, "left this behind. It was with his luggage."

He set the pouch on her night table and withdrew into the hall, the sharpness of his features receding into darkness.

"No matter what path you choose, it will serve you well."

"Thank you," she said. "For everything."

"You are most welcome."

He closed the door behind him, and for a full three minutes Eleonora stood with her back to the open window, staring into the darkness of her bedroom as she worked over her plan. Then she closed the window, undressed, and slipped into bed. Before snuffing out the candle, she untied the soft leather pouch and peered inside. There were two ten-kurus coins and five hundred-pound notes. She was not very good with money, but she knew that this would suffice.

Lying in bed, Eleonora listened to the sounds of the house die, the creak and swing of doors giving way to smaller, outside sounds, the wind blowing through leaves and animals pattering in the gutters. The moon rose like a distant city on the horizon, illuminating her desk, her armchair, and her dressing table with the white light of late summer. She would miss this room, just as she missed her room in Constanta, but she could not stay. She just could not. When the moon was at its full height and the house was silent, Eleonora slipped out of bed and muffled across the floor to her closet. She pushed her dresses aside and took down the pair of pants, shirt, fez, and suit jacket she had noticed that first day in Stamboul. She dressed herself in it as best she could. With pins in her hair and a bit of kohl dust under her eyes, she was able to affect a rather convincing image of an errand boy with delicate features.

Next came the note. She removed a piece of paper from the middle desk drawer and, dipping her favorite pen in its inkwell, wrote a single word across the top of the page. *Good-bye.* Below this, she signed her name. Her heart was beating faster now and her breath came shortly when it came at all. She opened the top drawer of the dresser, removed her mother's bookmark, and placed it in the inside pocket of her coat. Stretching her toes and cracking her jaw, she slipped her father's leather pouch alongside the bookmark. Then, glancing at herself once more in the mirror, she poked her head out into the hallway and left her room behind.

At the top of the stairs, she stopped and gazed down on the antechamber. It was a cavernous room with dull corners and shadows flickering at the edges. Closing a hand over the banister, she crept down the stairs toe-to-heel, breathing through her mouth as she listened to the echoing of her own footfalls. When she reached the bottom, the house moaned, as if she had stepped on an open bruise. In front of her, the carpet stretched out like a lake of fire sparked by reflections of moonlight in the chandelier. She touched the pouch in her coat pocket and, with a shiver, continued on, down the main hall, into the women's quarters, through the stuffy black corridors, down the stairs, and through the small iron door, out into the heavy straw air of the Bey's stables. Leaving the door ajar, Eleonora crept past a team of nickering horses and through the stable gates.

She was outside. There was a wind at her ankles and only sky above her, a dark sheet pricked with glimpses of the firmament it obscured. A white cat skulked across her path and winked its single blue eye. She understood. The world was big, it was cold, and it reeked of possibility. Her flock had dispersed; they had no more business here.

Eleonora glanced back at the yellow grandeur of the Bey's house and, unsure whether she had glimpsed the stooped silhouette of Mrs. Damakan framed in her second-floor bay window, hurried down the main road. She made her way across the moonlit bridge toward the Sircesi Station. From there, she could catch a train to anywhere in Europe, to Paris, Budapest, Berlin, St. Petersburg, or Prague. She could stow away and slip, unnoticed, out of history.

Epilogue

On the thirtieth of August 1886, nine years and a week after Eleonora Cohen first came into this world, the city of Stamboul woke to find its oracle vanished. Purple-and-white hoopoes were sighted perched above the entrance to the Egyptian Bazaar, in the branches of an olive tree near Le Petit Champs du Mort, and passing over the Old Greek Hospital just outside the Yedikule Gate. One enterprising young boy in Balat captured a hoopoe in his mother's bread basket. Unfortunately, the bird died soon after its capture. The other hoopoes were sighted alone, heading in contradictory directions.

At the order of the Sultan, His Excellency Abdulhamid II, all traffic leaving the city was stopped and searched. The gendarmerie was put on high alert, and all the railway officials within a fifty-kilometer radius of Stamboul were given descriptions of Eleonora. The Bosporus was dredged and a pack of Sivas Kangals was given her scent. Moncef Bey was detained for questioning, as were Monsieur Karom and Mrs. Damakan. However, no one, it seemed, had any knowledge of Eleonora's whereabouts. She was gone, vanished, leaving no trace but a note and a closet full of dresses.

Eventually, a funeral was held and life returned to its natural course. Ruxandra went back to Constanta and her new husband. Reverend Muehler finished up his term at Robert's College and, with the assistance of his contacts in the Department of War, took a position at Yale. Moncef Bey went back to organizing his meetings at the Café Europa, and Monsieur Karom continued to provide the palace with reports on his master's activity. Mrs. Damakan left Stamboul to live with her niece in Smyrna. The Sultan resolved to dismiss Jamaludin Pasha, then agreed, at his mother's behest, to give him one last chance. A new girls' school opened in Zeytinburnu, the Yildiz Hamidiye Mosque was dedicated; plans for the Berlin-Baghdad railroad were scuttled; Robert Louis Stevenson published *The Strange Case of Dr. Jekyll and Mr. Hyde*; and the Statue of Liberty was erected in New York Harbor.

History marched on and the story of Eleonora Cohen was forgotten; a footnote to late Ottoman history, she slipped into permanent obscurity. Whether she fulfilled Mrs. Damakan's prophecy or escaped it, whether she was, indeed, the one who would set the world right again on its axis, the answers to these questions we will never know for certain. And so it should be. For the stones in the river of history look different depending on where you stand.

U.K.

London

Amsterdam

NETH.

Berlin

Warsaw

Brussels

BELGIUM

GERMAN EMPIRE

Paris

Prague

FRANCE

SWITZ.

Vienna

Budapest

AUSTRO-HUNGARIAN
EMPIRE

SPAIN

ITALY

Belgrade

SERBIA

Barcelona

MONTENEGRO

Rome

Salonika

Algiers

GREECE

Tunis

Athens

ALGERIA

TUNISIA

Mediterranean Sea

Tripoli

200 miles

OTTOMAN EMPIRE